"All these yea[rs] ... you, R.T."

"I've loved you, yes, but I've hated you, too. And I've hated myself for it. I'm tired of all the hate, can't you see? I'm tired of looking at happy people and grieving because I'm not one of them. And now I have a chance to start over . . . "

R.T. swiped a hand over his face. The gesture was so heartbreaking the Allyson flinched.

His words came with an unexpected tenderness. "You don't have to run away from me, Allyson. I'll stay out of your life if that's what you want, but—" he heaved a sigh "—you don't have to go away."

When she didn't reply, he moved to the window and looked outside, his shoulders rounded.

"I shouldn't have said that." He bent his head low. "You have every right to go. But—" he faced her unexpectedly, his expression haggard "—if you go, go knowing that I love you, Allyson. I always have."

Dear Reader:

We at Silhouette are very excited to bring you this reading Sensation. Look out for the four books which appear in our Silhouette Sensation series every month. These stories will have the high quality you have come to expect from Silhouette, and their varied and provocative plots will encourage you to explore the wonder of falling in love – again and again!

Emotions run high in these drama-filled novels. Greater sensual detail and an extra edge of realism intensify the hero and heroine's relationship so that you cannot help but be caught up in their every change of mood.

We hope you enjoy this Sensation – and will go on to enjoy many more.

We would love to hear your comments and encourage you to write to us:

Jane Nicholls
Silhouette Books
PO Box 236
Thornton Road
Croydon
Surrey
CR9 3RU

LINDA SHAW
One Sweet Sin

Silhouette Sensation

First published in Great Britain in 1993 by Silhouette Books, Eton House, 18-24 Paradise Road, Richmond, Surrey TW9 1SR

© Linda Shaw 1990

Silhouette, Silhouette Sensation and Colophon are Trade Marks of Harlequin Enterprises B.V.

ISBN 0 373 58764 3

18-9303

Made and printed in Great Britain

Other novels by Linda Shaw

To Staff Sergeant Gerald Brown
and Sergeant Eamon Riley
of the United States Marine Corps.
My sincere gratitude for helping breathe life
into Major R. T. Smith.
Semper fidelis.

Prologue

It was as Daniel Wyatt was struggling his way up the snow-blinding embankment of Highway 3, a mile north of the sign that says Welcome to Nakatak, An Alaskan Fisherman's Paradise, that he saw the truth: Life was a bitch.

He had always thought it was, but recently certainty of that hypothesis had escalated dramatically. His first proof had been two days ago when the ski-masked fiend broke into his Vancouver apartment and fired six shots into his empty bed. At that point Daniel decided to leave Vancouver for Alaska—on the outside chance that the gunman hadn't miscalculated and broken into the wrong place by mistake. He had taken his two-week-old Porsche 911 Turbo Cabriolet and had done a lot of thinking on the drive up, mostly about his ex-wife and his best friend.

Now his Porsche was wrapped around the trunk of an ice-crusted spruce that grew along Highway 3. A 4 × 4 had come out of the darkness from behind and rammed his bumper, sending him skidding and careening sideways in slow motion like a clumsy swan on a frozen lake. With its engine screaming, the Porsche had plunged over the bank, and he had gotten the message and seen the Truth of Life at the same time: Old Ski Mask had not made a mistake, and Allyson and R.T. had been in love from the beginning.

"And they call you a genius," Daniel said as he scrambled out of the car, his legs churning like pistons through drifts that reached his knees. He reached the embankment and crouched behind a sapling, his heart pounding like a tom-tom. He wouldn't last ten minutes in this blizzard if he didn't keep moving.

Above his head, headlights slashed the 4:00 a.m. darkness. Had Allyson and R.T. slept together?

Daniel wasn't sure he wanted that much truth in his life. As the 4 × 4 stopped prowling, he remained very still. Snow was whistling down from Mount McKinley through the Matanuska Valley in killing sheets, blurring his footprints. Here, the world was eerie. The purr of the 4 × 4 was the only man-made sound.

A figure skittered over the embankment and aimed a beam of a light at the Porsche.

Another truth, Daniel thought with a strange detachment, was that genius wore two faces. One of them was incredibly stupid. If he hadn't been so stupid, he would have realized fourteen years ago that he had lost Allyson. Maybe he'd never had her. Wasn't it ridiculous that he kept thinking about R.T. and Allyson now?

A drowning man's life passing before his eyes, he supposed, and shrank deeper into the drifts until the spotlight stopped searching and finally disappeared up the embankment again.

With his heart hammering, he waited to the count of fifty. The engine of the predator revved and grew louder, then softer and was gradually swallowed by the keening wind.

Daniel peered furtively upward, to the sapling beside his head. Grasping it, he heaved himself up. Above the sapling grew another one. He handed himself up the slope. As he neared the top, the spindly twig bent double.

"Oh, no!" he groaned, and slid to the bottom of the embankment again.

Ten minutes later, after grueling work, gasping and heaving, cursing and repenting, Daniel lay panting beside the ice-crusted highway. For some minutes he hardly dared raise his head. He saw nothing except the white world of snow. Standing, he shook himself in an attempt to get the blood flowing again and, keeping an ear sharply tuned for the sound of an engine, he started off at a lumbering trot toward the Chevron station he'd seen before going over the embankment. Twenty minutes later he reached it and when he burst through the door, no one appeared the slightest surprised to see him.

It figured, Daniel thought. After fifteen-hundred and twenty miles of the Alaska Highway, the surprise would have been if the stranger *hadn't* stopped at Nakatak with trouble. A rock missile shattering the windshield, perhaps, or a cloud of suffocating dust, a mud bog to the axles, treacherous gravel, an unexpected snowstorm. Usually it was just a matter of too much highway and not enough gas.

No one asked if he'd been born a fool to bring a Porsche into Jeep and Bronco country, either. They probably assumed he'd been snorting the white powder that city boys were so fond of.

He asked if there was a telephone handy and the station attendant jabbed a disinterested thumb toward the plate-glass window.

"Yep," he grunted with frostbitten economy, and proceeded to clean the grease from beneath his fingernails. "Pay phone. Over there."

On the wall beside the window was a grimy dial phone and a scribbled-on calendar with a picture of a leaping, wide mouth bass and an advertisement for Scuddy's Bait and Tackle Shop.

"Thanks," Daniel said.

Two other men had come in from the early-morning cold. They were huddled around a gas heater, stamping and shuffling and slapping themselves to offset the frigid November temperature outside. One had found a yellow dinette chair whose stuffing was bursting through atrophied vinyl splits. The other roasted his backside while he flipped through a finger-stained *Sports Illustrated*.

Through his haze, Daniel wondered if they drove a 4×4. They didn't say, and he didn't ask. They returned to the pressing business of thawing out, and he pulled off a glove with his teeth.

His hands shook as he unzipped his jacket and fished a scrap of paper from his shirt pocket. He squinted at a number written in his own scholarly hand. Blowing on his fingers, he dropped one of his dwindling supply of coins into a slot. He didn't dare use a credit card. Credit cards were traceable.

He punched a series of numbers.

Presently a bland voice came on the line. "Thank you for using A T & T."

Daniel guessed he had a concussion; he was having trouble standing up. "I want to speak to, uh..." Touching his temple, he stared, wide-eyed, as his fingers came away bloody. "I want to speak to Allyson Wyatt. Collect, please."

"The number you're speaking from, sir?"

Giving it, Daniel blotted the cut on his head while the call went through.

No one answered at Allyson's apartment. Puzzled, he said, "Could you try another number? Global Defense in Seattle. I don't have that, I'm sorry."

"Hold, please."

Nothing seemed alive outside except an occasional pair of approaching headlights that gleamed out of the brumelike eyes of some unearthly creature craving human warmth. Daniel wondered what he would say when Allyson came on the line. He should never have run from Vancouver, of course, but aside from being a genius, he was a coward.

He shivered. The worst weariness he'd ever known was creeping up the backs of his legs now. Nausea was rising in his stomach. Beneath his jacket, a trickle of sweat was traversing the length of his spine.

He wet his lips before covering the receiver and inquiring of the station attendant, "I don't suppose I could find someone with a wrecker?"

The man shrugged. "Guess so. How far back are you?"

"A quarter mile, maybe."

"Much damage?"

Not much, Daniel thought, except that the entire rear of the Porsche looked like crumpled Christmas wrapping.

He daubed his wadded glove to his temple, and the floor shifted gently beneath him.

The man nearest him lit a cigarette and waved away the backwash of smoke. "Hey, you okay, mister?"

"Sure, sure." Grimacing, Daniel braced his shoulder against the plate-glass window. "I'm fine."

He must make the best use of his time now, he thought. If old Ski Mask and 4 × 4 had their way, there were things he must do. There were loose ends to tie up, wrongs to be made right, the past to be faced, regrets to be reconciled, debts that he owed Allyson and R.T. They had loved him more than they loved themselves. They deserved better than they'd gotten.

It wasn't so bad, really—facing eternity. Eternity gave a man a sort of dignity, a control. What was the saying? About how a man didn't have a choice about dying, but that he could choose *how* he went?

And perhaps where? It all depended, he supposed, upon the Justice Department finding Hickson and Hickson finding Grant and Grant finding Ski Mask and Ski Mask finding him and he finding... what? Truth?

There were worse things.

Part One

Chapter 1

In her right hand Allyson Wyatt palmed two aspirin tablets, in her left she swirled a cup of cold coffee laced with dregs.

It was seven o'clock in the morning and her mouth tasted of rust. Her headache had long ago progressed from the nagging stage to the four-star-splitting category. Her eyes, gritty as the Sahara, were more red than green, and for the past six hours an entire regiment of Lilliputian men with bows and arrows had been using her shoulder blades for target practice.

Allyson was on the thirtieth floor of the Melbourne Tower in downtown Seattle. At this moment she hated her office, and the feeling was mutual. The wall at her back was lined with canisters of magnetic tape, one of which was whispering through a machine whose monitor sat beside her chair. Her bookcase contained a whole army of computer manuals, some of which lay open on her desk and scattered on the floor, mocking her now that she needed them.

She tossed down the aspirin and chased them with coffee dregs and a sigh.

"Okay, Pandora..." She narrowed her eyes at the IBM 3270 with the fervor she usually reserved for two-week-old broccoli in the crisper of the refrigerator. "I'm through playing around now."

With her finger holding a place in a troubleshooting manual, she held her breath, punched in a command and waited.

Bleep. "Document not found." Blink, blink, blink.

"Aggh!"

Allyson slammed the book shut and slid low on her spine, pressing her burning eyes. Until today, she had never hated a computer. During the drab years between her divorce at twenty-six and this job with Grant Melbourne at thirty-two, she had actually loved a few. They had a sort of understanding, she and the machines; she wouldn't curse them because she had crawled into a hole and successfully hidden from life. They, on the other hand, would not hound her for making such a mess of things. Friends didn't do this to each other, damn it!

"Sorry to disturb your beauty rest," George had said when she dragged the telephone receiver to her ear at one o'clock in the morning and her brain had taken a moment to catch up with her body.

"George?"

"A file's disappeared," he said.

Open eyes. Find light. Don't panic. "You're kidding."

"You know I have no sense of humor."

She made a subhuman sound as she flailed about, searching for the lamp. "Where are you?"

"The Tower."

"Which file?"

"Bolten."

"Oh, no!"

Her eyes snapped open and she flicked the lamp switch. Bolten was one of the largest accounts on the computer. The Bolten Company was the Big Mac of wholesale weaponry. Bolten was *the* U.S. outlet for everything from graceful, feminine derringers that complemented Elizabeth Arden skin tones and Balmain gowns, to the army's official hand-held weapon of choice, the Beretta, to land-to-air Stinger missiles that were guaranteed to blow a jumbo jet out of the sky in two easy lessons. Bolten had taken months to set up. It couldn't have vanished into thin air!

"Well, at least we have the backup," she said on a shaky note of hope.

"Not anymore, we don't."

"Ohhh." Allyson swung her legs off the bed. Grant Melbourne would kill her. "A virus? Grief, George, Global's whole backup?"

"No virus, just Bolten."

"How can Global Defense be all right when . . . Never mind. Is Satellite okay?"

"It appears to be. 'Course I haven't checked it all. I've been working on Bolten since midnight."

"I hate this job, George."

"So you've said."

Global Defense was a new company, the bastard son of its prestigious parent, Satellite Communications, Incorporated. Wade Melbourne, an old college friend of her father, both prestigious and now dead, had built SCI from nothing. SCI was an admirable example of the good old American know-how when television had been a baby and computers were tucked neatly away in some scientist's DNA. Only after Wade's death did his son Grant create Global Defense. Wade definitely would not have approved.

Now Allyson fixed Pandora in a stare. It didn't pay to talk too disrespectfully to a machine. They never forgot, and they had an infinite variety of ways to get even. She drummed short, practical nails on the desk.

"This isn't becoming behavior for someone of your intelligence, Pandora," she reminded. "Now, for the last time, where's the file?"

She made another entry of keys and waited.

Bleep. "Document not found." Blink, blink, blink.

Allyson dropped her head upon the terminal and a tousle of blond hair swirled about her face. This is what happened when a person went against nature. The Randolphs were never meant to deal in weapons. The Randolphs became philanthropists and hospital administrators and museum curators and ambassadors to countries whose name you couldn't pronounce. Randolphs became social reformers, medical researchers, starving artists and alcoholics. They did *not* marry Daniel Wyatt, get a degree in art, get pregnant, have a baby, get divorced and go to work for Global Defense to keep from starving to death!

It had been her mother, Kaye, who had said after being made a widow, "Allyson, if Joe Kennedy can be respectable with whisky money, the Randolphs can certainly be respectable with Berettas. Take Grant's job, dear. We need the money."

So she'd taken the job and Kaye didn't have to sell the house. Greg, her brother, could keep painting his pictures that didn't sell, and she could put her six-year-old Michael into an expensive school for gifted children.

But she was leaving. Oh, yes, she was going to do it. Grant Melbourne didn't know it yet, but for the last year she had been working on this move. Like a cat burglar planning a diamond heist, she'd been sneaking down to Atlanta and interviewing with Earl Kolpechy, the director of broadcast graphics at CNN.

Kolpechy had taken a hard look at her résumé. "I'm going to go out on a limb for you, Mrs. Wyatt. Though your credits don't prove it and a number of people would do anything for this position, my gut tells me you can do the best job for us. Are you interested?"

Interested? She would have done graphics for Saturday-morning cartoons for the job!

So in three weeks she and Michael would be exchanging Seattle and its unhappy memories for Scarlett O'Hara country. Her letter of resignation was typed and in her desk. She was ready to close a real-estate deal in Atlanta and had already begun packing. Her mother... well, Kaye was still in a state of shock.

"You know, George," Allyson told her technician when he now appeared in her office doorway, coffeepot blessedly in hand, "Pandora has a warped idea of loyalty. She likes to see me suffer."

George didn't show the wear and tear of having been up all night. George always looked as if he'd been up all night. Rarely did he venture out of his world of cathode rays and phosphor dots long enough to recognize that people didn't operate from computer chips.

"Stop frowning," he told her cheerfully as he filled her cup with a brew as black as the circles beneath his eyes. "You'll make the lines in your face worse."

Laughing, Allyson balanced the heels of her sneakers upon her desk and stared at the extension of long, slim legs clad in rumpled jeans that she'd dragged from the dryer at one o'clock in the morning.

"This isn't my opinion of a quality-time investment, George," she said.

"Just preparing you for what they'll say upstairs." George slurped happily. "You know the name of that tune. When in doubt, blame the programmer."

"Who told you that, R2D2?"

"Hey, I trust him more than I trust my own father."

"He probably was your father, George."

Straightening, Allyson dropped her feet to the floor and sloshed coffee on her knee. "Did you call Phoebe?"

"She's on her way."

"Then go away." She blotted the coffee with the elbow of a plaid shirt, also rumpled. "Conjure up one of your spells to get me out of this mess. Once the building fills up, this office will be a junkyard."

"Hey, Al," George bellowed over his shoulder as he went out, "maybe this is just a hacker feeling his oats. Ever think of that?"

In the computer world, a hacker was a mischievous vandal, an over-bright computer nut who had seen *War Games* too many times. Years ago when she and Daniel and R.T. were only dabbling at life, she'd been a hacker herself.

Then, after three hackers were arrested for selling passwords and codes to the Soviets, *hacker* became a dirty word. Global Defense wasn't all that high in the popularity polls, either. The company was currently under investigation by the Department of Justice. Conspiracy to commit fraud, they alleged. Global Defense was supposed to be guilty of using insider knowledge to procure government contracts. Not only had Global used insider knowledge, it had had the cockiness to pad the bills!

Allyson considered a pack of cigarettes that she kept hidden beneath the Scotch tape in her desk drawer. Smoking was forbidden around the computers. Besides, she'd quit. Twice.

Rising, she strode to a darkened window and leaned all her five feet six inches upon its cold surface. "This is no hacker, George. It's a crasher, an out-and-out thief. And when I find him, I'm going to crash his ass."

"You have my blessing."

Beyond Allyson, Seattle was yawning and stretching itself awake. Across her superimposed reflection lay Puget Sound, where she and Daniel and R.T. had held hands and run barefoot across the hot sand and roasted their slim adolescent bodies upon the deck of the Wyatt's narrow-hulled thirty-two footer. There was Sea-Tac International Airport and the Space Needle.

Memory. It could sort through tons of impressions with lightning speed, yet preserve so few. An entire year could be reduced to a phone call on a blustery winter evening. Childhood could be the slap of a screen door or the smell of gardenias, waves lapping at the wharves of the Sound, the squawk of gulls. In her sophomore year, Daniel had carried her books. In the next, the smell of cold had been in R.T.'s hair. The three of them had shared a single Hershey bar at a football game. A Hershey bar with almonds.

Using a fingertip, Allyson drew an abstract design in the condensation of her breath on the glass. She should have left Seattle years ago. She might be over R.T. by now if she'd moved on.

At her desk, the telephone growled like a beast straining to be unleashed. Returning, she sank into her chair and tucked the receiver beneath her chin. Her attention drifted to Pandora's screen as her fingers began a new series of diagnostic checks.

"Wyatt," she said.

"Allyson Wyatt?"

With a montage of apprehensions, Allyson sat straight in her chair. "Yes?"

"A collect call from Daniel Wyatt. Will you accept?"

Phoebe, another technician, was coming through the outside door into the computer room—savvy, short-skirted and shaggily moussed. "On a Tom Skerritt scale," she called to Allyson, "last night's date was a skinny three. What's up?"

"Tempers," Allyson answered, covering the mouthpiece. "I'll explain later." She waved Phoebe to her desk. "Yes, operator, I'll accept the call."

"Go ahead, sir."

One of the mysteries of Allyson's life was why she'd never been able to cut the cord with her ex-husband. She liked Daniel, and in some ways she supposed she still loved him, but he refused to leave the nest. He kept returning to it—a Capistrano swallow at the change of seasons. She wished he would find himself a nice, kind woman who could bear living with an IQ of 180 and settle down.

"Daniel?" Her hand began an automatic exploration inside the desk drawer for the cigarettes. "What's the matter?"

"Allyson," he laughingly chided, "has anyone ever told you that you've got a suspicious mind?"

"All the time."

"I haven't talked to you in months, and here you are accusing me of being in trouble."

"Try a year." A year and two months, to be exact, she thought, frowning.

"I called to wish you a happy birthday."

A glance at the calendar proved him wrong. "You're premature, Daniel. Not for six days yet."

"Ahh. Just think, in six days you'll be thirty-three."

"Gee, thanks, Daniel."

"I didn't interrupt anything, did I?"

"No, no," Allyson lied. "I'm not busy. Did you know a man from the Justice Department was looking for you?"

"He found me. How's Michael?"

"Michael's fine."

"Has he gained any weight?"

Allyson heaved a sigh, pushed a button on her keyboard and propped her hand on a fist. "Daniel, why do we have this conversation every single time? Some children are naturally thin. It doesn't mean they're sick. What did he want?"

"What did who want?" Daniel asked.

"The man from the Justice Department!"

Daniel hesitated. "Nothing much. Look, Allyson, I was just thinking, just wondering, actually... Say, you haven't heard from R.T., have you?"

Without warning, Allyson's body seized like the parts of an engine that had suddenly outlived its usefulness. She didn't move. She didn't blink. She didn't breathe as images spattered violently upon her mind—the three of them that last innocent summer, laughing as R.T. wrapped himself around her and showed how to slam the eight-ball into a pocket, the three of them standing arm-in-arm to peer down at the world from the Space Needle, the three of them sprawling on the floor at Daniel's house and poking pizza into each other's mouths. The whole future had belonged to them that summer, dangling from heaven in all its sun-drenched promise, ripe, begging to be picked.

God, how in love she'd been! Only with the wrong boy.

Chapter 2

R.T. Smith and Daniel Wyatt should never have been friends.

R.T. Smith was the perennial bad boy. Every neighborhood produced at least one, and R.T. passed every test with zinging colors. R.T. was the seventies teenager with his hair forever too long, the one with the cocky swagger and acetylene-blue eyes. He wore shabby jeans and had Alice Cooper painted on his Levi's jacket. A cigarette dangled sultrily from his mouth, and he was in and out of juvenile probation so many times, everyone just knew he was bound straight for Attica or the fires of hell, whichever came first.

By the time he was fourteen, R.T. could outhustle every pool shark on the Seattle docks. He could also outdrink, outyell and outfight them. At fifteen, he plowed a Harley-Davidson into the side of a Mack truck and lived to tell about it. The bad girls whispered to the good ones about the scandalous things they let him do, and he bloodied his fists when anyone, but anyone, dared call him Rathmore Tennyson.

When Officer Darrin Hollister instructed the ambulance to take Eva Smith's body to the county morgue, he sensed something in the fierce, dark-haired teenager who stood biting his nails and refusing to shed a tear. Without any thanks and even less encouragement, Hollister went out of his way to get R.T. reinstated in school—a decent one this time, out of his neighborhood and across town: Cardinal Heights.

"Is it true that the boy found his mother?" the teachers asked in the main office when R.T.'s file came through.

"In the bathtub," someone said. "I remember from the papers. She didn't even leave a note."

"Oh, dear."

"He lives with his grandmother, it says here. Poor woman. First her daughter-in-law, then her son."

"What happened to her son?"

"He's doing hard time." Reavis Smith was a longshoreman with "Bad to the Bone" tattooed on his shoulder, who wore steel-toed safety boots and sold dope to school children.

"Do we really want this boy at Cardinal Heights?"

"At least he isn't a dope dealer."

"Not yet," someone said.

"I don't know. He's not the kind of boy we like at Cardinal Heights."

Daniel Wyatt was the kind of boy they liked at Cardinal Heights. With the golden beauty of Godunov and an intellect so phenomenal that his teachers only guessed at it, Daniel was beloved by everyone. At sixteen, he had taken the Yale entrance exams and made three perfect scores. He was president of the Junior League of Achievers. He headed the staff of the school newspaper. By the time he was a sophomore, Daniel had won two drama scholarships.

In a symmetry no one ever really understood, Daniel and R.T. proved the old adage of attracting opposites. Over the years, R.T. slowly found the missing parts of himself in Daniel, and Daniel, ironically, had his eyes opened to the real world.

At first R.T. admired Allyson Randolph because she was "Daniel's girl." But as the months stretched into years and their lives became inseparably plaited, R.T. had no choice but to accept the bitter truth about his life: He was in love with Allyson Randolph himself.

It wasn't a thing he had meant to do. He didn't find Allyson particularly beautiful, but to simply look at her, to watch her slim, graceful walk or see her turn, to accidentally touch her hair or brush her fingertips or hear her voice could raise gooseflesh on his arms.

Her eyes hypnotized him with their tiny fronds of gray promise in the green. Her skin glowed with a warm apricot sheen, as if the sun had played upon it a bit too long. She was by nature a happy girl, laughing, always ready to see the good, and there were times when he thought his heart would surely break with love.

Primarily because of Daniel, R.T. came to be tolerated by Seattle's society. He developed a sort of maverick, rough-diamond style. He learned how to conduct himself and how to dress. He stopped biting his nails and learned how to negotiate a grudging standoff with the power structure.

Kaye and Orin Randolph possessed a strong sense of their family's place in society. Into their children they instilled a sense of duty and responsibility for the good of all. Allyson was expected to pick and choose a better class of friends than "that long-haired punk" from across town, it was said, and Kaye never missed an opportunity to let R.T. know he wasn't welcome in her house.

Upon Orin's death when Allyson was seventeen and Greg, her brother, was eighteen, Kaye Randolph began, subtly and eventually not-so-subtly, to impress upon her daughter what an attractive catch Daniel Wyatt would make.

"There's nothing wrong with marrying straight out of high school, you know," Kaye liked to say.

"At eighteen?" Allyson's dreams were of doing something useful before she married, though she wasn't certain what that something might be.

"I married young." Kaye had not forgotten how painful it was to be born pretty and dirt poor. "If you wait too long, you'll turn around and find that all the really good men have been taken. It pays to be careful, dear. It's time you looked at life realistically, responsibly."

Without Allyson really realizing it, the decision was made for her. An August wedding to Daniel Wyatt. That way, Kaye said, the Wyatts would be obliged to help with the cost of Allyson's college education, which was nothing to sneeze at, considering that Orin hadn't bequeathed his family much beyond respectability.

By the time Allyson realized that she was in love with R.T., the wedding plans were engraved upon tablets of stone. Torn, confused, not trusting her own instincts and daring even less to disappoint her mother, she convinced herself that her feelings for R.T. were nothing more than an infatuation. They would die and blow away like dust of another lifetime. A future with R.T. Smith was worse than no future at all. Everyone knew that. She had heard about Eva and Reavis Smith and all the talk about juvenile probation and the Harley-Davidson motorcycle. It was simply unthinkable—R.T. and herself. Not in her plans at all.

Allyson and Daniel planned to leave for Yale immediately after their wedding. R.T. had no money to attend college, but that wouldn't prevent him from being Daniel's best man, to Kaye's horror.

So, the last days of summer were desperate, desperate to be happy. Yet things grew strangely awkward between the three of them. Allyson spoke to R.T. only when forced to, and then in the snappiest of tones. She went out of her way to show affection for Daniel in front of R.T. and lifted her face for Daniel's kiss. She made a show of straightening Daniel's collars and calling him darling.

Yet if R.T. even so much as mentioned another girl, she grew killingly jealous, raging at nothing then apologizing and bursting into violent tears that left everyone helpless and confused.

It had been Daniel's family's idea for Allyson and Daniel to drive up to Cavanaugh Lake to see Aunt Maud.

"Such a lovely gesture, dear," Daniel's mother, Idabell, said as she fingered the brooch that had once belonged to Virginia Wyatt of the Massachusetts Wyatts and which she planned to give to her new daughter-in-law as a wedding present. "Maud is the family matriarch, you know, and it never hurts to have someone in your corner when you're starting out.''

But Maud took ill the moment Allyson and Daniel arrived and was rushed to the hospital with a nasty attack of gallstones. The family sent word for Daniel to remain at the hospital until they could arrive. Disappointed, Daniel called R.T. and asked if he could come for Allyson and drive her back to Seattle.

For Allyson the trip was a nightmare. The last days had taken such an emotional toll, she shrank against the door of his battered pickup, disagreeable as the business end of a fishhook.

The heat was stifling. The highway seemed to melt as it unreeled beneath hissing tires. The muffler roared embarrassingly loud, and R.T. drove much too fast.

The neck and arms of his T-shirt had been slashed out, and Allyson could hardly bear to look at him, he was so virile. The openings showed sweat-sleeked ribs and wispy curls below his throat, beneath his arms. There were several irregular scars that she had seen many times, one on the curve of his biceps, another near a dusky nipple, a third upon his right wrist—capricious whorls of white.

He braced an elbow across the open window, and aviator sunglasses obscured the eyes that could change instantly from a summer-sky blue to hot lightning. She really didn't know why she cared. R.T. wasn't handsome. One of his center teeth had a small, half-moon chip on its bottom edge, and his hair was so unruly, no comb could badger the cowlicks into submission. The slant of his mouth was naturally cocky and had been known to provoke instant wrath in adults. His nose had been broken so many times, even he couldn't remember, and as for his attitude, there wasn't much she could say about *that* that hadn't been said by everyone a hundred times over.

But when he smiled—oh! It was moonlight flashing through the shadows! It was gold in a miner's pan, a tear in a lover's eye. His smile was the thing she lived for.

By the time they reached the outskirts of Seattle, darkness lay upon the sweltering day like a welcome weight. Al-

lyson had hardly moved from her door. She was exhausted.
Her legs ached and her hands throbbed from clenching them
so long.

R.T. had hooked his sunglasses upon the neck of his shirt,
and he flashed his sunny, high-noon smile. "It's been a long
trip."

She crossed and uncrossed her legs and moistened her
lips. "Yes."

"Tired?"

Think of something disgusting about him, Allyson's logic
warned. *Think of how he would look in the morning, all
whiskery and rumpled. Think of him grungy, think of him
smelly and dirty. Hate him. Be sick to death of him.*

He glanced away, then back, noting, Allyson was certain, the obvious way she was twisting her engagement ring
round and round her finger.

"Are you thirsty or anything?" he asked.

"I suppose," she said with a sigh.

"I've got this real addiction going with Pepsi." He
chuckled as he braked for a traffic light. "Every four hours,
on the spot."

"What happens if you don't get it?"

Keeping his eyes riveted upon moving traffic, he leaned
over and pretended to take a juicy nibble of her neck.
"Aghrr. I turn into Dr. Jeckyll and devour innocent young
virgins."

Goosebumps pebbled over Allyson's body, and before she
thought, she blurted nervously, "That lets me out, doesn't
it?"

The sudden gauntness of his face only confirmed what
Allyson had guessed was true, that Daniel had told R.T.
about those nights. She didn't know herself why they'd
happened so easily—a desperation to love Daniel when the
feeling wasn't there, she supposed, when she wasn't sure
what the feeling should be. Making love was expected of a
fiancée, wasn't it? And Daniel was an honest and gentle
lover.

A muscle knotted in R.T.'s jaw as he swung the truck up
to the window of a fast-food drive-through. He skidded to

a stop. After taking their order, the cashier rang up the ticket.

Scowling at his twenty-dollar bill, she said, "Don't you have anything smaller? I'm low on change."

To reach into the pocket of the skin-tight jeans, R.T. had to brace his boots on the floorboard and breech upward—a commonplace move, thighs straining, buttocks flexing as his fingers groped along his groin for the elusive coins. When he sucked in his stomach, though, Allyson's eyes went straight to the telltale ridge.

With a jolt, their telepathy connected. His gaze slammed guiltily into hers, then jerked away. Allyson ducked her head and stared blindly at her own knees. With a ragged breath, R.T. dumped the money into the cashier's hand and snatched back his twenty. He thrust the paper cup into Allyson's hand.

Her brain delivered a series of instructions: *hand about cup, lift cup, sip from straw, swallow, smile, pretend to be sane.*

"Haul it outta here, buddy!" a man hollered from the car behind as he blared his horn.

Allyson snapped like a crossbow that had spent its arrow.

"Goddammit," R.T. muttered as, with a tortuous squeal of tire rubber, he sped out of the parking lot and into a busy street.

Nothing about Allyson seemed to work. She couldn't swallow. She couldn't speak. Her heart was beating a deafening knell. A cup holder was perched beneath the dash, and she fit her cup into it then stared savagely at a thread on her skirt that had worked free. In her agony, she began picking it.

Without a word, R.T. drove them out of town and down streets she would never remember. He took them past the Southside Drive-In where they'd seen all the nauseating teenage movies with Daniel.

Allyson could sense him sifting through his experiences in search of a finesse he didn't possess. *"Casablanca,"* she

mumbled because at this point she must say something or
snap like skeins of a cobweb.

"What?" He followed her indication of the theater. "Oh,
yeah." He cleared the rasp from his throat. "Yes."

"Have you seen it?"

His shrug could have been yes or no or drop dead. "Have
you?"

She pushed back a drooping wave, but her fingers returned to their task of plucking convulsively at the thread.
"Not in a long time."

"They're good, the old ones."

"Yes."

He warmed to his subject. "Do you know, that old Bo-
gart line 'Play it again, Sam' isn't even in the movie?"

"Really?" Plucking, plucking, plucking.

"Uh-huh."

Allyson's pause was the final second before jumping off
the high dive into the pool for the first time. Turning, sitting on her hands, she took that last, death-defying gulp of
air.

"We could go see it," she whispered, and was immediately caught in a free fall from a terrible height. Why in
heaven's great mercy had she said that? What could she do
to unsay it?

R.T. turned into the street where she lived—a staid, gentle
lane as respectable as her Great-grandfather Randolph, after whom it was named. The streetlamps were a soft glow in
the lacey branches. Majestic oaks, a long-time planted,
bordered the walks on both sides, their great limbs embracing over the pavement like phantom lovers out of the past.

Swerving to the curb, R.T. left the engine running. He
grew rapt with his hands opening and shutting upon the
wheel.

"You mean," he whispered as though he couldn't quite
conceptualize it, "just the two of us?"

Saying it made it ugly: treacherous, unforgivable. Daniel's ring was on her finger. The wedding invitations had
gone out. Allyson distractedly combed her hair with her
fingers. What thirsty demons were pressing her on?

She shook her head in regret for what she could not change.

"I didn't mean to...I shouldn't have said...I only thought...what with..." She bent over her lap and covered her face with her hands. "Oh, me."

Her tears came then, with all the frustrated sting of eighteen-year-old failure. They slid off the tips of her lashes and spilled—throwaway diamonds—onto her hands.

Turning off the engine, R.T. slid his arm across the seat and leaned toward her.

"Hey," he said in a raspy whisper as he started to touch her but stopped, a hand poised above her head. "Hey, it's okay, Cricket. It's okay."

But it wasn't okay, and Allyson thought her love would kill her, and she really didn't care anymore. "Please take me home," she wept.

His hand moved, mothlike, over her shoulder. "Shh, it's only a movie. It's not like it would be a crime or anything. Right?"

The bridge of his broken nose was what Allyson saw through her prism of tears. And the ridge of muscle framing the hard sensuality of his mouth, the muscle in his jaw that bunched over and over. How many nights had she gone to sleep fantasizing about that mouth fastened upon her own, searching for her breasts, moving over her, hot and wet, that hungry, persuasive mouth cajoling all her secrets?

When he inched his arm along the back of the seat and bent nearer, she caught a whiff of Ivory soap and Old Spice, the sweetness of the Pepsi he'd sipped, his own skin's drugging, masculine smell.

A thrill of yearning exploded along her nerves. She attempted unsuccessfully to smile. "Not unless movies have suddenly become against the law."

"They weren't yesterday."

"They probably won't be tomorrow, either."

Gradually then, their eyes drifted to a searing point of contact on the seat. There was on her face, Allyson knew, a silent plea for him to understand why she had placed him in this position, on his, a conflict that was completely out of character with his wild reputation: undefined honor shadow dancing with the forbidden.

She could smell her own desire.

"What would we tell Daniel?" he asked on a dazed breath.

She hardly recognized her strangled voice. "Would we have to tell him anything?"

The silence had its own chorus of accusing voices.

Then, his tortured whisper. "He's my best friend, Allyson. In all the world."

Yes. Daniel was everyone's friend. She was a traitor, a monster.

"Oh . . . forget it," she wailed, and twisted away. "I can walk home."

"No, dammit!"

He grabbed her by the arms, his hands manacles of steel. Allyson fumbled desperately with her door, but it refused to open and he refused to let go. She had nothing left but the cold ashes of defeat.

"I didn't mean to do this," she grieved, hugging herself and rocking back and forth. "I swear, I swear."

With gentle clumsiness, he attempted to comfort her and his fingers moved helplessly over her back. They traveled the curve of her spine, and when they reached the softer flare of her hips, he sucked in his breath and gazed at her in an inquiry so burning, so branding, Allyson thought they could have been slowly undressing each other, one garment at a time with its own quivering damnation.

"Is this it, then?" he whispered. "Have we come to this?"

His lips were moving nearer, reaching ever-so-tentatively for hers. As he slowly closed his eyes, Allyson could see the sultry fringe of his lashes coming between them.

The kiss was as fragile as stardust, nothing like the bad girls had whispered about. He coaxed her trembling lips with a seduction so careful, Allyson imagined herself to be a butterfly, nothing existing of her body except the fluttering wings of her lips as they clung to his.

Her whimper, when it bubbled from her throat at last, seemed to burst some dam in him. He muttered her name in a low, half-animal groan, and then his arms went around her like a vise as he began pulling her down in the seat.

Their hunger was savage and undeniable as only young hunger could be. Once he possessed her mouth, Allyson's logic turned to mist. He was on fire as he arched against her, grinding the vibrant ache of his worship into her warm, cradling hollow. Down, down, down they were sucked into the pool of the guilty embrace.

Of course *she* had been the one who suggested the motel that night. *She* was the one who took off her blouse, *she* stepped out of her shoes and unhooked her bra and dropped it to the floor, gliding to R.T. on whispery stockinged feet and, with her breasts pale and trembling, lifted her arms to twine lovingly about his neck.

"I've wanted this for so long," she whispered as she clasped his head and drew it to her own, pressing her parted lips to his.

At that moment, time ceased. It became nothing more than a slurred tattoo filled with sighs and rustling wonderment. For a moment they forgot that what they did was forbidden by all the rules and almost-grown-up laws they lived by. They were simply two bodies joined in a seam of burnished, chafing flesh. She lifted herself against the half man, half boy whom her heart had chosen, and printed herself there. Even their whispers jarred the air, their startled murmurs of pleasure, her soft groans as she sought more, ever more.

But later, in the tarnished reality of the present, the future broke apart. Allyson opened her eyes and saw the tawdriness of the motel and knew there was no hope. Despair was all around her, passing into R.T.'s body and back again as she struggled to find a way to salvage something, anything.

"We'll be all right," she kept whispering as her logic searched for a door in a wall. "We'll be all right. We'll work it out. I'll find a way to make it work. I'll think of something. It'll happen, you'll see."

But he held her from him with desperate trembling. "It wouldn't work, Allyson." His voice was harsh as he saw her paleness, and he caught her again in his arms and pressed his lips to her ear. "We couldn't live with it. This can't ever happen again. It's not right."

Not right?

Allyson's humiliation hung poised like a flare in its bright apogee, long enough to see her own mocking nakedness. And then it fell, hissing and sputtering to earth. How dare R.T. speak to her of right and wrong? He who had come from such sordid beginnings? He who had failed every test that society had ever given him? How dare he reject her?

She fought herself free and tried to cover her breasts, to cover everything while he attempted to take her again into his arms. "Please, Allyson. Try to understand, please."

"Don't touch me," she wept, self-loathing congealing in her heart. "Just ... don't touch me."

In that moment her hatred was an abyss. She grabbed up her skirt, unable to see for the tears streaming down her face. What a fool she'd been! What a stupid, stupid little fool!

"Try to see what Daniel's given me," R.T. was pleading as she furiously dressed herself. "He's been my friend when everyone thought I was trash. You think I could go anywhere if it weren't for him?" He covered his face with his hands. "For years I crawled because I was ashamed of where I'd come from, of who I was. For years I hated it, and it made me mean. But Daniel changed that. He signed for me at the bank to get my truck. He's been a brother, Allyson. More than a brother."

She couldn't wait to wound him. "You give him too much credit, R.T.," she said viciously. "You think Daniel's a saint? You're the only saint around here."

His features were distorted, haggard, suffering, and he swung around, knocking the lamp to the floor so that it shattered.

He shouted his agony. "You think it's been easy, watching you all these years? Do you? Dreaming about you at night when the lights are out, feeling sick to my stomach because I've had to smile when he's told me how much you love him? He told me some of the words you said, and I wanted to yell at him, to smash his mouth. 'I don't want to hear it! I love 'er, too.' But I can't, Allyson. I don't have the right, dammit. No right!"

His voice broke under its bitter weight, and her thrill at learning R.T. actually loved her was lost in the swamp of her own speechless regret. As his hands closed about her shoulders and he jerked her nearly off her feet, her head snapped back upon its axis.

Ugly white ridges stood alongside his mouth. His blue eyes were pits of torment.

"Daniel's shared everything with me." He hissed the words as though he were ripping them from human flesh. "Fifty percent. Right down the middle. And I can't pay him back by taking his girl!"

Now Allyson stared at the crumbled Virginia Slims cigarette in her palm as silence weighed upon the telephone connection between Daniel and herself, heavy with misplaced dreams.

"Why should I have heard from R.T., Daniel?" she said when she recovered her balance. "Whatever gave you that idea?"

"Nothing," he said quickly. "Nothing. No problem."

Sighing, she dumped a confetti of tobacco and paper into the wastebasket and brushed crumbs from her hands. At least one of them had no problems.

But Daniel couldn't be blamed for not knowing what was going on at Global. He couldn't know how atrocious his timing was. Or could he? Was it possible that he had something to do with the disappearance of the Bolten file?

Of course he knew! The disappearance of Bolten wasn't a theft at all but another of Daniel's demented, egotistical, hacker's tricks! It was his way of amusing himself!

"This isn't funny, Daniel," she snapped. "You really take the cake, you know that?"

"I don't know what you're talking about."

"You know exactly what I'm talking about. Dammit it, Daniel, I'm tired of you breaking into this system just to prove you can do it. You've made your point, okay? You've breached my security. You're smarter than I. You taught me everything I know, I admit it. Now, what did you do with my file?"

"What file?"

"Honestly, Daniel! I could be in real trouble here." She strangled the receiver as if it were his neck. "Did it ever occur to you that there's a federal investigation going on in this company? Now, get out of this system before I report you to the FCC!"

Daniel surprised her more when he lowered his voice and spoke like a normal human being. "Don't get hysterical on me, Allyson," he soothed. "Be cool. Tell me about Michael."

Allyson rubbed her forehead in bafflement. Her headache had returned. A screw was burrowing into her temple. This was making no sense at all.

"Michael's fine," she said. "Why do you keep asking me that? Are you going to put back the file or not?"

"Where is he?"

"In school, Daniel, where every six-year-old is supposed to be."

"I thought you said it was seven o'clock."

"I did."

"Then how could Michael be in school?"

"My mother is going to take him to school, you idiot. I've been here most of the night."

"She's going to drive him herself?"

"Of course. What d'you think?"

"And then she'll pick him up?"

"I don't know, Daniel." Allyson brushed repeatedly at tobacco crumbs that weren't there. "I might even get reckless and pick him up myself, who knows? I'm only his mother, for crying out loud."

"Well, that fancy school is particular about the kids. I'm sure they'll take precautions."

His engrossed concern finally got to her, and she blinked. Since when had Daniel worried so about his son? When was the last time Daniel had asked about R.T.?

"Daniel—" apprehension crowded her "—how did you know to find me here? At seven o'clock in the morning? Where are you, Daniel?"

"Nakatak." His hand was cupped about the receiver, she thought, and she could imagine him looking over his shoulder. "I don't have much time, Allyson."

"Nakatak? Alaska?" Allyson changed the receiver to her other ear. "What cloak-and-dagger thing have you gotten into? What's going on?"

"Will you listen to me?" Desperation edged his words now. "Just once? This is important. I want you to get ahold of R.T."

"I can't." She shook her head, mocked by her failures. "Call R.T. yourself. Don't ask me to do it."

"I don't have time. He'll be offshore, and by the time I get a message through the military red tape... Allyson, will you just call him? He's got to come get me out."

Allyson honestly didn't know if her reaction was because Daniel's paranoia had finally gotten to her or because talking about R.T. could still tear her to pieces.

"What's happened to you?" she demanded, trembling.

"I wrecked my car. No, actually I got hit from the rear. This guy...well, I kind of hit my head. Will you just call R.T.? And don't tell anyone else about this. And don't call R.T. on that phone."

Old guilt rose in Allyson like silt from a stagnant pool. Poor Daniel. Poor, sweet Daniel. Why hadn't his need for her been enough to make their marriage work? He trusted her. He counted on her.

"All right, Daniel, I'll call R.T." She fumbled for a pen and pad. "Tell me where you'll be and when. I'll do the best I can, but I can't promise anything."

"Olsen Tracking Station. You know the one."

"You're crazy, you know that?" She was scribbling as she talked. "You've crossed over that thin line I always warned you about."

"I'm going to walk over and see if they don't have an infirmary. I guess I'm not making sense, but things are so—"

Allyson's heart knocked at her ribs. "Daniel?"

"Jesus, Allyson, think about what's happening. Think of the overall!"

As if a puppetmaster had given her strings a yank, she jerked up in her chair. So, he *did* know! He *had* taken the file! How could he?

She could have punched him through the phone. "Look here, Daniel—"

"I can't talk anymore." His words tripped over each other. "I love you, babe. I always did. I still do."

Allyson's chest constricted with a dread that no longer needed a reason. "Do you have money?" she blurted. "Give me a phone number, Daniel. Something—"

He dropped the telephone. Or at least, she thought he dropped it. She heard the eerie but unmistakable shatter of glass. Not breathing, she sat for some seconds, her hand reaching outward, her fingers splaying as if she could find him at the end of the world and, like Allah, grasp his hair and pull him up into Paradise.

"Daniel?" she whispered, trembling, dreading. "Are you there?"

Men's voices. Agitated voices.

Adrenaline spurted through Allyson's veins. Her voice raised in a shrill panic. *"Daniel?"*

"Around!" she heard a voice shout. She covered her free ear and strained to hear. "Get him around. This way!" The masculine voice grew abruptly louder, as if bursting out of a tunnel.

An ominous rustle. A fumbling. A click.

"Daniel!" she gasped, horrified.

The dial tone buzzed rudely in her ear.

Chapter 3

When a reporter from the magazine section of the *Seattle Herald* once asked R. T. Smith why he had joined the Marines, R.T. made a disparaging remark about the man's mother and said he admired the esprit de corps.

That was a lie. He'd enlisted because of the rain. Where R.T. came from rain was different from rain anywhere else in the world. In a poor neighborhood, the streets were never washed clean or the sky rinsed fair. The gardens never smelled of wet wisteria or medallions of roses. The factories vomited moldy gray poison and it sluiced down the gutters and made the sidewalks stink and the alleys vile until the odor permeated the walls of the buildings and seeped into the seams of a person's clothes. Whenever it rained, his spirits had immediately taken a gravitational slide downward.

Today, the sky was weeping a steady drizzle, and the old familiar blues had found R.T.

"Aww, come on, Skipper," Jesse Hurlburton was cajoling as they all walked, four abreast, across the fenced parking lot of Sand Point Naval Base. "One for the road. One lousy beer at Red's. I'll even talk Sam into telling his top-less-dancer story. You can't ask for better.''

R.T. and his buddies were a quartet of tough, expansive career Marines. They were wearing regulation cammies and heavy fatigue jackets and carried duffles and scuba gear and garment bags draped over their shoulders. The heels of their spit-shined boots clicked in unison across the rain-spattered lot. They had been ashore from the *USS Jason* exactly one hour and twelve minutes. Major Smith's recon unit was responsible for security aboard the *Jason*.

R.T. was the tallest man of the team. His military record said the top of his head was exactly six feet three inches above his feet. R.T. was actually a half-inch shy of that. He weighed in at one hundred ninety-five pounds, which cost him a run of five miles each day. His records also made note of a bullet that was lodged deep in his right hip too near his spine to tinker with and random shrapnel that was still peppered across his back.

With the exception of the silver oak leaf pinned to his jacket, R.T. dressed no differently from his men. He had a smooth, coordinated way of moving, however, that radiated power the way some men wore their wealth, impossible to pinpoint but there—coiled, formidable, deadly. Nothing about him was contrived. There was no false bravado, no strutting. At thirty-four, Major Smith was simply an extremely capable man who could do whatever needed to be done.

"Aw, I don't know, Jesse," he drawled, and showed a mouth of strong white teeth, one of which had a small half-moon chip in its bottom edge. "I was kind of looking forward to a nice hot fire and *Murphy Brown*."

"*Murphy Brown!* Come on, big dog. That's takin' purity a little too far, ain't it?"

R.T. laughed. "You've got better plans?"

Jesse came to a stop and the other men gathered round, grinning.

"You bet your sweet bustle I have," Jesse declared. "I'm going to find me a sweet young thing who wears that sassy goop on her hair, and I'm going to put my hands behind my head and get this big grin on my face.''

Letting his gear slide to the ground, R.T. slapped the outside of his jacket until he located a cigar. Removing it, he peeled off the cellophane and drew it beneath his nose. The last thing he intended to do was go to a dingy bar and grill that had become the traditional watering hole for men fresh off the ship.

"Sam, my man," he clapped his arm about the man who stood behind Jesse, "I think it's about time for one of your lectures on safe sex. Jess, take a good look at Sam. When you look at Sam, you're lookin' at one safe Marine."

Sam McDivitt could shoot a man's buttons off at a thousand yards with an M-16, but he'd been cursed with a woman's shy blush. He had yet to live down the night he'd been caught in a police raid in Manila only moments after having been dragged to a tabletop by a half-naked exotic dancer.

Turning red, he growled, "Up yours, Hurlburton, for starting this mess."

"Tell you what, Jess," R.T. said as he worked the cigar to the other side of his mouth and jingled through his pocket in search of a lighter, "I'll hang out at Red's for a while, but only on the condition that we go in my truck."

R.T. indicated the other side of the parking lot and the men exchanged grins. Around the base R.T.'s truck was known as the Beast. The night before high school graduation, Allyson had spray-painted the name across the driver's door, and the writing was still visible in spidery black letters: THE BEAST.

The Beast, though its bumper boasted a coveted array of decals—Jump Wing, Ranger, Airborne, Scuba Bubble— was not a classic vehicle. It wasn't even in the process of becoming a classic. No one was quite certain what the Beast was or what it was in the process of becoming. It was all quite complicated, and R.T.'s pet peeve was getting hassled about it.

Jesse considered his own Acura that was parked, apple bright and rain speckled, near the fence. He hurried forward to give it a quick once-over and checked all fenders and the chrome on the doors.

He rubbed a spot with the elbow of his jacket. "Damn tree," he mumbled, and plucked a soggy leaf from the windshield.

Jack O'Banyon, the corpsman of the unit, whom they called Jack the Knife, but never to the black medical man's face, said to R.T. under his breath, "I know people who don't get treated as good as that car."

"I could bring you back to the base, Skip," Jesse was offering. "I'd be real happy to."

The snap of R.T.'s lighter sent a flame dancing to the cylinder of tobacco, and he puffed briefly before anchoring the cigar between two fingers.

"Oh, I don't know, Jess," he said, and removed his cap briefly to stroke a bushy stubble of black hair. "I draw the line at ridin' in a Tonka toy. I keep bumpin' my head and messin' up my hair."

As R.T. considered the white ash of the cigar, Jesse said earnestly, "You know, Skipper, that truck of yours died back in seventy-nine. You really ought to bury it."

"Bury the Beast?"

"No self-respecting body man would come near it."

R.T. was counting on that. Allyson had once grazed the left front fender against a street light. She'd been sixteen and her driver's permit was so new, the paper wasn't creased.

"You're going to kill me," she'd wept when she threw herself into his arms one fragrant autumn day when a chill was biting the air and a rasp was in the leaves rustling about her feet.

He'd laughed down at her with eighteen-year-old glee. "How d'ya want it, Cricket? Hanging? Poison? I could drown you in Puget Sound. I got it! Death by machine gun." Rearing back, he proceeded to mow her down with an imaginary Uzi.

She pummeled him with her fists. "I told you I couldn't parallel park. I'll pay to have it fixed. Will you please just don't tell my mother. And for heaven's sake, don't tell Daniel!"

Then she had laid her head upon his shoulder and he closed his eyes in shock—not at her hair that was perfumed with the change of seasons or her softness that reminded him of honeysuckle blossoms or her breasts that would have filled his hands exactly. He was shocked at the violent pooling of blood in his groin. A breath from her would send him over the edge.

He hardly remembered how he'd gotten out of it without making a fool of himself. Perhaps he hadn't. For almost as long as he could remember, he'd been making a fool of himself over Allyson Wyatt, and he had never stopped loving her. And he'd be damned if some paint-and-body man was getting his hands on that truck!

"What you don't understand, Jess," he said as Sam and Jack pasted a sudden solemnity upon their grinning faces, "is that the Beast is an antique. What we have here is a classic, an artifact. Those dents are history."

Picking up his gear, R.T. balanced his duffle lightly on his shoulder and gripped his scuba equipment. "It's an unnatural act to screw around with history, Jess. Have a beer for me. See you in six weeks."

As the other men of the unit piled into Jesse's Acura, R.T. unlocked the Beast and climbed into a world that was totally his own. Here the silence was absolute, like the bottom of the sea. His camaraderie with his men was washed away and he was once again R.T. Smith, the loner, the maverick who had haunted the Seattle docks and hustled for a dollar, the son of Reavis Smith.

With a twist of his key, the Beast roared to life. R.T. smiled bleakly. The body of the Beast might be prehistoric, but he had rebuilt the engine with his own loving hands.

He reached into the glove compartment and removed a well-handled, peeling photograph. Allyson smiled radiantly back at him, wearing her going-away suit at the wedding. In a guilt-ridden moment years ago, he'd sliced Daniel off with his pocket knife, leaving only her. The photographer had captured the gold of her hair, the music of her laughter, and he could hear it now, silver and sweet. *Allyson, Allyson.*

The Acura torpedoed out of the lot, and R.T. looked up. Jack O'Banyon was leaning out the window, his black arms waving as he pierced the air with a whistle. Pretending to laugh, R.T. waved them on, but the whistle lingered in his ears, echoing on and on and on....

Standing at the corner of a street in Angola, dragging mechanically on a cigarette, a young enlisted man is waiting to cross. Behind him are two other men, both Americans, both Marines, both young. Without warning, rockets are bursting around them. A magazine is emptying its ammo amid a high cacophony of bullets overhead. Before the eyes of the three men, buildings begin to go down. Automobiles explode. Streets erupt. A school is blown to pieces. Cries of children rend the air. Stunned into action, the first young Marine throws down his cigarette and plunges into the inferno of the school. In seconds, flames shoot to the power lines overhead.

At Camp Pendleton, when R.T. was twenty-one and sergeant's stripes marked his sleeve, the military doctors told him, "Flashbacks are perfectly normal, sergeant. In time they'll take care of themselves. Try to be patient."

But on the parking lot of the Sand Point Naval Base, patience was a little hard to come by for Major Smith. After Allyson and Daniel had married, R.T. had left the old neighborhood and signed up for his first tour. The hard regimen of the marines had appealed to him. He could turn off his mind and put his body through punishing discipline, and nothing in his past seemed to matter. A civil war in South Africa? A nasty one that would affect the world?

Perfect. He volunteered straight out of boot camp and shipped out for Angola, an underling attached to a detail of advisors.

In Angola, R.T. witnessed unbelievable suffering, but it didn't affect him. Nothing would ever affect him again, he swore. He wouldn't love, he wouldn't hate, he wouldn't feel, he wouldn't think.

"What the hell?" he told Archie Swan. "We're not even here. Right?" He wasn't going to get all screwed up like GIs had in Nam. No, not him, no siree.

And then he was standing on the street corner and rockets were blowing up the school.

Exactly how he and Archie had gotten into the thick of it was unclear. R.T. only remembered running back and forth through the rain until he couldn't run anymore, crouched low, as if by getting his head down far enough, he could avoid the artillery. He lost track of how many children they carried out that day. They simply ran until they couldn't run any longer. He carried them until he could no longer feel his arms. Sometimes they died there, in his arms, their blood staining his shirt and their hearts silent and still.

A man always knew. There was no weight like the weight of a lifeless body. He laid them gently beside the street and went back for others, pulling them from beneath the rubble while mothers ran screaming from their houses and knelt upon the ground and tore their hair, keening for their babies.

Archie had been caught across the legs by a burning timber. It was as he was trying to free Archie that R.T. was struck from behind. He didn't remember getting shot or shrapnel peppering the backs of his legs. He didn't know when the corpsmen got Archie out. Or himself.

Later, they started calling Angola another Vietnam. And worse. R.T. asked the commanding officer if he had to accept his decorations.

"If you want to have a career in the Corps, you'll accept," he was told.

So he accepted the stripes and became a sergeant and worked himself up to major. He had stood at rigid attention to receive his glory at the expense of dying children. He never discussed the shame he felt, not even with Archie. There were no words, no tears, only the flashbacks.

Now R.T. shook his head clear. The taillights of Jesse's Acura were winking at him from faraway as it pulled out of the lot.

Smiling briefly, caressing the photograph with his thumb, R.T. replaced it, not in the glove compartment but in his wallet. Then he groped beneath the seat to locate a bottle of Jim Beam whisky. Spinning off the cap, he tipped back his head and let a long rush of liquor sear his throat. He sucked his breath between his teeth and replaced the cap. As the whisky smoothed the edges of his nerves, he focused on the other side of the chain-link fence, where one of the skinniest, scrawniest pups he'd ever seen was creeping along the wire, sniffing out a scrap to eat.

The dog didn't look like much except a mutt, but by the size of his feet he would be a big mutt—if he didn't starve or was picked up and put to sleep. He pawed and sniffed through the clutter that had blown against the wire. Unsuccessful, he dropped to his frail haunches and looked around.

Well, hell! Driving off the lot, R.T. parked, stubbed his cigar and walked back to the fence. When the pup saw him, it hunkered down and shivered, whining.

"Hey, Manny," R.T. said gently, stooping and holding out his hand and letting the frightened pup cautiously sniff him out. "What's happenin'? You lost, hmm? Or don't you have anywhere to get lost from?"

Already the dog had collected enough sorrowful expressions that a man would have been a monster to resist.

"Quite an act you've got going there," R.T. said, and grinned when the animal was finally confident enough to venture out and wag his tail.

"There you go," R.T. said.

The dog whined, and R.T. made the fatal mistake of picking him up.

The pup sat neatly in the palm of his hand and wiggled beneath his chin for warmth. "Well, so I'm a sucker. Maybe I'm even a little drunk. We'll blame it on Jim Beam and the rain."

R.T. dumped Manny into the truck, and the dog promptly scuttled under the seat. "You remind me of someone I used to know," R.T. said as he drove down the street, mufflers rumbling, and paused for a traffic light. "Hang loose, Manny. Everything'll be okay."

Only Manny's moist black nose showed from beneath the seat, and R.T. drove across town to a loft apartment where he sometimes went to when life got especially hard. A woman answered the door, a tall, beautiful, slim-hipped woman with long hair drawn back from her sleek head. Her cheekbones were high and her eyes turned delicately up at their corners. She took one look at his face, and without a word, stepped from the door and let him in.

Chapter 4

Gossip had it that on occasion some of Grant Melbourne's employees had been known to refer to him as a jerk. Some had even called him a sleaze, it was rumored. Several of the more brave souls had gone so far as to call him a son-of-a-bitch.

No one called Grant anything to his face. Grant Melbourne was president of Global Defense and senior vice-president of Satellite Communications. *Vanity Fair*, when it included Grant in its spread of up-and-coming executives on the West Coast, mentioned that the successful weapons dealer had broken with family tradition by developing Global Defense. Grant's company, the article said, mirrored his personality in that it had outgrown the parent.

The reporter was careful not to estimate how much money Grant was worth, though. Money as old as Wade Melbourne's was difficult to pinpoint, and money as new as Grant's was gun-shy.

The real truth about the Wade fortune was that the bulk of it was beyond Grant's grasp, willed to Grant's step-mother, Joan, who had become Wade's bride when Grant was a mere seventeen years old.

Grant had never doubted why Joan climbed into his own bed the minute she returned from her lavish Parisian honeymoon: insurance. Joan liked to have the bases covered. Wade was never to know, she told him, that he had married one of the most expensive call girls west of the Mississippi. No one was to ever know, and if Grant was especially good and no one found out, baby would be rewarded with candy.

Over the years Grant never betrayed Joan's secret. Yet after the reading of the will, he wondered if Wade hadn't suspected that he and Joan were cuckolding him. Eventually it ceased to matter, and though Grant chafed at Joan's tight hold upon the purse strings, he nonetheless continued to haunt her bed. He was determined to retire a multimillionaire at fifty. He had four years to go.

At ten o'clock in the morning, on the thirty-second floor of the Melbourne Tower, Grant Melbourne stepped from his office into that of his secretary and considered Amelia Wickes's slim ankles. He sometimes wondered why he'd never had an affair with Amelia. She was the perfect secretary—blond and discreet—and he happened to know that she kept a small packet of prophylactics hidden beneath her ink pad in her righthand desk drawer. Besides that, she loved opera, as he did.

But today Grant's ulcer felt as if Mount Saint Helens had taken up residence in his stomach. Even Amelia's dainty ankles had lost their appeal.

"Hold my calls, Miss Wickes," he said irritably as he headed back to his office.

"Yes, sir." Amelia Wickes followed him with an adoring expression on her pretty face.

That was why he'd never made a move, Grant thought as flames bathed his stomach. Amelia was too nice, too willing. Nice was for friends, not lovers.

"That's a lovely bracelet," he said, and pressed his abdomen with a wince.

"Oh, thank you, Mr. Melbourne." Amelia beamed as she lifted her wrist so that the antique coins twirled beguilingly from their chains. "My mother—"

"Is there any Maalox around?"

"Right away, Mr. Melbourne."

"Thank you, dear."

Letting the heavy door click shut, Grant moved soundlessly across his carpet toward the Jacobean desk that loomed as big as a battleship. He allowed only a few carefully selected pieces in his office—an antique pedestal near the draperies on which sat a priceless, carved jade urn; a Vermeer on the wall opposite the window; his framed diplomas: one from Stanford University and another from Harvard.

He adjusted one of the frames a millimeter and picked up a small framed snapshot that had been taken a few months before Wade's death. Joan was holding a piece of cake to Wade's mouth. At fifty, she wasn't a particularly beautiful woman, but she had the most remarkably preserved body Grant had ever seen.

Grunting with discomfort, the price a son paid to break with the tradition of a prestigious father, he waited until the ulcer settled down. He removed a tape player from a drawer, placed it beside the telephone and dialed a number.

A feminine voice answered, and he said curtly, "Put Joan on." Then, when she answered, "Can you talk?"

"Go ahead," Joan said.

Grant dropped a tape into the slot and pushed a button. Lowering the telephone, he turned up the volume so that the conversation between Daniel and Allyson Wyatt was distinct.

When the conversation ended, with Allyson agreeing to find some unheard-of Marine and Daniel being cut off, he returned the receiver to his ear.

A thin line of sweat had beaded his upper lip. His palms were clammy. "What do you make of that?"

"I want to see you," Joan snapped angrily. "Don't keep me waiting."

Wade Melbourne and Orin Randolph had traditionally organized the drive to raise money for the Children's Rehabilitation Center. Allyson's annual duty was to attend. When she was eight months pregnant and had just filed for divorce, she danced the last waltz with Grant.

The Christmas Eve benefit had been held at the Lake Highland Country Club that year, and a ballroom of floor-to-ceiling mirrors made the chandeliers come alive with their thousands of dripping crystals. Here the most elite, old-monied women in Seattle twirled beneath them in their Chanels and Galanos and Pauline Trigeres.

At her table with Kaye, Allyson found the occasion unbearably tedious. Her mother's friends kept strolling by and patting her hand and murmuring, "Poor dear." With Joan on his arm, Grant sauntered over, resplendent in his tuxedo and red-velvet cummerbund. Joan kissed her, and Grant adjusted his cufflinks and asked her to dance.

Lunging to her feet, Allyson blurted, "I'm divorcing Daniel. I filed yesterday."

Grant's smile rivaled Joan's diamond choker for sparkle. "Does that mean you don't want to dance?"

"It's my fault," she sighed as Grant led her onto the glittering floor where they chuckled about the logistics of combining her pregnant middle with his tall frame and three-quarter time.

"I thought it was a good marriage," Grant said.

"A mistake from the beginning. A person should never hold on too long."

"Well—" leaning back, he laughed down at her "—I have to say one thing for your timing, sweetie. It's a pain."

"Oh, you noticed, did you?"

Grant pressed his cheek against hers. "Daniel may be a genius, Allyson, and his name alone could get him a place on any university staff in this country, but he'll never cough up child support. You'd have to swear out a warrant. Let's face it, you're on your own, sweetie."

Allyson made a whimpering sound. "I've had to move back home."

"Oh, God," he groaned.

"Exactly."

Then he had held her at arm's length and asked, "Would you like a job at Global?"

Allyson had looked at him as one who had just obtained proof-positive that Santa Claus lived.

As she now drew a circle around the number for the U.S. Marines in the yellow pages, Grant strolled into the computer room. He was, Allyson thought, as handsome now in his single-breasted Aubert suit and candy-striped shirt with a silk square peeping from his pocket, as he had been that night at Lake Highland Country Club.

But his timing couldn't have been worse. She hastily copied the Marine's number on a scrap of paper and sat creasing it with her fingernails as he came through her door.

His sweeping glance took in the manuals strewn over the floor and her desk, which was in chaos. His eyebrows made her cringe. Grant was such a stickler for neatness.

"Well, well," he said, laughing as he struck a handsome pose by bracing his hips against her desk. "I hear you've been having a little trouble. I adore your hair."

Pulling a clownish face, Allyson playfully threw her pen at his head. *Please leave quickly.* "Don't rub it in, you monster. Let's see you shampoo at one o'clock in the morning."

"Things must be worse than I thought." He polished the onyx of his pinky ring on the lapel of his suit.

"That isn't possible."

"You're considering joining the Marines."

Glancing down at the number she'd circled, Allyson felt her cheeks turning crimson. "Well," she shrugged, "you know what they say to do when you're desperate, Grant."

In unison, they chanted, "Call in the Marines."

"They are looking for a few good men," she giggled.

"Honey, no one could ever mistake you for a man."

"Keep talking, Grant." She grinned. "You get better as you go along."

Their laughter was more than the joke deserved, and Allyson's smile threatened to dissolve as she raked her fingers through her dirty hair. She considered explaining everything, right down to her suspicions that Daniel was at the bottom of her trouble with Bolten. But Daniel's panic was still ringing in her ears.

Please, please go. "About Bolten..." she began uneasily.

"No need to explain." Giving her hand a reassuring pat, Grant retrieved her pen from the floor and replaced it in its holder. He gazed over the computer room outside, which was teeming with people, most of them women who angled wishful, feminine glances his way.

"I haven't the slightest doubt that you'll fix it, Allyson," he said. "Who did you put on it?"

"George, mostly. He helped me set up the file. But Phoebe's working on it, too. You know, Grant, Global is much too vulnerable. I've always said so. Too many people use these files. There's no way I can put decent security on them."

"You should probably change what you have, though. What d'you think? You're the expert."

Melting back into her chair, Allyson plucked her lower lip. "I've already started. We'll reconstruct Bolten from what we've got on tape. In the meantime, maybe I can figure out a way to debug it."

"But not today." He fixed her with an affectionate grin. "Today, you're tired."

Allyson laughed. "That's the understatement of all time."

"Take the rest of the day off." Taking out a pair of nail clippers, he removed a sliver of skin and snapped them shut. "Phoebe can hold things together."

Surprised at his generosity, considering the circumstances, Allyson shrugged and pointed to an empty chair. "Sit down, Grant. No, on second thought, take my chair. Would you like a pint of my blood?"

He laughed. "Good blood?"

"The safest around." She groaned in mock chagrin. "Grief, it is ever safe."

Grant looked at her as if it didn't surprise him. "What I really came for was to ask you to lunch."

In her nervousness, Allyson had picked up the telephone book and she held it to her chest in surprise. "What?" she said, confused. "Sorry, what did you say?"

Peering deeply into her eyes, he flashed one of his thousand-watt smiles. "Lunch, my darling. You know, lobster salad? Glass of wine? No prices on the menu?"

Allyson frowned. Grant Melbourne never asked underlings to lunch. Besides, he didn't eat lunch; he attended power luncheons.

"The truth is, Grant..." She had no wish to offend.

"No matter. Lunches are a drag, anyway." His chin strained at the knot of his tie. "Oh, I meant to tell you, if the Justice Department should ever contact you—"

"You know they did. Some guy named Lord called me, asked what I did here, all that."

"What did you tell him?"

"Nothing. I don't know anything about defense contracts."

"It's such a drag to have Global's name in the paper all the time."

"Better Justice than the IRS."

Chuckling, he adjusted his cufflinks. "That's true. How's Michael?"

Desperate for him to leave now, Allyson began collecting the computer manuals. "Better since I put him in a gifted children's school."

"That's what happens when two people like you and Daniel have children. You're just asking for trouble. At least Kaye's there for you. Allyson, why don't you and Daniel come over to the house for dinner?"

Flabbergasted, Allyson dropped the manuals to her desk. "Grant—"

"Let's say...eight o'clock?"

She felt as if she had missed a step. "Grant, what's wrong with you? Daniel and I are divorced."

He closed his eyes in horror. "How could I be so stupid? I'm sorry. Then, tell Daniel I asked about him, the next time you see—"

"I don't see Daniel all that often, Grant."

"Oh? I thought you kept up with him quite regularly."

"Not really."

"Allyson, you really aren't looking well to me."

If she looked like Grant was making her feel, Allyson thought, she looked ghastly. What was the man's problem? Why did he persist in talking about Daniel?

She shook her head. "I'm just tired."

Taking her shoulders, he pulled her emphatically to her feet. "Then it's settled. You take the day off, and more, if you need to."

"But—"

"Take off the rest of the week."

"But—"

"I insist, Allyson. We've got a rough time ahead of us if this grand jury gets a wild hair. I can't afford to have you getting sick. Do as I say."

She nibbled her lip. "Are you sure?"

His smile was blinding as he smoothed his suitcoat and tucked his silk tie beneath its lapels. "Absolutely. George and Phoebe can always call if they need help. And I'll drink to your health at lunch."

Before she could protest, he was backing away from her desk, waving at some of the girls nearby. On his way out, he stopped at their desks and flirted the proper amount, then moved on. Admiring smiles followed him to the door. Once there, he turned and waved.

"Give Joan my best," Allyson called lamely from her partitioned doorway.

"And if there's anything you need . . ."

As he was opening the door and stepping into the corridor, Allyson had a sharp sense of alienation. Phoebe and George were staring at her. She waited for . . . what? The other shoe to drop?

It didn't matter. Nothing mattered right now but getting ahold of R.T. But that she would do at home, and she swiftly fetched her coat, shoved the number of the Marines into a pocket and touched base a final time with George and Phoebe. On her way out the door she kept hearing Daniel's words: "R.T.'s got to come and get me out."

Out of what? she wondered as she struck the elevator button with a gloved fist.

Madison Street, where Allyson lived, had been nicknamed "Widow's Peak." It was a friendly old birch-lined avenue with swing sets in the backyards and geranium planters beneath the stoops. Almost to a brownstone the surviving spouses had grown up listening to the fireside chats of FDR. Most of them, gray-haired and house-slippered, rented out their rooms in various combinations of walk-up apartments and singles.

After her divorce, Allyson had considered living with her mother permanently in Emerald Hills. But Wednesday nights of eating Kaye's curried chicken and listening to her brother's unrealistic aspirations were enough familial dues, she'd decided.

So she coughed up the rent each month along with Michael's expensive tuition. She consoled herself that no matter how much she disliked working for a weapons manufacturer, she could at least park her ten-year-old Mercedes at the end of the day, climb the wide steps of the brownstone, turn her key in the lock and disappear from the world into the 1940s, right down to the light fixtures and toilets that worked by pulling a chain.

This afternoon she paused only long enough to pick up her mail inside the front door. It consisted of a bill from Michael's school, a bill from the dentist, a bill from the garage for installing new brake drums on the Mercedes and a bill from American Express that reflected two round trips to Atlanta.

Depressed, she looked back as her landlady's door opened.

"Allyson, my dear," Doreen exclaimed as she clutched her crocheting and peered over the rim of glasses that had slid to half mast on her nose. "Whatever is the matter?"

Elegance was not a word one would ever associate with Doreen Penn. Her clothes, though nice and well-made, looked like a banana peel trying to conform to a pear. Her hair waged an unflagging battle with its pins. Losing twenty pounds might have helped, but Doreen was an excellent cook. She often turned up at one door or another with a tureen of soup or a casserole that she "just happened to have left over."

Allyson consulted a mirror that hung above the table where the mail was placed each day. "What? With me? I don't look that bad, do I?" She saw nothing more alarming than the general dishabille that had stared back at her from the plate-glass window in her office.

"You're home in the middle of the day," Doreen said, and poked her incorrigible hair with a crochet needle.

"Yes, well . . . I went to work in the middle of the night." Allyson pulled off her gloves and shoved them into her pocket, then unwound a long trailing scarf from her neck. "My boss took one look at me and said his insurance premiums would go up if I stayed any longer."

"Then I forgive him for getting you out of bed at one o'clock."

"Grant means well, Doreen. He's just out of touch. Can you believe he forgot that Daniel and I are divorced?"

Leaning over to sniff one of the chrysanthemums on the table, Allyson sneezed. *Please don't gossip today, Doreen.*

Doreen plucked a tissue from her pocket and thrust it at Allyson. "Well," her tone dripped bereavement, "you won't be burdened with Grant Melbourne much longer, will you, dear? And you won't have to live in this old, run-down brownstone. You'll be moving into one of those glass-and-chrome things in Atlanta where no one knows your name."

"Doreen—"

"You haven't told Mr. Melbourne, I suppose? That you're leaving us?"

Dropping her chin to her chest, Allyson shook her head. "Today was not the right time to announce anything, Doreen, much less resignations."

"I wish you weren't moving."

Allyson sighed. "Please don't start that again."

"I know, I know." Doreen retrieved one of the tissues she'd given Allyson and bravely wiped her eyes. "Life goes on. And you'd be foolish to turn up an opportunity like

CNN. But it'll be like losing my children when you and Michael do go away.''

As Doreen broke down into sobs, Allyson folded her arms about the woman and patted her back. ''You're going to have me crying in another minute if you don't stop this, Doreen. Everything's going to be all right, you'll see. That Ellen Whoever will be a lovely tenant. She'll adore your eggplant casserole and you'll adopt her. I promise.''

''Go along, then. Have a hot bath and a nice cup of tea. I'll bring you a salad I have left over from lunch. Can't have you coming down with a sinus, can we, just when you're getting ready to move?''

With a laugh and a shake of her head, Allyson kissed Doreen's cheek and waited until the woman's door clicked shut before she dashed up the stairs at top speed. Once inside her apartment, without removing her coat or turning on the light, she leaned against the door, her heart a trip-hammer. *Hey, it's okay, Cricket. It's okay.*

Her apartment was in the process of being torn apart for the move, but it was organized confusion. The contents of the bookshelves were being packed and neatly labeled. The kitchen cabinets were being emptied. Dozens of boxes that were already labeled were stacked wherever there was walking room.

The phone was hiding behind a stack of books. Finding it, Allyson placed it earnestly upon *Webster's Collegiate Thesaurus.* What magical power did R.T. possess that he could loom so eternally in her mind? Since the wedding, she could count on one hand the times she'd seen him. How did he infect her with some paralyzing expectation so that she seemed to be waiting for something? Waiting to hear his laughter again? Waiting to see his crooked smile that could melt her heart?

At the last second, her nerve failed.

''I don't need this, dammit!'' she said, and strode defiantly across the room, jerking the drapes open. ''I don't need it and I don't want it.''

But even the sunshine betrayed her by having died. Heavy with bleakness, she found the number of the U.S. Marines in her coat pocket and knelt before the stack of books again. After ten minutes of being transferred to one office after another and after covering the whole piece of scrap paper with doodling, she finally obtained R.T.'s home number and scribbled it down.

Her palms were sweating now and she punched a three instead of a four. She struggled for a deeper balance and then stopped breathing altogether when a receiver clicked.

"I'm sorry," R.T. said, his sandpapery chuckle clashing across her existence like a sword hungry for blood, "things are their usual war zone around this place. If you'll leave your name and number..."

Crumbling, Allyson squeezed her eyes shut. No, no, no....

The beep at the end of R.T.'s message brought her back, and she straightened with a stern resolve and wet her lips. Before she could speak, however, a strange man's voice came on the line.

"Hello?" it said.

"Yes," Allyson said and blinked like a politician who's been unexpectedly asked to take a stand. "I'm trying to find R.T. Is...well, I mean, is he not there?"

"No, but he's due home pretty soon. Tonight, actually. Would you like to speak to Liddy?"

R.T.'s grandmother was still alive? She lived with him? "No, no, thank you. That's all right. I can...uh..."

"Could I take a message?"

"It's rather complicated." Allyson found her nervous laughter embarrassing and she drew a border of troubled hearts around R.T.'s number. "As a matter of fact, it's very complicated. Who did you say you were?"

His voice was reassuring. Whoever he was, she could see him settling back in a chair and crossing his legs.

"Archibald Swan," he said. "A sort of man Friday. When anything goes wrong, you can always yell at old Arch. Convenient, huh?"

Allyson laughed. "I think I need an Archibald Swan around my house."

"You do a lot of yelling, do you?"

"No, but something's always going wrong. You live with R.T.?"

"For the past ten years." Implied was, *But I've never talked with you*.

"You must work nights, Mr. Swan. I woke you. I'm sorry."

"I'm a veteran. Disabled. And the name's Archie. Mr. Swan is some white bird and Archibald is one of those geezers who runs the bingo game down at the American Legion."

The word *disabled* flashed a whole new series of pictures into Allyson's mind. "I'm sorry, I didn't mean—"

"Pardon me if I'm out of line, but this wouldn't be Allyson, would it?"

Allyson's knuckles whitened. R.T. had told this man about her?

Her voice cracked. "Ahh, look, Archie..."

"Tell you what. I'll hang up. You can redial and talk as long as you need to. I'll tell R.T. to listen to the machine first thing. How's that?"

The apartment was very still, very foreign. Reality was no longer here but was somewhere in the past, in racing clouds and R.T.'s strong, brown back in the sun.

"The truth is, Archie," she said, "I haven't seen R.T. in a long time."

He laughed. "I know the feeling. We don't see him very much around here, either."

"I really don't have the foggiest notion of what's going on in his life. I mean, we sort of grew up together, but then I got married and lost track, you know? He's doing well, I suppose?"

"To a Marine, if you're alive, sober and not in jail, you're batting a thousand."

Archie didn't volunteer much information. Over and over Allyson scrawled R.T.'s initials on the paper. "Actually, Archie, I was a little surprised when you answered."

"Are you askin' if he's got a wife, Allyson?"

All Allyson could do was open her mouth. She couldn't make a sound.

"No wife," he said.

Thinking she would be forever grateful that the man couldn't see her face, she managed to eke out, "I, uh . . . I think I'll hang up now, Archibald Swan. Thank you. Thank you very much."

He laughed his wonderful laugh. "You're very welcome, Allyson Wyatt."

"It was nice talking to you," she whispered after she had pressed the disconnect button and sat cradling the receiver as if it were a creature she had accidentally killed and must now bury.

Her heart was drumming in her ears. Beneath her arms, her shirt was soaking wet. Her knees were shaking. She had to go to the bathroom!

She slammed down the receiver and peeled off her coat and fanned herself. After washing her face, she once again faced the telephone in a battle stance. She hated this! And she could only hope that Archie had the good manners not to listen.

Once again R.T.'s sexy voice came on the line. She steeled herself not to care and repeated the words Daniel had given her to say. She stammered her way through a scanty report of her own but wound down slower and slower. What would R.T. think as he heard *her* voice? Had the things he'd told Archie been kind or vengefully soul cleansing? Did he remember drawing her down on the seat of his old truck, the way she had hungered for his lips and placed her hand inside her blouse?

"Don't ask me if he's exaggerating," she said in a desperate rush to finish. "You know Daniel. But something happened before he hung up. I don't know what. I think he's in trouble this time."

When it was done and she had fastidiously avoided touching on their stolen time together, Allyson wondered if she hadn't, in sidestepping them so widely, magnified the memories and brought them into the present.

It hadn't been her fault! she wanted to shriek—the failure between Daniel and herself. No one had tried harder to make a marriage work. She couldn't be blamed. Could she?

Oh, yes. Much blame. "I wish I could drive you to your knees," Daniel had said when divorce seemed the only way out of their mutual tragedy. "Then you'd know how much you've hurt me."

She sat in a boneless huddle on the floor. With irrational vengeance, she wadded R.T.'s phone number and threw it at her coat.

But there were some recompenses that could not be delegated, there were some sins that could not be transferred. Her decision, when it came, was amazingly calm. Certain that her guilt over Daniel was not disproportionate, she redialed R.T.'s number.

She drummed her fingers until the announcement was finished and the beep sounded. Quickly, before Archie could come on the line, she said, "R.T.? This is Allyson again. Forget that other message—I'm going to Nakatak myself," she said as the strength of the decision poured nervous energy through her. "I'll be all right. I'm sorry to have troubled you. Uh . . . thank you. I mean, good luck. Bye."

Hanging up, she called her mother. Trying not to alarm Kaye, she barraged the woman with ludicrous lies of why she had to make the trip—SCI's hopes to develop a better satellite system; Grant's need for her to research.

By the time she groped along the top shelf of her closet and found a black nylon bag, tossed it onto the tousled bed and crammed garments into it willy-nilly, she was sure she was doing the only thing left. Once and for all she had to place "paid in full" on the debt she owed Daniel Wyatt.

Part Two

Chapter 5

When Allyson stepped off the plane in Anchorage, she had three choices. She could experience a nice, dignified Aunt Pittypat swoon. Or a mild heart attack. (Dying wasn't out of the question.) Or she could turn around and go home.

People were *everywhere*! Wall to wall people—standing, sitting, spilling into the aisles and packing the walkways. College students were sleeping against the walls using ski parkas for pillows as they waited for standbys. Stubble-bearded roughnecks were chain smoking as they tried to return to the North American Pipeline before the bad weather. Worried businessmen in pin-striped suits clutched attaché cases as they stood in line for telephones. Homesteaders, lumberjacks, priests and Third World entrepreneurs were battling to make connections—a kaleidoscope of seething humanity, all of them desperate to fool Mother Nature.

On the flight up, when everyone talked in hushed tones about the weather, Allyson had told herself that her white fur hat would be adequate. Her long Judith Leiber coat, though not new, was perfect. Her calf-length skirt was toasty wool, and her green silk blouse, the exact shade of her eyes, had long sleeves and a high collar. Her boots were tough suede lined in shearling and her gloves, Portolano. And, a vital point, she hadn't left home without American Express.

Now she was jostled from behind and stepped on by a man wearing a clerical collar. "Watch—"

"Sorry." Without looking at her, he darted away.

A woman passed, prodding an Eskimo toddler who was dragging a life-size Winnie-the-Pooh by one arm.

The child peered over her shoulder at Allyson with dark, knowing eyes.

Smiling sympathetically, Allyson quickened her pace. Olsen Tracking Station, she had been told, was reached by way of Talkeetna.

She fixed the clerk with a no-nonsense stare and asked about train service. "You mean the train doesn't even go to Talkeetna today," she exclaimed when she heard the news. "But this is an emergency!"

The clerk looked perfectly innocent until she smiled. "Everything's an emergency today, madam," she said, and showed sharp little vampire's fangs. "Look around."

"When does it go?"

"Anchorage to Fairbanks on Saturdays and Fairbanks back to Anchorage on Sundays."

Sighing, Allyson had visions of Daniel's body stretched out on a slab in a morgue. "Great."

"An air taxi would be your best bet. If you can get one."

An air taxi? Planes might be to Alaska what yellow cabs were to New York City, but any two-star movie buff knew the chances of a New Yorker catching a taxi during rush hour.

Allyson hurried to another booth. A well-combed gentlemen who looked as if his name should be Willingham Havendash Van Steed III, told her that there, indeed, was air taxi service to Talkeetna.

"But the weather, madam," he politely advised, and gestured to the window that was dripping condensation, "is becoming prohibitive, as you can see."

Allyson arranged a seasick smile.

He appeared willing to overlook her vast ignorance. "Bush pilots are an option, madam. A rather remarkable breed of men who accomplish, so I've been told, some rather incredible things. It might be to your advantage to give them a try."

"How would I go about doing that?"

He caressed the flawless part in his hair. "Charter pilots are out of my department. You may acquire a list of them at the next window."

"Thank you." Allyson began shuffling away.

"But one really should exercise discretion, madam," he warned. "Just because a pilot is on the list doesn't necessarily mean he's certified. If you wish that information, a list of certified operators is available from the Federal Aviation Administration."

"Thank you very much."

"The Federal Aviation Administration *is* my department."

Allyson wearily retraced her steps and lowered her head belligerently.

He smiled politely. "I also have the telephone number of the Flight Standards Division. You might call rather than go downtown."

As Allyson took a harder grip on sanity and stuffed her gloves into a pocket, rummaging for a paper and pencil, he produced a gold Cross pen and a pad with Anchorage, The Crossroads Of The World embossed on one side. Preparing his hand with a series of maddeningly slow circles, he wrote down a number in script so perfect it could have been printed by a machine.

"If you change your mind and want to go downtown," he generously informed, "that address is 701 C Street."

Before he could write that down, too, Allyson slipped the list from his hands. "I'm sure I can remember it."

"Very well, madam. Will there be anything else?"

There really wasn't unless, in his lavish efficiency, he could tell her that Daniel was alive and doing well. Or unless he could hold back the weather so she wouldn't waste precious days of her moving preparations. Or unless he could miraculously replace the Bolten file in her computer. Or erase the echo of R.T.'s dusky voice that echoed in her head.

As she was turning, the public address system boomed, "Allyson Wyatt, Allyson Wyatt. Will Allyson Wyatt please call the operator? Allyson Wyatt, please call the operator."

Daniel! Her heart somersaulted. It *had* to be Daniel! He was all right. Thank heaven!

"Allyson Wyatt, that's me!" With a laugh, she looked over her shoulder at the clerk.

"Very good, madam," he said, and laughed with her.

No sooner had she reached the house phones than a voice said over her shoulder, "Ma'am, are you Allyson Wyatt?"

"Oh!" Dropping her bag upon her feet, Allyson tipped up her face.

The black patch covering his left eye was the first thing a person saw. Its straps were fastened into a blond, naturally curly Afro. His one good eye was brown, not much older than her own, and she had the distinct impression that the patch wasn't because he was blind but because he was scarred; a terrible burn started at his temple and spread partway across his cheek.

The scar and patch lent him enormous charm. His rawhide boots, the kind movie costumers invariably found for leading men in swashbuckling movies, were splendid with his jeans and leather bomber jacket.

"Who wants to know?" she asked with a grain of suspicion; his one eye was flirting shamelessly.

"Steve Grosvenor." Swiping a knitted red cap from his head, he stuffed it into a back pocket and thrust out a large, friendly hand. "I had you paged."

"Ah. Have we met, Mr. Grosvenor?"

"No, ma'am." He grinned and said the magic words, "I'm a pilot."

A pilot? But she hadn't even called one yet.

Allyson scanned the clerks at the opposite side of the terminal. Apparently Steve Grosvenor had a lucrative private arrangement.

"Actually," she said carefully, not wanting to blow a good thing, "I've been advised to make sure any pilot I hired was certified by the Federal Aviation Administration, Mr. Grosvenor."

He chuckled. "You've been talkin' to Percival."

"Who?"

"Percival Hamlish. The old codger at the counter who looks like he should be knighted."

"Exactly." She laughed, then sobered. "Yes, well..." She swept up her bag. "He said that a pilot would have to be starving or crazy to go up in this weather. Which are you?"

"Both." He touched his eye patch the way some men would stroke a mustache. "And call me Steve. Would you like some coffee?"

As if they had been friends for years, he reached for her bag and slipped it from her arm onto his. A possessive man, Allyson thought as she trailed alongside him. But irresistible.

They wound up at Chicken Lickin', where fresh coffee and fried drumsticks competed with packaged food, hamburgers and french fries at the next booth. He glanced at the food prices of both places.

Allyson stopped in her tracks, confused. "I'm sorry. I don't have time to eat, Mr. Grosvenor."

"Steve."

"If I don't reach Nakatak before the weather moves in, I'm in trouble. I have to be back in Seattle by day after tomorrow."

"That's really pushin' it, Miz Wyatt. Nakatak's landing strip is for sh—well, it's not very good. Are you sure you don't want somethin' to eat?"

"Just coffee, thanks."

"Gotcha."

He deftly ordered two coffees and two tissue-wrapped drumsticks from one counter and three granola bars and two Tiger Milk bars from the other. He also bought two cinnamon rolls that he stuffed into a side pocket while he poked everything else into any pocket he had available.

"But you *could* land at Nakatak, couldn't you, Mr. Grosvenor?" Allyson asked.

"Ma'am . . ."

From his pocket—the only one he hadn't placed food into—he removed a wallet and gave it a flip of his wrist. A vinyl packet of credit card holders unravelled halfway to the floor. They contained flying credentials from the U.S. military to federal organizations to private commendations.

His look asked, Good enough for you?

Amazed, Allyson made a sound of apology and said, "I'm impressed."

His smile didn't rub it in. He congenially added, "If it's got a square inch of dirt, ma'am, I can land on it." He elbowed them some standing room at a food counter. "The military's got a decent strip up at the tracking station."

"Well, there you are!" She laughed with relief.

He emptied three packets of sugar into one of the coffees. "Sugar?"

She shook her head.

He unwrapped a cinnamon roll and politely offered her a bite before wolfing it down. "Rather unsharing people, the military," he said, and neatly wiped his hands on a napkin.

Figuring he was holding out for some terrible amount of money, Allyson dropped her shoulders in a sigh. "Then it's back to square one, I guess."

He didn't reply.

You wouldn't have treated R.T. this way! she thought in exasperation, and began trudging off like a failed dragon slayer.

His voice trailed after her. "I gotcha, I gotcha." He was tossing away clutter when she looked back, and coming toward her, hastily blotting his mouth. "But I want you to know goin' in, the landing could get a little rough."

"Then we have a deal?" she said.

"You don't want t'talk money?"

"Are you going to rob me blind?"

"Oh, no, ma'am."

"Then we have a deal."

"I'll check the weather. You wait right here." With his last candy bar, he stabbed at the place where she was standing and made a backward, long-legged retreat into the terminal, raising his voice as he went. "Don't wander off and get lost, Miz Wyatt. In this crowd, we wouldn't find you till spring."

"Gotcha," she mumbled under her breath.

After a half hour, Allyson was resigned that she had, by some revolting innocence, been hornswoggled by the man. She hurled her coffee cup into the trash, and her place at the table was immediately filled by a young Japanese man with a diamond in his ear.

"Damn you, Grosvenor," she sputtered, and doggedly began retracing her way to Percival Hamlish, seething with every step. "And damn you too, Daniel, for getting yourself into this mess in the first place. You, R. T. Smith, most of all."

Steve Grosvenor loomed abruptly in her path and Allyson gasped. "You didn't stay put, Miz Wyatt, ma'am," he scolded mildly, and wagged his finger.

She could have punched him. "Mr. Grosvenor," her boot tapped the floor impatiently, "is money your problem? If it is, name your price. The sky's the limit."

"Miz Wyatt—"

Reaching into her bag, she groped for her wallet and, finding it, snapped open her checkbook. "How much?"

"Miz Wyatt—"

"If you'd rather have cash..." She pulled off the cap off her pen with her teeth.

"I gotcha, Miz Wyatt, but—"

She spat the cap into her hand. "I can get cash."

With a dashing flair, Steve Grosvenor swept off his red cap in surrender. "What I've been tryin' to say, ma'am, is that it's all been arranged. Talk to that man."

Even as Grosvenor pointed and Allyson spun around, some sixth sense told her that in this churning potpourri of humanity, R. T. Smith would be elbowing his way toward her and the waters would part before him.

She knew she would look up and see his arrogant, loose-jointed stride, his cocksure smile and his blue eyes chasing hers like heat-seeking missiles. He would be strolling back into her life as if he'd never left it, and there would be nothing she could do, nowhere she could escape, nowhere on God's earth that she could hide.

She clutched her pen as if it were some magical promise that could deliver her from herself.

But it wasn't, and it didn't. He occupied more space than she remembered. He seemed taller, more rangy with his duffle slung lightly over his shoulder and his head towering above everyone else's.

A mustache framed his mouth now. His long hair was gone, in its place, a cross between a lanky wallpaper brush and a curry comb. Its black ends spiked in all directions beneath a camouflage cap that was settled emphatically on his brow.

His name was stenciled across a fatigue jacket that swung open: MAJ. R. T. SMITH, USMC. Beneath the jacket, a navy sweater hugged a waist that was as trim as it had been fourteen years ago. The jeans were gone, too. In their place, sharply creased cammie pants were tucked into aggressive, lace-up military boots. Virility was in every muscle that moved—driving but harnessed, barely.

Yet, it was the mileage on his face that made Allyson's mouth go dry, a lived-in face of hard, thrusting cheekbones and harsh hollows, one that had seen too much. Major R.T. Smith was a man's man now, and while he might do hard things in the name of duty, he was not a man for sale. Anyone who ignored that would do so at their peril.

As he came to a stop, he scooped his cap from his head and stuffed it into a hip pocket.

"Well, now," he drawled as he looked from her head to her toe and back up again, "what have you gone and done, Allyson Randolph Wyatt?"

His duffle slid, unheeded, to the floor.

"I'm not sure," Allyson said, and she had a sudden desire to turn and run.

When he leaned forward and grazed her cheek, the kiss was so brief it almost didn't exist. "You've grown up on me."

Allyson's hands tightened their desperate hold upon the pen. How foolish she'd been not to predict this. If Daniel had wanted R.T.'s blood, R.T. would have asked where he could spill it.

"Did you think I would stay a girl forever?" she said, matching her smile to his.

He grinned. "All I can say is, as much as I liked the girl, the woman is fine, Allyson. Really fine."

"Well, you haven't changed much either." She urgently busied herself with her bag, returning her pen and her wallet. "You're just as outrageous a flirt as you always were."

"You think so?" Chuckling, he returned his duffle to his shoulder and opened his other arm in an invitation that she should walk alongside him. He sent Grosvenor a tacit signal. "At least I don't turn that pretty shade of pink when I receive a compliment."

Was she blushing?

"Neither do I—" she indicated that she could manage her own things "—when I receive one."

He tipped back his head and laughter poured out of him, so richly, so infectiously, people who were passing glanced with envy. *But you don't know!* she wanted to shout at them. *This man broke my heart!*

"There are some things you can always depend on," he said as his laughter dwindled into a lazy chuckle. "Have you talked to Daniel since you called me?"

Allyson shook her head and couldn't believe that this was the famous greeting she'd imagined—how R.T. would vow that his life had been no good without her, how he would mourn that he'd been a fool and how he would do anything if only she would forgive him and give him one more chance. He wasn't devastated at all, the bastard!

"Where're we going?" she asked.

But he had turned aside to say something to Steve about ceilings and whiteouts. When he looked back, he peered up at a rank of terminals to make note of arrivals and departures and checked his wristwatch, a heavy one designed for underwater use.

"I can only assume that you didn't get my last message," she said.

His consideration was quick and sizzlingly thorough. "I got all your messages."

"There were only two, R.T."

"Really?" His arm drew her out of the way of two pilots. "I would have sworn there were more."

Allyson stopped in the flow of traffic and people had to walk around them.

"R.T. . . ." Her poise refused to stay intact. "This is why I put that last message on your machine. I can do this on my own. I appreciate you coming, I really do, taking time from your furlough, but I—"

He pretended to miss the point entirely. "I was glad to do it."

"But—"

"Archie caught me at the door the minute I walked into the house. He said you two had a nice chat, by the way."

"R.T.—"

"I couldn't believe my answering machine. It made me feel sort of like Luke Skywalker, though, getting a glimpse of Princess Leia and not being able to get the picture back again."

Allyson slumped with dejection. His mind was made up. Nothing would change it, certainly not her. Behind them, eavesdropping shamelessly, Steve Grosvenor was smiling. What magic spell did R.T. cast that he could inspire such mindless devotion in men? In everyone?

She pulled a dreary face. "There always was a larger-than-life aspect to you, R.T."

"Not really." For an instant, so quickly she almost didn't see it, the boy flashed through the man. "I let you get away, didn't I?"

Allyson stopped breathing. Why couldn't he have said that fourteen years ago? Why couldn't he have given her the slightest shred of hope before she walked down the aisle in her white gown? Why couldn't he have said, just one time, that he wanted to try?

"I wouldn't worry about it," she said woodenly. "You seemed to have come out with a very healthy attitude, R.T."

"Hell, yes. I'm just chock full of attitude."

A distance away, her small face large with watchfulness, the Eskimo child was sitting beside her mother, swinging her legs and wearily hugging her Pooh bear.

I know exactly how you feel, darling, Allyson thought.

All the way to Anchorage R.T. had rehearsed his speech to Allyson—the fourteen-year-old one about how she had him all wrong, about how he wasn't that long-haired punk anymore who had roared down her street in the Beast and appalled her staid, highbrow neighborhood. He was a Marine, he would tell her, an officer and a gentleman.

Not exactly, but he was, as the saying went, a man of means now. His farm was free and clear, which wasn't bad for the son of Reavis and Eva Smith. He had friends and family. He had the reputation of being a man to be reckoned with. He was even considered, in some circles, to be a catch.

But the rehearsal hadn't taken into account opening-night jitters. Things were written on Allyson's face that he hadn't been prepared to read. He had looked into her eyes and seen the mistakes of his youth traced in the fine lines that framed them, his own rash behavior in the nervousness of her hands.

Déjà vu kept placing him back in the Beast when she'd stood outside the door with the moon plundering her hair, her pride dripping blood. They had been young enough then to believe that life would work out and dreams would come true. Hadn't she promised to haunt him for the rest of his days? Well, she had, far and above her wildest expectations.

"I've been right behind you," he told her now as they weaved their way through the crowded terminal. "The whole way. I called Steve to find you and hold you here until my flight could arrive. I chartered a plane immediately."

Astonished, Allyson glanced at Grosvenor, who had heard his name and taken it as permission to step up and join them. "You mean," she pointed from one to the other, "you two are..."

"Only a small conspiracy, Miz Wyatt," Steve said, and patted his jacket for something to eat.

She pulled a grimace. "A real powerful union you've got going, Mr. Grosvenor."

"We're rather proud of it."

With one eye for the weather and another for the pilot's irresistible charm, R.T. disengaged himself from the banter, but after a few minutes, when it showed no sign of waning, he drew his eyebrows bluntly together.

"Shouldn't you be checking the weather or something, Steve?" he mumbled.

But Steve wasn't seeing past the sparkle in Allyson's emerald-green eyes. Bending, he scooped up a magazine that had worked free of her bag.

Allyson all but gave the man a curtsy. "Why, thank you, Mr. Grosvenor."

"You're welcome, ma'am." Grosvenor unpeeled a candy bar and offered it. "Wanna bite?"

She laughed. "Thank you, no."

R.T.'s temper began to simmer. Steve, the jerk, was grinning at Allyson as if he'd fallen into a vat of whiskey.

"Steve," he said.

"The weather's okay, Skip." The pilot leaned closer to Allyson. "About the way I left you standin' at Chicken Lickin', Miz Wyatt. I was afraid to explain for fear you'd think I was a lech or somethin'."

"You?"

Allyson's laughter was so lyrical that R.T. envisioned his hands about Grosvenor's neck.

"A lech?" She pulled a face. "Come, on."

"Hey, fly-boy," R.T. growled. "The weather?"

She laughed. "Compared to the men I usually deal with— and we're talking major lechery here—getting stood up at Chicken Lickin' is one of the highlights of my life."

Steve's one good eye was smitten. "What kinda fools live in Seattle, anyway?"

"Grosvenor!"

Being no fool, Steve looked at R.T., held up his hands and stepped backward, nearly treading on a woman who was pulling a cart of shopping bags.

She called him a jerk and told him to watch where he was going. "Pardon me, madam." He doffed his red cap. To Allyson, he said, "Miz Wyatt, ma'am, it's been a slice. If it's all the same t'you, Skip, I think I'll just mosey on over and check on the weather. And I'll put in a call to Olsen while I'm at it and see if our man got there."

Before Allyson could say a word, the pilot had located some chewing gum in his pocket and had struck out for parts unknown.

The silence, after he had gone, left Allyson and R.T. with only their past between them.

"You'll have to forgive Gros," R.T. said dryly as they were forced to move out of the way of loading courtesy carts. "The man's shy. The thing about it is, if you encourage him, he gets over it."

But Allyson's effervescence had disappeared, and he couldn't get it back. Why couldn't she laugh so easily with him? Why couldn't she come running into his arms as she had on a fragrant autumn day when the wind was blowing her hair around her face like a gold silk shawl and lifting her skirt and helping it between her legs?

"You really shouldn't have gone to the expense of chartering a plane, R.T.," she was saying with a dull formality. "You know this could be one big wild-goose chase. It could be nothing more than one of Daniel's moods."

"Maybe. But I couldn't take the chance. Could you?"

"I'm here, aren't I?"

"Oh, yes. You're here." She was very here. But then, she wasn't here. Quickly, he added, "You didn't give me much on the tape."

"There wasn't much to give. Daniel was talking and then he stopped. Someone was there. I could hear men yelling, but they couldn't hear me and I didn't have a number to call. There was nothing I could do."

"Daniel keeps in close touch with you?" A drop of sweat had found the curve of R.T.'s spine.

"Daniel gets in touch by breaking into the security on my computer."

"Our Daniel's a clever lad."

"Computer security is a joke with Daniel."

"Really?"

"It's his style of macho. Except that this time he took a file."

"I didn't know that was possible."

"Oh, Daniel can do that." Her awkwardness was momentarily forgotten and she spoke as if the years separating them did not exist. "You know, R.T., I got the idea he was trying to tell me something. I asked him what, but he started asking about Michael and . . ."

Her shrug was full of self-blame. R.T. wondered if she knew that Daniel still loved her. A woman had to know. And how did she feel about Daniel after all these years? They shared a son. Even when two people stopped living together, the bonds of children weren't broken. Too, she was here, out of her element, dealing with unwieldy odds simply because Daniel needed her. If he were in Daniel's place, she wouldn't have come for him.

What the hell difference did it make? Their own history was written in blood, and that was his fault, not hers.

"How's Michael?" He stared broodingly at the door where Steve had disappeared beyond them. Their steps had become slower and slower.

"He's fine."

"I always wanted to come see him, Allyson. But it was . . . you know, awkward."

In the wonderful way of mothers, she mellowed and asked shyly, "Would you like to see a picture?"

R.T. laughed. "You think I'm suicidal? Of course."

Stepping out of the way of three hurrying stewardesses, luggage trailing like pets on a leash, she moved into the protection of a pillar near the windows. She rifled a zippered pocket of her bag, flushing as she removed the magazine.

"I thought it was here..." She tucked the magazine beneath her arm and her pen between her teeth, then shifted everything to the other arm until she finally located her wallet. "Ah..."

Removing the pen from her mouth, she flipped the wallet to a compartment of snapshots and held one extended.

R.T.'s throat felt as if he'd swallowed a stone. Taking the picture, he stood nearer the window and moved his thumb across the figure of a thin, gangly youngster with gleaming blond hair and Daniel's beautiful, fair features. Michael had the same clear-eyed intelligence as Daniel, the same high forehead, the same sweetness as his own photograph of Allyson in her going-away dress. But his frailty made his joints seem too large for his frame. He was wearing shorts with a drawstring and a shirt with a Space Needle decal on the front. One of his socks had drooped toward the top of a white, high-top sneaker.

He should have been our son, R.T. wanted to say, and catch her close. *I should have been there when he was born. I should have held you.*

"He's great, Allyson," he said around a painful, unwieldy knot in his throat.

"He's six now, you know."

Pride was golden on her face. Unexpectedly, R.T. remembered when she'd tossed her face up to the summer sun, her hands on her hips, laughing as he plowed up through the waves and waded ashore, dripping, his soggy bathing suit plastered to his body so that he dreaded what she might guess or what Daniel might see.

"Yeah," he said. "First grade, huh?"

"He's a genius."

"Naturally."

An airliner took off nearby, and the roar gathered momentum as the power vibrated beneath their feet. She tucked a mother's sweet smile into her collar and replaced the picture.

"He's shy, though," she admitted. "He doesn't make friends easily."

"He'll grow out of that. I did."

Her laughter was silver, embracing him. "I'm not talking about spray painting obscene words on the school water tower, R.T."

He hadn't forgotten being suspended from Cardinal Heights for three days for spray painting the humorous obscenities. Maintenance had had to repaint the thing. Chuckling, he almost feared to speak for fear of breaking the spell.

"You remember that, do you?"

"R.T., all of Cardinal Heights remembers that."

She unbuttoned her coat and shrugged out of it. As he helped, R.T. found himself suddenly confronted by the backs of her legs and her hips—slopes and curves that he could but imagine, and their nested secrets that brought the swift taste of desire to his lips. She was no longer the slim, tomboyish girl who'd raced up and down the Sound, clad in the bikini that had set him burning. She had ripened. She was a woman with all her consummate temptations.

A violent tremble gusted through him. Muscles ridged along his back, tight with tension.

She retucked a silk blouse into her skirt so that it smoothed artlessly over her spine. He remembered dropping kisses upon that spine!

Turning, she looked at him with such unwitting honesty, her eyes reflecting his secret lust, that R.T., in an effort to calm himself, plowed his fingers through his hair in an explosive gesture.

"You know, R.T.—" her eyes danced as she rose on her toes to skim her palm across his wild stubble "—it doesn't have to stay like this. There're things you can do. Marvelous new products—shaving cream and razors—are coming onto the market all the time."

Before he could stop himself, he caught her and pulled her to him. Her bag jostled his side. Her lips parted in surprise, and she leaned back against his arm, her wide eyes curious, her lips pinkened.

"God, you're pretty," he whispered.

Her hand slipped from his hair as if she'd touched something hot. Before she could escape completely—what did he have to lose?—he caught her hand. "We have to deal with it, Allyson," he said quickly, as he replaced the hand on his jaw. "It hasn't gone away. You know it hasn't. If it hasn't gone away in fourteen years, it's not going to."

Her protest was a series of tiny gasps. "I don't know what you're talking about."

"You know exactly what I'm talking about. It's in every breath you draw, Allyson, every look you give me. You haven't forgotten, and I damn sure haven't."

She tried to conceal her alarm, but it only made her more transparent. Unshed tears sparkled as she dropped her hand.

Unhappily, R.T. let her go. He dropped his duffle and patted the front of his jacket until he located his cigarettes. Lipping one, he replaced the pack, thumped the cigarette on the lighter and gave the lighter a flick.

"Who's keeping Michael?" he said, knowing he could not follow where she had retreated inside herself.

"My mother." She stared gravely at another jet taking off, penetrating the cloud cover that was becoming more and more threatening.

"Ah, Kaye. Our very own." Kaye Randolph was living proof that he could truly never rise above his beginnings. "And how is your dear mother?"

"Don't start, R.T."

"Me? Start something?" He tipped back his head. "Hell, I like a good thriller. Keeps the fear up."

"Your manners haven't changed, either, I see."

He picked a shred of tobacco from his lip as she stared at the white cylinder between his fingers. "You?" He looked from the cigarette to her. "A vice? I don't belive it. Allyson the Pure?"

"I was never that pure." Pulling off her fur hat, she gave her head a shake so that a gilded cloud swirled about her head and shoulders.

"I thought you were," he muttered.

"Well, now you know."

He offered her the pack, but she shook her head and found a pack of trail mix in her bag. She nibbled a piece of coconut.

"Tell me something, Major," she said.

"Shoot."

She opened her mouth, then closed it again.

"What?" he prompted.

She shook her head. "You'd just yell at me."

"Yell? Me? Nah, we're not married."

With a smirk, she threw an almond at his head and missed. "Actually, that's what I wanted to ask you about."

"If I'll marry you?" He grinned. "Absolutely. I was hoping you would ask."

Her frown was shyly coquettish. "Why *didn't* you get married, R.T.?"

As he stooped for the almond, R.T. thought how easy it would have been to marry after he returned from Angola. Life could get halfway tolerable when you had a few medals. Bankers who'd once shut you out could be eager to loan you money. Women with a quarter-millon in diamonds circling their throats could invite you to parties. Some could even ask you to stay.

"There's no need to look at me like that," she said with a defensive huff. "It's a legitimate question."

"I just didn't get married, that's all," he mumbled testily, and tossed the nut into the ash tray by the wall. It was none of her business.

"I always wondered why you enlisted without telling anyone," she mused. "I mean, right after Daniel and I got married."

"You think I joined because of you?"

"I didn't say that."

A series of flights was announced and neither could speak over the reverberation. She fanned herself with her hat. Her blouse matched her eyes. The tiny seed-pearl buttons that locked its front would prove difficult for a man's blunt fingers. His blunt fingers?

"I wasn't going to college," he said guardedly. "Why not join up? Why did you divorce Daniel?"

Flicking him a non-smile, she turned her hat over and over in her hands. "You know the answer to that."

"I only know what Daniel told me."

"He wouldn't lie."

"Would *you*?"

"What?"

"Lie to me?"

"About Daniel?" She threw a shank of hair back from her face but refused to look at him. "No."

"There's something I want to ask you," he said, and stubbed his cigarette. "You don't have to answer if you don't want to."

The look she slid him was detached, regal. "I'll answer any question you ask."

"Do you...do you ever imagine how it might have been like between us if you and Daniel, I mean...if you two hadn't...?"

There was a saying about how only those you loved could make you suffer. Everyone else could only be nasty. But there wasn't a saying, R.T. thought, for the exquisite pain of seeing someone whom you loved suffer because of what you had done.

Allyson had turned to stone. Tearstains glistened upon her cheeks and her regret consumed R.T. with guilt.

"I shouldn't have said that," he said quickly, damning himself. "Forget I said that." He stretched his hand to her face but let it hang suspended, not daring to touch, not daring to say what he felt. "It's all right, Cricket. It's..." He shrugged helplessly. "It's all right."

With sudden ferocity, she blinked away her tears. As jets screamed across the sky, she caught up her hair and twirled it into a rope that she coiled savagely about her head. Before it could fall, she yanked on her fur hat and proceeded to stuff tendrils viciously beneath the furry rim.

"Oh, you do such have a habit of saying that, R.T." Her voice dripped venom. "And it never is all right. Never."

He didn't deserve this, R.T. thought. Not now. Not after he'd forced himself to keep away all these years. Not after her divorce, all those thousands and thousands of times he'd

wanted to call, even to write. He'd given her what she
wanted from him. Which was nothing!

"Oh, I don't know," he said, and placed a terse military
space between his feet. "You haven't done too badly for
yourself, Allyson. Except for the divorce, you have everything you want—your yuppie life-style, your uptown job,
your smart little red Mercedes." He squinted. "Michael's
fancy private school."

Staggered that he should know such things, she gasped.
"You spied on me!"

R.T. closed his eyes. He was renowned for his control. No
one got to him. Then why did this one woman invariably
send him over the edge?

"It wasn't really spying. I knew you moved out of your
mother's and into the house on Madison, that's all."

"I suppose my mother told you that?"

"Not exactly."

"Oh." The sides of her mouth tipped mockingly. "I see."

"No, you don't." He sighed unhappily. "I called her,
Allyson. Hell, I told her I was taking a census for a city di-
rectory and asked for you. Like some kid. And she believed
me. She said you didn't live there anymore."

"How interesting."

"I picked out a couple of the best schools around, figuring that you'd put Michael in a good one. I watched them
until I saw you pick him up one day. Then I followed you
over to Madison."

From the public address system came more flight an-
nouncements. More than one angry voice was arguing with
an agent. Steve Grosvenor was coming down the corridor
now and, turning to find them, waved that everything was
in order. Signaling with a salute from the bill of his cap,
R.T. indicated miserably to Allyson that they must go.

In silence they walked toward the hangar that was sepa-
rate from the accommodations of the big jets. There was no
field manual to help him survive battles like this one, R.T.
thought. He was caught in a one-on-one with the person he
least wanted to fight.

"Did Daniel tell you?" he said, knowing she would misunderstand and needing, on some bitterly familiar level, to make her share the pain he was suffering. "Did he tell you that I have a son, too?"

Chapter 6

The single-prop airplane crouched on its snow skids inside the hangar, looking, R.T. thought, like a prim spinster with two vents for eyes, a cold red hub of a nose, and a small, astonished mouth.

Steve sat at the instruments in the cockpit, talking to the control tower. Men in thermal jumpsuits moved about, their boots echoing through the vast, cathedrallike space. They would wheel the plane around so it could taxi onto the runway.

Allyson had soaked up dejection like a stowaway and was standing some distance apart, her slumped shoulders making R.T. feel, as he mirrored her moroseness, as gray as the burgeoning clouds outside.

He shouldn't have spit out the news about Kahn as he had. That she still cared enough to react didn't make him feel better. He should have explained his family—those folded, spindled and mutilated rejects he had taken to the farm: Liddy, his grandmother, whose mind was slowly slipping away; Archie, who had left his legs in Angola; and Kahn, whom he'd found at the VA hospital after the boy was taken off a Cambodian refugee vessel bound for North America.

Grosvenor was climbing out of the cockpit to check the landing gear.

"Hey, bud," R.T. said glumly, walking up.

They both glanced at Allyson, still at a self-imposed safe distance.

"Hey, yourself," Steve said as he squatted to inspect the plane's chocks. He rubbed grease between his fingers and sniffed it.

R.T. squatted, too, as if they were old-timers about to share a chew of tobacco and swap tales about marauding Indians. "Tell me more about what the Tracking Station said about Daniel Wyatt," he said.

Steve plucked a shop towel from his hip pocket and methodically wiped his hands. "Pretty well what I told you and Mrs. Wyatt, skipper. Wyatt's all right, but since there was a shooting, they're not about to give out any information until an investigation's been made."

"It doesn't figure." R.T. raked at his mustache with his lower teeth. "Daniel's a bookworm, a real cerebral guy. It's just not logical that he should be involved in a shooting."

"Well, you're not going to find out anything from Olsen. You know the military."

R.T. grinned. "Bitter, bitter."

"What d'you mean, bitter? I'm not bitter. I just think it sucks, that's all."

R.T. laughed, then deflated as he viewed Allyson's inaccessibility. He cleared his throat and tugged his nose. "Ahh...hey, I, uh...I'd like you to do something for me, Steve."

Swiveling, the pilot drew the patch from his scarred eye as a teacher would consider a troublesome pupil. "Oh-oh."

"Tell 'er she can't come, Steve."

"Cripes, skipper!" The pilot straightened, his curls missing the fuselage by inches. Stuffing both hands into his front pockets, he hunched his shoulders and considered Allyson with a frown.

R.T. drew in the cold, acrid smell of the hanger, the diesel and grease and solvents. It wasn't too much to ask. They had gone through boot camp together—Steve and Arch and himself. When the gasoline engine had blown up in Steve's face, he and Arch had been beside his bed when he'd come to. Steve was a brother-in-arms.

He absently retied a boot lace. "All she's ever heard from me is no. I can't tell her she can't come." He rubbed at a smudge on his boot, then looked up. "But it would be easy for you, Steve."

"Sure," Steve retorted, and mauled the patch over his eye. "I like pulling the wings off butterflies."

Rising, R.T. walked to the open hangar door. Clouds were thick, their undersides swollen with snow. Across the runways, the lights of the main terminal were diffused in the rain. This part seem more distant somehow, more cold. They could have been some lonely space station on another planet.

Allyson had turned up her collar and was stealing glances. When she caught him looking, she jutted her chin and skirted the grease stains on the hangar floor, heading straight for the plane.

Steve had climbed into the cockpit and was talking to the control tower again. She stopped beneath his window, and when he poked his head outside, she said, "I want to get in."

Hesitating a moment, Steve nodded. "Watch the slippery steps." Extending her a hand, he hauled her up into the copilot's seat.

Feeling a pique of neglect, R.T. stuffed his cammie cap into his pocket and strode toward them. Allyson was rubbing the pane of the tiny window. She was laughing, but her laughter faded as she saw him.

R.T. jerked open the door and waited like a sizzling parent. *Gee, thanks, Gros. You're some help.*

"We're running out of daylight," he grumbled, and reached behind Allyson for her bag.

She had folded her foot underneath to sit on it. How many hundreds of times had he watched her sitting so, her long skirt swirling to the floor? Maps filled her lap. From a portable tape player in the back, Waylon Jennings was nostalgically singing "Luckenbach, Texas."

Sourly R.T. heaved his own duffle into the back. "Being out at night in a snowstorm in one of these little jobbers isn't my idea of a good time."

"There isn't any real danger, is there?" Allyson quickly inquired of Steve, eyebrows aloft. "I mean, aside from the usual?"

"Well, let me put it this way—" Steve's good eye winked as he pushed his headset aside "—if a regular pilot was going out in this soup, I'd say he was suicidal. But me? Ole Flyin' Jack? The Red Baron, himself?" He held up a thumb. "Piecea cake."

R.T. wanted to hit them both. Why couldn't Allyson trust him as easily as she believed the pilot?

When he held out a hand, she blinked at it as if he were an enemy soldier offering a grenade.

"What?" she said, incredulous.

"You have to get out now, Allyson." He clasped her hand firmly.

Bristling, she jerked free. "Oh, no you don't." She shook her head emphatically from side to side. "I'm going with you. Steve?"

Steve, lilly-livered coward that he was, became conveniently involved with the controls.

"Come on, Allyson...." R.T. cajoled.

Her jaw was set with a stubbornness that R.T. was no stranger to. "I'm not getting out of this plane and that's final." She gripped the seat so hard he wouldn't be able to pry her loose with a crowbar.

R.T. placed a military space between his boots and planted a fist on each hip. "I knew you were gonna give me a hard time about this."

"A hard time! I'm not one of your greenhorn recruits, R.T. I happen to be grown up now, in case you haven't noticed."

"I noticed."

"Yes, well . . ." Her sniff was aloof, regal. "I'll get in the back."

A spasm of temper ripped through R.T. as she prepared to climb from the copilot's seat to the cramped space behind. That he should now be forced to spread out their past failures before Steve Grosvenor was an even larger embarrassment.

"My *job* sweetheart—" his syllables had a biting edge "—is to keep greenhorn recruits alive. Something you obviously haven't given much thought to. This weather isn't playing around."

"Neither am I, Major!"

"Allyson, honey—"

Passion blazed in her eyes, turning their green to the shade of damp moss. "I'm not your honey, R.T.!" Bitterness furred her voice. "So save that for the mother of your son!"

"Oh, brother," R.T. complained softly to the hangar's cathedral ceiling.

When he looked back, she was jutting her chin, daring him to push her an inch farther. He briefly considered the possibilities of knocking her flat with his fist, but he clasped her wrist instead and dragged her out of the cockpit. In a display that he would not have forgiven in anyone else, he forced her to slide against him all the way to the floor.

Her hat tipped askew and fell at his feet. Blond hair spilled about her shoulders. She slammed a boot to the floor. His grin was one of his best son-of-a-bitch smirks.

The flurry had attracted the attention of the men in the hangar.

"I suppose that makes you happy!" she hissed, and pushed back a burnished tangle from her face. "Hmm? Major Smith? Tough Marine? Why don't you just pull a gun on me and poke me with a bayonet? Better still, blindfold me. And in case you mistake my meaning—"

R.T. felt like a fool. "Allyson, no one could possibly mistake your meaning."

"Then get this! You wouldn't even know about Daniel if I hadn't called. I could've come up here and you'd be sitting at home, doing . . . whatever it is you do. You know, it never ceases to amaze me, R.T., how you always let Daniel manipulate you. All he has to do is snap his fingers and you jump. He's like Spock doing a Vulcan nerve pinch. One touch and you just keel right over."

Everyone in the hangar was straining to hear the delicious argument between the pretty lady and the meathead Marine. R.T. wished he had never told Allyson about Kahn, and he wished he'd never said she couldn't come. He wished he didn't know anything about her and was a million miles from here.

"Darlin'," he said softly, and stalked her more doggedly against the plane, "far be it from me to contradict an intelligent, pedigreed woman like yourself, but you happen to hold the keeling-over championship of the world when it comes to Daniel Wyatt!"

"Pedigreed!" She tossed her head in mutiny, and her hair whipped her jaws. "I guess you've forgotten," she whispered with rancor, "why it was that I married Daniel, you, you—Rathmore Tennyson, you!"

Before R.T. realized it, he had grabbed her face with his hands and was looming over her. "Allyson—" he gritted his teeth "—I'd take it as a great personal favor if you wouldn't call me that."

"I am going to Nakatak." She gouged his name that was stenciled on his jacket. "So stick that in your cammie cap, Major, and—" she turned down the sides of her mouth "—and nerve pinch it."

Wasn't he to be forgiven one lapse of control? After years and years of taking crap from the military, wasn't he to be excused one small vindication? With a grip of her shoulders, R.T. swung her back when she turned away. He propelled her, stumbling, to the opposite side of the wing, where the fuselage afforded them a wedge of privacy. He pushed her into the corner and kept her trapped there, and when she attempted to shove him, he pinned her arms to her sides.

"What d'you think you're doing?" she whispered angrily.

"What does it look like I'm doing? Making an ass of myself. Now shut up."

Allyson didn't know whether to laugh in R.T.'s face or shrink into a dust mote and disappear. She had to be insane to harp at him like this. This man wasn't the long-haired hellion she could tease and browbeat and haggle into submission. He wasn't a memory or an ache in the middle of the night. He was a tough, strong-willed man who was perfectly capable of getting his own way, and as he pressed her, she wanted, illogically, to stop the craziness of what they were doing. She wanted to rise up on her toes, to run her fingers across the angry bristle of his mustache and whisper for him to please not be mad. She wanted to say it was good, so terribly good to see him after all these years, and she wanted to cling and press her face into his neck in one last memory of folly.

Her eyes found his stormy blue ones. "Why do we always do this?" she whispered. "Why do we snap and snarl?"

His breath shuddered as the planes of his face grew soft. His look was not one of anger but one of immeasurable longing.

Blood pooled inside her, low and throbbing until she was alive in a way that frightened her.

"Before I go to get Daniel," he said gently, "I have to explain about my son, Allyson."

She didn't want to know about his son. She didn't want to think about him loving another woman that much, of him coupled with a woman and holding her as he spilled his body and soul into her.

"His name is Kahn," he said.

Shrinking against the fuselage, she stared blindly at his name on the fatigue jacket. In her fantasies, she had never imagined this part. "Kahn is . . . Oriental?"

"Cambodian."

Cambodian! The last thing she would have imagined was R.T. impregnating a foreign woman and not marrying her. The same principles of honor that had driven him to sacrifice her for Daniel wouldn't have let him desert any woman who carried his child.

"You must be very proud," she said, and wanted only to go away now, to lick this most recent wound.

He caught her sleeve as she was attempting to move past. "Look at me," he commanded.

She couldn't. As she walked away, she mumbled, "What you do with your life is no one's business but your own, R.T."

She ducked beneath the wing and scooped up her hat and hurried out into the open hangar.

"Kahn is my adopted son," he called after her.

The ringing words took a moment to sink in. Allyson was already a distance away. Adopted? She spun around and as clearly as yesterday saw the girl she had once been, arching up to take this man into her deepest, most needful center. She saw herself riding him, climbing him, sating herself with his love, and it wouldn't have mattered if a hundred men had been watching as he walked toward her and she began walking toward him.

With a sound that originated somewhere in the past, she ran the last steps and threw herself into his arms. She didn't ask herself why it mattered.

"I'm so sorry, Allyson," he groaned into her hair as it floated about their shoulders in a mist. "I'm so very sorry for everything's that happened to us. I'm so sorry."

With her arms clasped hard about his waist, with her throat bursting, Allyson placed her mouth against his ear. Of all the people she knew, he must understand—this man, this hard, toughened man who knew the guilty secret of her life. He had to know why she must be here, why she must come with him.

Closing her eyes tightly, she whispered the words that she'd never said to another living soul. "He asked me for so little, R.T. I gave him exactly that. It wasn't his fault, it was mine. And the worst sin of all was that in all those years, I never once told him that I loved him."

So, hold me, just one more time, she prayed as her arms tightened around him, *hold me once more and let me find absolution for that sin in you, my darling.*

Deep inside, R.T. felt his heart swelling with pain. He had always known that part of Allyson still loved Daniel. Yet he had hoped—he was such a fool!—that she still harbored something of the love they had once felt for each other.

At this moment, however, in the cruelty of reality, he saw himself for what he was, the son of Eva and Reavis Smith, while she was the daughter of Kaye and Orin Randolph. How pathetic to hope that those two elements could ever mix.

When she pushed free and peered up at him, tears shimmering on her lashes and her lips pale and trembling, she whispered, "I have to go with you, R.T. Can't you see? I have to. You know I have to."

Steve was calling. The prop was sputtering. Time had run out and the sky was growing angry. Daniel's ghost was drawing closer, chains rattling.

"But you're not dressed for what we'll find up there, sweetheart," he argued.

But she was pulling the white hat about her face, her cheeks the color of one of Liddy's pale, pink roses. He would never be able to deny her anything. If Daniel was what she wanted, he had no choice but to see that Daniel was what she got.

He reached out his hand. Her smile was one of brimming gratitude. Then he boosted her inside, threw her bag inside after her and crawled in himself.

"Fasten tight," he said, and hoped he could afford the price he would certainly pay for this. "It's going to be one hell of a ride."

Chapter 7

"Sylvia, darling," Joan Melbourne purred to her private manicurist as they went through their biweekly pedicure, "do be an utter lamb and get me another drink."

From behind the white-fronted villa overlooking Puget Sound, surrounded by fluted columns and a railed gallery and eight acres of immaculately manicured lawn that represented only six of Wade Melbourne's millions, Joan found it hard to remember when Vincent Constanza had taken her off Sunset Strip.

At sixteen, she had been one of the best-paid call girls in the country. Even in the late sixties she had made anywhere from seven hundred to a thousand dollars a client. As Wade's widow, however, she wouldn't be able to pay her cosmetics bill on such earnings.

Sylvia Gifford's smile was a pouty twitch as she poured Joan's drink, and the knock at the door could have been synchronized to rise with the rich color of Louis XIII cognac in the glass.

"Mr. Melbourne," she announced a moment later, and waited to be told what to do.

Like a sleek cat, Joan swung her slim legs from the chaise to the floor.

"Leave us, Sylvia," she said with a flutter of fingers that dripped diamonds.

Entering, Grant Melbourne watched the beautician the way some people would ponder an insect in their path, but Joan was watching Grant. The day when Grant didn't have every hair in place was D day. Grant was more like his father than he knew—gullible, weak. But it wasn't to her advantage to allow him to suspect she thought so, not with the Justice Department poking its fingers into every nook and cranny of Satellite Communications and Global Defense. She needed Grant.

He was pouring himself a glass of straight Scotch and tossing it down. Gasping as it hit his ulcer, he waited several seconds before he tried to talk.

Joan stepped behind an Oriental screen and slithered out of her gown. For a moment she stood naked, reassuring herself that nothing had happened in the last hours to mar her superb body. The muscles in her thighs were still as strong as a girl's. There wasn't a trace of flaccidity anywhere, and she spent most every waking hour making sure it stayed that way.

Still the best around, she thought, and slipped into a pair of tight velour pants and a robe that covered her bosom but flared open from the waist to display the pants.

"You look awful," she said to Grant as she emerged. "I suppose I'm to assume that the problem still exists, that nothing has changed in the last half hour."

"Assume what you like, Joan," Grant growled. "You always do."

"I don't want excuses. You draw your salary so I don't have to listen to excuses."

"Well, you'd better hear this one, my darling, because if we don't solve *this* particular problem, your next one will be deciding what color to paint your jail cell instead of your toenails."

Pursing her lips, Joan kissed the air. "My, my, what a mood you're in. I do hate moods, Grant."

His expression grew ugly as he raked a finger beneath the collar of his shirt. "Tell that to the federal government if we don't find Daniel Wyatt."

The seconds passed with a dangerous energy, and Joan considered the on-going investigation. Global Defense maintained its own firm of lawyers, but lawyers drew the line at some things.

Opening a silver dish, she lifted out a cigarette and thumped it upon the end of the sidebar.

"I'm tired of opening the newspaper every morning and finding Global Defense plastered all over the front page, Grant. If you can't find the proper person to dispose of Daniel Wyatt, I can."

When she lit the cigarette, Grant filched it and took a drag, coughing and meeting her look with watering eyes.

"I had it under control," he declared flatly. "My man was taking care of things. He still is."

"How much does this Daniel Wyatt know?"

"A lot."

"Good going, Grant."

Her sarcasm was a needle in Grant's ribs. "What did you expect?" he stormed. "That Wyatt wouldn't put two and two together?"

"Why didn't you get someone less clever?"

"You don't just pick a man off the street and tell him to bury documents and fix computers so even the government's sophisticated equipment can't find them. It was very involved, Joan. Daniel Wyatt was the only one who could do it."

Joan stabbed her cigarette with a vengeance. "Then why isn't he dead?"

Grant spotted his reflection in the mirror, repaired his hair and straightened his tie. The liquor had made him brave.

"Hackers like Daniel Wyatt don't die, Joan," he said. "They can hide themselves in a computer if they want to."

Joan lay back on the chaise to think. "Your mistake was in not buying him off."

"Men like Wyatt have ethics."

"That's why he agreed to stealing and perjury, I suppose?"

"He accepted a dare. You don't tell a man like Daniel that a machine can best him. He was like a junkie willing to do anything for a fix. He didn't know it was for real."

"I'm sure he does now."

A smirk distorted the edges of Grant's mouth.

Joan poured herself another drink. "Just how much was our markup on the government contracts? Just in case Daniel Wyatt didn't bury them deeply enough?"

Grant spread his hand upon his ribs and closed his eyes briefly. "Anywhere from forty to one hundred percent."

"Then, you'll simply have to handle the problems, Grant. Both of them."

Leaning back, cocking his head at an angle, Grant slid her a disbelieving look and shook his head. "Uh-uh. *Prob-lem*, Joan." He held up a single finger. "One problem. Daniel Wyatt. That's all."

Reaching up, Joan loosened his tie and pulled it free, leaving it looped around his neck. She unbuttoned his collar and, taking hold of the tie, hoisted herself up so that her face was directly beneath his.

"Because you failed the first time, Grant darling, the interest is compounded. We have two problems now."

He briefly attempted to free himself of her. "Forget it."

"You shouldn't get so upset, Grant," she purred, and rubbed his stomach. "Think of your ulcer. You're not a kid anymore."

A pained expression flitted across his face, but Joan knew that he was smelling her perfume. Like clockwork, she could feel desire building in him.

"I never expected Allyson Wyatt, Joan," he blurted nervously. "Not a woman, not Allyson. Find someone else."

"There is no one else," she cooed. "Allyson Wyatt is as much of a danger to us now as Daniel. Tell your man to take care of both. It's very, very simple."

When she licked her lips, Grant twisted aside. "No," he said weakly, his neck darkly stained.

"Yes."

Quite suddenly, he bent his head into his hands and began to sob.

Joan smiled. "It's all right, baby," she whispered soothingly. "I'm here. It's all right."

"No, it's not. And I can't do it."

"You can," she said from deep in her throat. "You can and you will."

Connie Clements's laugh wasn't a giggle and it wasn't a guffaw. It wasn't even a knee-slapping cackle. As half owner of the Bear Cave in Nakatak, Alaska, and being the kind of woman who could clothe her six-foot frame in fringed rawhide, strap a knife to her belt and still manage to look normal, Connie's laugh was an event. It was thunder that rumbled up from her chest and brought her hands down hard upon her thighs so that the sound overpowered the jukebox in the café and the snapping pool cues and the short in the neon sign that hung above the cash register and sputtered Budwei-er Beer.

At such times Herb, Connie's husband, who did the cooking for the Bear Cave, would poke his balding head through the window that separated the kitchen from the rest of the cave. "Everything all right out there, Pussycat?" he would bellow.

Allyson was now standing beside the Budweiser sign, and she winced as Connie howled. When Herb yelled, "Everything all right out there, Pussycat?" Allyson guessed she would go down in history as the only person who didn't appreciate the finer points of the event.

Very little of the past hours had amused Allyson. Hardly had she and Steve and R.T. been airborne than the sky turned from a dirty, late-afternoon gray to a menacing black that swallowed them up.

"We're never going to get out alive," she had wailed when they plummeted earthward for the dozenth time and the wind slapped them around with giant paws.

"Hang on, troops!" Steve had shouted as the plane was finally caught by an updraft with only thirty feet between the fuselage and the treetops. "This is one wild bronco we're ridin'!"

"Don't worry," R.T. assured her devoutly, "once we land, I'm gonna kill him."

Of course, she ended up embarrassing herself, clinging to the one man in the world she should never have clung to and crushing his hand until it would probably never be the same again. When he crawled into the back and cocooned her in his heavy jacket, she burrowed gratefully into his sweater and hibernated until it was all over.

Once they landed, Steve was in maddeningly excellent spirits. He hired a Caterpillar half-track to get them from Nakatak's airstrip to the Bear Cave. Then Allyson, in all innocence, had said to Connie, "We'd like two rooms, please, Mrs. Clements. For one night."

When Connie finally stopped laughing long enough to catch a breath, Allyson made the mistake of trying to explain. "We'll be returning to Seattle tomorrow," she said. "I'm sure Mr. Grosvenor and Major Smith wouldn't mind doubling. You wouldn't mind doubling with Steve, would you, R.T.?"

And the woman became completely hysterical.

Even R.T. betrayed Allyson by leaning his hips against the counter beneath the Budweiser sign, bracing his elbows and crossing his ankles so that he could hide his face between the bill of his cap and the ribbing of his sweater.

"Well, excuse me," Allyson said, and spun haughtily around in search of a more faithful ally, Steve Grosvenor.

But Steve had plastered himself to a wall at the opposite side of the cave. At R.T.'s request, he was calling the tracking station again and had missed the whole thing.

"Hey," R.T. cajoled when Allyson started stomping through the café toward the pilot. "Don't go away mad." He snagged the belt of her coat and reeled her back.

Sniffing, Allyson refused to be mollified. "You aren't helping matters, R.T."

He placed a kiss into the vicinity of her fur hat. "I understand, but please don't tell this woman any more jokes. I don't think I can stand it."

Beneath his jacket, Allyson found enough flesh over his ribs to pinch, and she smiled sweetly as pain passed over his face.

Connie and Herb Clements had opened the Bear Cave in 1981. The business had originally begun by catering to the GIs from the tracking station. Soon it picked up the truck drivers who made the long, fifteen-hundred-mile haul up from Washington state. Since Nakatak wasn't particularly high on the tourists' points-of-interest charts, Connie also provided spirits and female companionship for both.

"Whiskey and women are my contribution to the mental health of the world," she liked to say, and considered it sort of like group therapy.

But now Connie was a spokesman for the whole town. Stabbing at them with her toothpick, she said to R.T., "I'll bet you're up here because of the shootin', aren't you, darlin'?"

Allyson told herself that nothing would be gained at this point by a nervous breakdown. She leaned over the counter toward Connie.

"What happened?" she blurted. "And how do you know what happened when we've called everywhere and can't find out?"

"Honey—" the woman gestured with her toothpick to R.T., whom she obviously saw as one who might be more appreciative of her position in Nakatak "—nothing happens around here that I don't know."

"Well?" Allyson demanded. "How badly was he shot? Is he still alive? Is there a proper doctor in this town?"

Connie's frost turned to ice, and R.T. laid his fingers upon Allyson's wrist.

She shook them off. "What kind of people are you up here?" she railed. "You go around shooting people the minute they get into town, then don't let their relatives visit them?"

"Herb!" Connie bellowed, cupping her mouth. "You better get out here."

"Oh, forget it," Allyson said, and twisted toward the front door in defeat.

Watching Allyson's temper with uncommon interest, R.T. pushed his cap to the back of his head and grinned at Connie as if she were his favorite aunt.

"Hell, Connie," he drawled, "we don't know what we're doing up here. Runnin' around on a wild-goose chase, likely as not. We'd have saved ourselves a whole lot of time and money by simply pickin' out a random number from the phone book and askin' 'em who the most savvy person in town was, and they would have said you—right? Unless I miss my guess, you know what goes down in this town before it goes down."

Connie's smile thawed a few degrees. "Damn tootin', I do, Major. Always have and always will."

Allyson felt compelled to mumble over her shoulder, "It wouldn't have hurt her to tell *me* that."

Connie punctuated her words to R.T. with stabs of her toothpick. "You can tell your friend over there that patience is a virtue."

Allyson wanted to crawl over the counter and rip the fringe off Connie's rawhide jacket, but R.T.'s mustache framed one of his dazzling, chip-tooth smiles.

"You two haven't been introduced, have you?" he said as if he'd known Connie for years. "Con, I'd like for you to meet Allyson Wyatt. Say, do you mind poppin' the cap off one of those Buds for me? Thanks."

Tipping back the bottle of beer so that half the brew sluiced down his throat, R.T. wiped his mouth on the back of his hand with a sigh. He flashed Connie another grin that sent Allyson's pique scaling to grander heights.

"Nice place you got here, Con," he said.

"We like it," Connie purred, and popped the cap on another bottle of beer for herself.

"Bet you're just sockin' those old dollars away."

"Well . . ." the proprietress laughed.

"This is just the kind of place I'd like to get me when I retire." R.T. leaned forward like a conspirator. "You'll have to overlook Allyson tonight, Con. Her nerves are a little on edge."

"I gathered that," Connie heartily agreed.

"Between you and me," R.T. confided behind his hand, "her son is real sick. Somethin' genetic on her side of the family, they say. Poor kid, he could wind up needin' a transplant. It gets real complicated. The man who was shot? He's Daniel Wyatt, the boy's natural father and a hell of a guy, by the way. He's the logical donor, should the worst happen, God forbid. We were comin' up here to find him, Con, just in case. Now all this business with the shooting..." He sighed heavily. "Mistaken identity. It's gotta be mistaken identity. But that happens, right? Daniel's got this face that looks like somebody you think you know. Anyhow, our Allyson's been bearin' up like a first-rate trooper, but every time she thinks of her little boy back there in Seattle, waitin' for his daddy to come home...tsk, tsk, tsk." He shook his head woefully and tugged his sweater down about his hips. "Damn fine boy, Con, damn fine boy."

Fearing that she would either explode with rage or dissolve with laughter, Allyson returned to the counter and gave R.T. a blistering scowl.

"Hon—" Connie took her aback by leaning over and giving her hand a maternal pat "—I just heard about your trouble. I'll remember you in my prayers."

Allyson smiled thinly through her teeth at R.T. and said, "Thank you, Mrs. Clements."

"Don't you worry one little sec, darlin'. Everything'll work out. At times like this, you just have to have faith." The proprietress of the Bear Cave motioned them closer with a crooking finger. "I'll tell you this much, there was gunfire. No, no." She waved her toothpick. "Your little boy's daddy is all right, hon, and that's the truth. This van drives past, see, and whoever had the gun shot the plate glass right out of the Chevron station. It was an awful mess, glass everywhere. They took your poor husband—"

"Ex-husband."

"Whatever. They took him to the infirmary over at Olsen, seein' as how we don't have a hospital." Connie returned to R.T. "Riley's gonna have some of the guys drag the car out of the ditch. It went off just past the bridge. Riley says he'll be good three weeks gettin' glass back in the window. It'll have to come from Anchorage, is my guess.''

"Daniel's all right?" Allyson asked.

"'Course he is, hon. The bullet just grazed his hairline, I heard tell. 'Course, I didn't see him myself, but Clara from the *Times* went over. She's Riley's aunt and an old maid who could probably catch herself a husband if she'd quit wearin' those god-awful shirtwaist dresses. Anyway, Clara said he was sort of vague about what he was doin' up here in that dandy new Porsche. Say, he don't snort up those drugs, does he?"

"What?" Allyson yelped in disbelief.

"I didn't think so, him bein' such a good daddy and all. Listen, you don't worry your pretty head one teensy bit. He's fine or I would've heard by now."

Smiling wanly, Allyson decided that with Connie's present mellow state, it was the appropriate time to ask again about a room. She adjusted her coat and smoothed her gloves.

"You do have a couple of rooms for rent, don't you, Mrs. Clements? For one night? We'll pay whatever you ask."

"Darlin'—" Connie shook her head "—you could have a million dollars, and it still wouldn't change the fact that I'll be feedin' you a week from now."

Allyson looked at R.T. in horror. The first day of her new job in Atlanta was in only *two* weeks. "A week!" she gasped.

"Hey, Herbie!" Connie boomed. "How long're they sayin' the storm'll last?"

"Could be a week, honey-love," came the reply.

The fringe of Connie's jacket jiggled as she chuckled. "A week, hon. I hope this won't mess things up for your little boy."

"What?" Allyson squinted in confusion. "Oh, yes. No, well, I'm sure Michael's...condition won't..." She whirled to face R.T. "They say it'll be a week."

R.T. was thoughtfully scratching his jaw. "That's the word I got, all right. A week."

Allyson could have hit that jaw with her fist.

"I'm just hopin' we don't have a bunch of busted water pipes so the toilets don't flush," Connie was musing. "As for the motel rooms, I can give you..." She held up her toothpick for time out and consulted her registration book. "I can give you one."

Calling the Bear Cave a motel was, in Allyson's opinion, a gross mutilation of the English language. It was a ramshackle café with eight tables and caneback chairs, plus three postage-size log cabins out back. The interior was heated by two gas heaters and a creaky paddle fan that circulated the warmth. Yellowed photographs covered the wall, and most of them were falling apart. Even the label "café" was generous. Connie's Bear Cave was a bar and grill, heavy on the bar.

Too weary to go another step or say another word, Allyson sagged against R.T. "Now, what?"

"What we will not do, my sweet love," R.T. murmured from the side of his mouth, "is look a gift horse in the mouth. Hey, Steve!"

With the telephone receiver glued to his ear, Steve was contemplating the moosehead trophy grinning down at him and the photographs that dated back to the gold rush at Nome in 1898 and Fairbanks in 1903.

"Grosvenor!"

Steve covered the mouthpiece with his hand. "Yo!"

"How're you doin'?"

Waving him away, Steve turned his back and spoke into the telephone.

"Tell you what," Connie offered magnanimously, "seein' as how your circumstances are what they are, I'll give you the best room I got. See Shokie over there at that table? He paid me an extra ten for the Honeymoon Cottage, but he's so drunk already, he won't know the difference. If you pay cash in advance, I'll even knock five percent off the bill and throw in a bottle of champagne. But don't try to eat the fruit on the coffee table. It's fake."

Steve strolled blithely up and said, "Count me out, folks. I'll take my chances at the hangar."

"But you can't do that." Allyson protested. She appealed to R.T. "He can't do that."

"He's a grown man, babe," R.T. murmured, and said more privately to Steve, "What's the verdict this time?"

"Now the CO's gone. The sergeant in charge is too sissy-pants to talk without permission. Say, ma'am, if you don't mind, I'd like a couple of those Milky Ways and a bottle of Bud."

Allyson jammed her fists into her coat. R.T. calmly thumped a cigarette from his pack.

"Try not to worry, darling," he murmured.

Try not to worry, darling? With an explosion that had been coming on all day, Allyson snatched the cigarette from R.T.'s hand, tore it into shreds and dumped it into Connie's ash tray that was made from a bighorn sheep. When Connie opened her mouth to speak, Allyson held up a warning finger.

"Did you know," Allyson said with parodied serenity to R.T. "that the Marine Highway offers a ferry system and steam-heated, cocktail-lounging accommodations and fresh Alaskan salmon on the menu?"

R.T. looked at Connie, who was gaping at Allyson. Letting out his breath, he frowned at a new cigarette, then arched one raven-colored eyebrow. "Was I supposed to?"

Allyson affixed a plastic smile to her face. "I could've taken the ferry." She didn't care that she couldn't possibly have taken the ferry and that Connie and R.T. were sharing looks of pity about how the weeks of strain had proved to be too much, poor thing, what with her little boy and all.

"Some people actually say you should drive through Alaska." She was talking faster now. "Well, Daniel proved the fallacy of that one, didn't he? On the plane, I read that Alaska had everything. Did you know it had everything, R.T.? Jewelry, sculpture, furs, down parkas, mukluks, baskets, gold nuggets, jade, ivory, native paintings? Everything but *freaking motel rooms*?"

She had grown steadily louder and more shrill, but Allyson didn't care. Around this place, loudness was a plus.

"Did I take the Marine Highway?" she shrieked. "Did I drive a car? Noooo. I'll tell you what I did. I flew up here in a kite with a lunatic and almost crashed three times. I came up here and found out that Daniel's lying in a perfectly safe bed and is probably having the time of his life catching up on his PC catalogs. And now I've gotten caught in a blizzard that's going to last a week! *I suppose it's of no interest to anyone that I had plans of my own this next week?*"

Connie looked sympathetically at R.T. while Allyson clamped her mouth and wanted to crawl under the counter. Holding one hand poised over the buttons on the cash register, Connie removed her toothpick and moved it back and forth.

"Last call on the room," she said. "Take it or leave it."

"We'll take it," R.T. said, and clapped his hand about Allyson's shoulders so vigorously that she stumbled forward and caught herself upon the counter.

Connie struck the button on the cash register. And then she laughed.

Chapter 8

The moosehead trophy over Allyson's head gave a perfectly vile grin as she telephoned Kaye in Seattle.

Allyson wasn't sure how much to tell her mother. When she had begun to weave her web of omitted truth to Kaye, she had only been trying to protect her mother. How could she now explain her fiasco? How she had come to Alaska and was squandering her precious moving time and still hadn't seen hide nor hair of Daniel or even talked to him?

Daniel had wrecked his car, had been shot at and was now being held in some kind of protective custody by the military while she was facing what promised to be one of the most harrowing ordeals of her life. The jukebox was blaring "The Race Is On," and through a cloud of cigarette smoke that set Allyson's nicotine craving on edge, Connie's girls were cheering wildly as Steve Grosvenor downed a pitcher of draft beer without taking a breath.

It was best, Allyson decided, to tell Kaye nothing.

"I don't think I can get back tomorrow, Mother." She had to shout over the bedlam, for Steve had said something funny and the walls shook with Connie's laughter. "No,

Mother. I'm in Nakatak, but so is a lot of bad weather. Getting a flight out is hopeless.''

"Speak up, dear," Kaye shrilled. "I can hardly hear you."

Allyson took a fresh grip on her deceptions. "I called to remind you not to tell anyone where I am or what I'm doing."

"Well, if you ask me, Allyson, the whole thing is totally ridiculous. I still can't believe Grant sent you up there, for goodness' sake! You're no technician."

"Would you tell Michael I'll talk to him tomorrow?"

"Don't worry about Michael. He and I are having a fine time. Did I tell you that Daniel's name was in the Seattle papers?"

"Ahh, no." Apprehension took hold of her. "What about?"

"The grand jury. Why on earth would Daniel be testifying against Global Defense, Allyson?"

"The paper said *that*?" Allyson peered over her shoulder, not knowing what she expected to find.

Kaye continued, "The bottom line was that the prosecuting attorney in the case against Global is in a public snit. Personally, I find it very boring. Daniel was the prime hostile witness, and now no one knows where he is. A regular manhunt's going on. They think Daniel may have left the country. Be glad you're not here, Allyson. It's all coming down on Grant."

"Grant! Why Grant?"

"It came out that Daniel once worked for Wade Melbourne. You remember that first summer after you two went away to college? Anyway, some dreadful reporter from channel 3 accused Grant of intimidating Daniel."

So *that* was why Daniel had left Seattle! So he wouldn't have to testify. The intimation that Grant was intimidating Daniel was ludicrous, of course, but someone obviously was.

"What's Grant saying for himself?" she asked, anxious for any scrap of information.

Laughter drifted from Kaye's end of the line.

"What do you think, dear? Grant looked down his nose and asked the reporter who she thought he was, some mafia boss who rubbed out witnesses? Isn't it delicious? He was wearing that camel-colored cashmere topcoat of his, and you know how much he resembles Ken Wahl on *Wiseguy*. Between us, though, Grant, isn't going to come out of this lawsuit looking very good. Even if you weren't moving, Allyson, you'd need to find another job. It goes without saying that Joan is absolutely beside herself."

"Grant needs his friends, all right." Peering upward, Allyson decided she could grow to really hate the moose. "Mother? One more thing before I go?"

"As long as it doesn't involve Doreen Penn. Honestly, Allyson, that woman makes me want to wire her jaws shut."

"Would you check my answering machine? If there's a message from Earl Kolpechy, I need to know."

R.T.'s voice came unexpectedly from over Allyson's shoulder. "Who's Earl Kolpechy?"

With pulses plummeting, Allyson spun around and tripped over R.T.'s boots. It was a collision he didn't appear to mind as he kept her from falling and seized the opportunity to add an involved appraisal of the flesh revealed by a gap in the neck of her blouse to his growing list of sins.

"What're you trying to do?" she gasped as she clapped one hand over the mouthpiece and attempted to fend him off with the other.

He made a kissing motion with his lips. "Are you quite sure you want to know?"

"Allyson?" Kaye's voice was reedy from where it was smothered in Allyson's coat.

Bending as far from R.T. as possible, Allyson replaced the phone to her ear. "I'm here, Mother."

"You sound like you're in a well, dear."

R.T. affixed himself lazily to the wall behind Allyson's back. "Who's Kolpechy?" he asked, and pulled off her hat to blow a stream of electrifying breath into her ear.

"No one." Shivering, she thrust him away with an elbow. "A man about a job. Shh!"

"A new job? In Seattle? Doing what?"

"This is my *mother* on the phone, you idiot!" Allyson hissed, and cupped the mouthpiece as she said into it, "Just a minute, Mother. There's someone here who wants...to use the phone."

Another lie! She wouldn't live long enough to be forgiven for all of them.

"Dear, dear," R.T. murmured as he toyed with her earring. "Your mother. Shall I slit my throat?"

"Why bother?" she sniped. "You've already slit mine."

Chuckling, he rested his chin upon her shoulder. "A most delicious throat." He nibbled it lightly. "I only regret that my name is Von Helsing."

"Allyson—" Kaye's voice was exasperated "—I really think we have a bad connection."

"I need to go, Mother." Allyson strained to keep R.T. at bay. "Just...don't forget my answering machine, okay? And if you can, keep Michael from reading about his father in the paper. I'll explain everything when I get home."

As Kaye hung up, Allyson sagged against the wall, her face pressed to a photograph of two men in fur coats who were posing with gold nuggets for a turn-of-the-century photographer.

Her finger was still pressing the disconnect button, and the receiver was crushed against her bosom. She swore that if R.T. so much as breathed upon her one more time, she would shatter into pieces so small they would have to sweep her out with the snow that was blowing through a crack in the window.

He plucked the receiver from her hands and replaced it, then lifted a lock of hair from over her eyes.

"So," he said, "rumor has it that you're going to quit your job?"

"Word gets around," she muttered dejectedly to the picture frame.

"What'll you be doing?"

"Graphics, if it works out."

"Ah. Sounds interesting."

"It beats the heck out of Stinger missiles."

"You'll keep living where you are, then?"

Not answering, for one more lie would surely reserve her a place in burning torment, Allyson faced him but kept her back nailed to the wall, just in case her legs decided to betray her, too.

He was twirling her hat on his finger like a Globetrotter showing off with a basketball. The café was buzzing with its own momentum now, and much of it was surely about them, for Connie Clements's "waitresses" kept sidling by, their hips swaying in their tight jeans as they surveyed R.T. up and down.

He had to be aware of how much sex appeal he reeked with his cammies and his boots and spiky hair like the Terminator's.

"Correct me if I'm wrong, dear—" his voice was huskily laced with sarcasm now "—but you're not going to tell me about this new job, are you?"

How could she? He would start hounding her with, Why Atlanta, why Atlanta? And then she would start defending herself, and he would wreck her dream as he had wrecked it once before. She had too much invested in this move—many, many dollars. Earl Kolpechy had gone way out on a limb, having turned down Marsha Levine from Fox when the woman's credentials were legendary.

Allyson nervously pushed hair back from her face. "It's not your concern, R.T."

With a tomcat's grin, he replaced her hat on her head. "That's what I like about you, Allyson." He adjusted the angle of the hat. "Your penchant for sweet talk."

Snatching off her hat, Allyson jutted her hip. "Why is it that every time you open your mouth, R.T., I wind up in a crisis?"

"Me? A crisis?" He turned down the sides of his mouth. "Nah. The Highway Patrol, maybe. They've closed the road to the tracking station."

R.T. hadn't been quite sure how Allyson would react to the news. She might be stubborn, but everyone had a breaking point. There were a lot of things he didn't know about her life now, and what he didn't know made him nervous.

She dropped her lashes, and a slow sigh slipped past her lips. "They can't do that."

"They just did."

"But I've got to talk to Daniel. I don't care what they told Steve."

"You're dealing with the military, sweetie. They think they're keeping Daniel alive until he can make a statement. Maybe they are."

Frustrated, she stamped her foot and pressed her fingers into her eyes.

R.T. wondered what she would do if he leaned over and kissed her, right now, here, in the full sight of heaven and Connie Clements.

"There must be something we can do," she said with a shake of her head.

"It wasn't my idea for you to come."

Her eyes snapped open and she lifted her chin, her nose crinkling until she resembled a kitten that had been watching a rubber mouse for hours only to discover that the vigil wasn't working out. With a stamina R.T. had to admire, she pursed her mouth and stood thinking, reevaluating the situation and shifting her priorities. At one point she opened her mouth to say something, but shut it.

Then she huffed a great sigh of resignation and accepted her defeat so gracefully, he wanted to hug her. "We-ell heck! Lead me to this famous Honeymoon Cottage, then, Major Smith. If I don't get a shower soon, I'm going to mildew."

Under different circumstances, the trio of cabins behind the Bear Cave would have been charming. Small, rustic and quaint with their chimneys and porches and hand-carved totem poles that served as posts, they were something that might conceivably have been on a picture postcard.

Parked before two of the cabins were a diesel semi that was hauling Affiliated Food Products and a Bronco with hulking Goodyear snow tires. An electric cord disappeared beneath each hood—heaters to keep the engine blocks from bursting.

The cabins shared the parking lot with the café. Two gas pumps were set off by a sign that flashed OPEN every few seconds. But the flash glanced off the windows of the cabins, looking, Allyson thought, like the beacon in a lighthouse warning of danger, and the sodium-vapor light wasn't doing a good job of lighting the steps.

Steve Grosvenor had returned to the hangar while he still could. As they watched him leave, R.T. murmured that the food on the *USS Jason* didn't look so bad after seeing Connie's menu.

"Herb does all the cooking," he said, and unlocked the cabin nearest the café and threw open the door.

As he stepped back, his duffle thrown over one shoulder and her own luggage draped across the other, a black tomcat appeared from nowhere, bounded up the icy steps and darted between his legs into the room.

"Oh!" Allyson gasped, skidding and grasping on to one of the totem-pole posts to save herself.

"Easy," R.T. said, stepping back to help.

She waved him away as she regained her balance. "No, no. I'm okay, I'm okay."

No sooner were the words out of her mouth than her feet went in different directions again. With an awkward arabesque, she twirled off the porch and landed in a snowdrift.

R.T. sent their luggage sailing into the room after the cat while Allyson thrashed her way out of the drift. He stood over her with an amusement that Allyson found rude in the extreme.

"Gee, I wish you hadn't done that, Allyson," he said.

"That cat and you are obviously in collusion," she sputtered. "At this rate, I'm not going to get out of this state alive." She clawed her way to her knees and extended a hand. "Help me up."

He pretended to mull over the matter as a glow from the parking lot spotlight wreathed his head. "You know, a man never knows what to do when a woman falls at his feet. It's really quite unnerving. He can either pretend he hasn't seen and let her flounder, or he can help her up and wreck her ego. I'm confused.''

Allyson wondered that the heat of her temper didn't thaw the snow where she lay. "If you don't help me up, you wretch, you're going to think confused!''

In an attempt to stand, she grabbed the side of his leg and gripped a back pocket of his cammies. His pants listed dangerously, but he held out a well-meaning hand. She tripped on something beneath the snow, however, and toppled into the shrubs.

This time she took him with her. They both wound up sprawled in the snow, him half on her and half off, his cap a foot away and her own topping a sprig of the shrubs like a pretty Christmas angel.

With a grunt of discomfort, he picked himself up and crawled over to fetch his cap. When he looked back, snow was crusted upon his eyebrows, clotted upon his mustache and dusting his stubble of a beard.

"If you say, 'I wish you hadn't done that,' '' Allyson wheezed, covered with snow, "I'll kill you, R.T. Right here.''

"Gotta hand it to you, Cricket.'' He fit his cap blandly onto his head and leaned back upon his heels. "You really know how to get a man's attention.''

"If my behind wasn't freezing off,'' she chattered, glaring furiously, "I'd be even more clever.''

"Well, hell, we can't have that now, can't we?'' Rising and anchoring his boots, he grasped her hand and hauled her up and walked her safely up the steps.

"Actually,'' he said as he stomped clumps of snow from his boots, "thawing out behinds is my métier. I'll bet you didn't know that, did you?''

"R.T.!'' Exasperation swelled in Allyson's chest as he commenced brushing the snow and ice from her coat, "I didn't know you were acquainted with the word *métier*.''

"I daresay there's a lot about me you don't know, Miss Priss.''

Bending, he shocked her more by scooping her up in his arms in a swirl of her skirt and a flash of leather boots.

"What're you doing?" she squeaked as she grabbed his neck. "Put me down."

Vapor exploded from his mouth when he laughed. "Here?" He pretended to drop her in the doorway.

"Philistine!"

"I'm carrying you across the threshold, my sweet. In some circles that's still considered a romantic thing to do."

With his heel, he sent the door crashing shut behind them. Leaning against the light switch, he nudged it on with an elbow and the cabin's interior came to life with approximately twenty-five gloomy watts of electricity.

"Ugh." Allyson's spirits sank. She looked around. "I have a really bad feeling about this place, R.T."

"Cheer up. Now we have an excuse to use the candles."

A fireplace had been built for some former time, and now a gas heater had been installed in its cavern. The entire mantel was lined with candles—fat candles, skinny candles, white ones and red ones, some in battered brass holders, some in glass, in wood, in saucers and one in a tin pie plate.

"A commentary on the state of the utilities in this country, no doubt," he said. "You don't suppose there's an omen in the cat's being black, do you?"

"It's probably a good thing I don't play trick or treat anymore."

"Well, I do." With the look of a pirate, he considered the way she was cradled to his chest. His voice dropped to a rumbling tiger's purr. "Depending upon the treat, of course. I'm a great lover of treats."

Allyson's pulse took a thudding leap as he let her slide slowly to the floor. When he touched the light switch and the gloom disappeared, leaving only the softer, more gentle glow of the flame in the gas heater, she clutched her coat tightly about herself.

"Much better," he said as he gazed around. "In this case, ignorance is bliss."

The room was small and its ceiling low, but it had been remodeled recently. The double bed had been pushed against a wall, and blue and green pillows were scattered over it. Running water was simmering in the bathroom pipes, at least for the time being, and reasonably clean rugs covered the wood floors. The table with the bowl of fake fruit sat near the door. On another table was an electric coffee maker, two cups turned upside down on a tray, as well as paper napkins and packets of sugar and artificial sweetener.

"But a motel . . ." Allyson started to say, then stopped.

The abrupt silence was filled with the wind keening in the eaves.

"We started in a motel, Allyson," he softly reminded.

Allyson didn't move. She couldn't move. He was touching her now, really touching her. And it wasn't a touch of friendship or affection as their embrace in the hangar had been.

"You know we have to do this and get it out of the way," he said quietly.

He laid the back of his hand against her jaw.

His glance sees everything, Allyson thought, from the too-quick rise of her breasts to the throbbing pulse beneath her ear. Trembling, she parted her lips in an unhappy protest. "We ended in a motel, too, R.T. Remember?"

"Maybe we shouldn't have," he said.

His lashes threw shadows upon the hard angles of his cheeks. With the unrelenting tenacity of his eyes riveted with hers, he reached for the zipper of his jacket.

Its rasp burst through the silent room like a chain saw, and Allyson quickly stared at the preening cat. "I wasn't the one who ended it."

"Then one baby step won't matter either way, will it?"

He returned her face to his with a finger prodding her cheek. Never had Allyson been more aware of him. Nor had she ever been more helpless than when he speared her hair and closed his hands about her skull. Her body felt like a reed in a high wind. It shouldn't be so easy for him, she thought.

"Would you fight me?" he asked huskily.

Don't let this happen, a voice shouted in her head. *You'll be sorry. You'll be sorry.*

Then he unbuttoned her coat and drew her closer. He captured the lobe of her ear in his teeth and her knees buckled traitorously. She sank against him.

"Maybe you play trick or treat, after all," he muttered into her hair.

Allyson's lashes drooped low upon her cheeks. She shook her head. "But this isn't…" she tried to say. "You can't…"

He drew her hand beneath his sweater, and, not daring to look at him, she skimmed the planes of his back and found the gullied scars and ridged slopes. With a sound of anguish, she grazed the whorls of hair on his chest and shuddered when he made sweeping excursions of her sides and her waist and the span of her belly.

"No tricks, then." His whisper feathered her senses as he nudged her face upward to his. "This is as honest as it comes, Allyson."

Allyson really didn't know what she'd expected. For too many years her fantasies had been those of revenge. She wanted to say that she couldn't give what he was asking, that there would be nothing left of her, no future, no way of surviving the slow death of her dreams.

But his lashes were lowering and he was wrapping himself around her—a reaper gathering the harvest that had been allowed its time in the sun. Tighter and tighter he reaped until she was part of his flesh, inside his bones and rushing in his blood.

"A million times I've wanted to tell you," he choked as he branded her throat with fiery kisses. "I never meant to hurt you. God, Allyson, I was just a boy, a foolish boy. The past is gone. Don't judge me, because I can't bring it back."

But the past was what she needed now, with its bludgeoning power. "We have to be sensible," she heard herself protesting between his kisses.

He wasn't listening. He was bringing them around and drawing her down upon the bed, sliding alongside and fitting her into his side. Her hair was between them and he buried his face in it, pressed her hand into the juncture of his legs, moving, moving against her.

Even as a boy, R.T. had been able to say as much with a sound as with a touch. Allyson swore he was crooning her into surrender as he raked her hair away and his breaths fanned her cheeks and his low moans of hunger filled her head. Was she really kissing his hair? Were her own lips reaching for his ears and his eyebrows? They couldn't be, and she couldn't be stroking the urgent, straining proof of what had existed between them from the beginning.

This was the story of her life, then! All this man had to do was come back after fourteen years and she melted. She couldn't be alone with him for five minutes before they were taking off their clothes!

"No!" she gasped, and fought free of him to scramble away, kneeling upon the bed and covering her face, bending low until she was a whimpering knot of regret.

Outside, the wind was shrieking in the eaves.

He didn't say a word, and presently she looked up to find his stare haggard with blame. This was not his fault, his glittering eyes accused; it was hers. Oh, he was so free with such looks!

Cursing herself for a fool, she flung herself from the bed and dashed in a frenzy for the door, but his big boots struck the floor before she got two feet.

"Dammit it, Allyson," he choked as he captured the flying sail of her coat and twirled her back into his arms.

In her frenzy Allyson brought her fists hard upon his chest, pummeling his shoulders with a blind despair. "I loved you, R.T. I told you I did. But then, I told you, and you put him first. First, first! You're still putting him first, and now you want—"

He all but jerked her from the floor, and she writhed between his hands.

"Don't put motives to my actions, Allyson," he ground out. "I don't put him first."

"You wouldn't be here now if it weren't for Daniel!" She kicked uselessly at him and wriggled, striking anything she could connect with.

"Will you stop that?"

"So you can tell me how it's hurt you all these years?" she railed on a rising note. "So you can tell me how much you love me? That a mistake is a mistake and you can't keep paying for it? I've heard it all a thousand times from Daniel."

With a growl of self-disgust, R.T. released her and moved back. But the duel was already understood now. The terms had not changed, nor the cause, only the cost. He was certain he could overpower her and, given time, he could probably change her mind and make her say the words his heart was bleeding to hear.

He didn't want her that way—a body, a brief entry, a withdrawal, then nothing.

He drew his thumb across his jaw in dismay. "You've seen the worst of both of us, haven't you?" he said dully.

"The worst!"

She walked to the bed as if she were in pain. She eased herself down to sit and bent over her knees until her forehead came to rest and her words resounded like a stone dropped into a well.

"You can't just walk into my life, R.T." Tears filled her throat. "Not as if you'd never left it. I'm only groping my way through as it is." She covered her head with her arms. "You can't—you can't just . . . walk in."

R.T. had grown too accustomed to the predictability of a soldier's blacks and whites. He felt as if he'd befriended a kitten for years only to have it grow into a lioness, turn on him and bite off his head.

"I'm sorry," he said, and moved to the mantel and leaned dejectedly upon it. "I should've asked if you had someone else. My fault."

Without looking, he knew she was glaring at his back. "You think I have a lover?"

He didn't know if she did or not, but it hardly mattered now. The last thing he wanted to do was hurt her again. Peeling off his jacket, he flung it onto the bed beside her.

"That," she accused him with a stabbing finger, "is utterly ridiculous. Didn't you learn anything during those times when you spied on me?"

"I wasn't spying," he countered. "I was…making sure."

"Sure of what? That you would approve of any man who might take me to bed?"

The bones in R.T.'s face felt as if they would pierce his flesh. A pain knifed his temples and settled low in his groin. He was exhausted. He wanted to bathe; he wanted to sleep.

"I was making sure you and Michael were safe," he mumbled. "I was…" The anger drained abruptly out of him and he turned hard on his heel so she could not see the depths of his love for her.

He picked up a candle and gouged a groove into the wax with a thumbnail. "I was making sure, that's all."

The sounds of her movement attracted his attention, and he saw her rifling the pockets of his jacket like a wife on the trail of a suspected philanderer. Without apology, she found his pack of cigarettes.

"If you must know," she said as she plucked one out, "I do not have a lover. Not that I haven't wanted one on occasion, I just haven't had the time. And there hasn't exactly been a procession of desirables knocking at my door. You know what I mean?"

"How have you managed for sex?" he asked baldly.

"You don't have the right to be that personal, Major Smith."

Her hands were shaking by the time she tucked the cigarette between her lips. Keeping her head angled, she found his lighter, but it refused to work. Filching it, R.T. struck the flint with a rasp.

A flame danced in the cup of his palm. She reached for his hand as the flame cavorted.

"Are you sure you want to do this?" he asked with a wry query. "It's a nasty, filthy habit."

"There are nastier, filthier habits." Holding his hand still, she leaned toward the flame and inhaled.

As her eyes closed, her face screwed up. She coughed once, then twice. Chuckling, R.T. plucked the cigarette away, took two deep drags before he stubbed it and blew smoke at the ceiling.

"Give it up as a lost cause, Allyson. Your lungs'll love you."

"Don't worry about my lungs," she managed to croak.

He worried about everything where she was concerned, but he could not tell her that. He could not explain what it was like, loving Allyson Randolph Wyatt from so far.

Sitting down beside her so that they looked like Tom Sawyer and Huck Finn deciding their next move, he gave a great sigh and placed his arm about her shoulders. When she surrendered her head to his embrace, his heart twisted with tenderness. *Ah, Allyson, Allyson, my sweet Allyson.*

The cat was watching them with wise, thoughtful eyes.

Presently Allyson whispered, "You know we can't do this, R.T."

"Do what?"

"Live together."

"I'd hardly call it living, darling. More like sharing the same foxhole."

When she pulled her coat about her legs, R.T. continued to hold her. He lost track of how long they sat without moving, without talking. Sometime later, when her head grew heavy and her breaths level and deep, he dipped his head to find her asleep. He laid her lovingly upon the bed.

He had lost her again. Was this, then, the constancy of his life? To live in the shadows of his love? To feel the pain but know none of the peace?

She stirred briefly as he folded the bedspread over her legs and back.

"It's very cold in here," she whispered.

"I know," he said. His eyes misted as he pushed ringlets of hair from her face. "Rest now, my sweet girl."

But he didn't think she heard him.

Much later, somewhere around midnight, R.T. thought, his eyes snapped open.

Had he slept? He was sprawled out in the chair before the hearth. From a long-established habit, he remained perfectly still until his sleep-drugged eyes could orient themselves in the strange surroundings. Shadows were crowding in from the corners. Pain was stabbing a bayonet into the back of his neck. His body was stiff, and the cat was sitting patiently beside his boots where he'd placed them on the hearth.

The animal meowed to be let out, and R.T. unfolded, rose and stretched the kinks from his back.

"You don't have to come back," he said when he let the cat out into the evil weather.

Allyson was curled in almost the same position, one slim arm crossed protectively over her breasts, her hair spilled over the pillow in a wild tangle, its waves catching the elusive twinkles of the fire. He should have taken off her boots.

As if she dreamt he was watching over her, she sighed and turned onto her other side, her lips parted and her cheeks flushed as rosily as a child's.

Part of R.T. hated her for coming back into his life. What would he do when she left it again? How would he fill the lonely nights? Did he dare hope that he could change the rules? That he could change the course of the future?

He couldn't bury himself in that particular pit again. The cat scratched to be let in.

"This is your fault," he told the haughty creature when it pranced in on snowy paws. "You could teach Garfield a thing or two. And don't bring me any more bad luck. I've got enough as it is."

The cat forgave such an insult by stropping his legs.

With clumsy attempts at silence, R.T. went to the bathroom, then tiptoed around the bedroom, removing the fake fruit from the coffee table and butting the table, length-wise, against the chair. Glaring at the monstrosity that happily promised him one of the most torturous nights since the hospital in Angola, he wished for a good, stiff drink.

It was a perfect night for getting drunk. He could smell her perfume on his clothes, on his hands. God, he hoped he didn't dream about the war.

After smoking a cigarette, he stretched out upon his bed of nails and told himself that he deserved to suffer. Maybe it would bring him to his senses.

He wasn't even sure how to go about helping Daniel. He needed to know more. What did Daniel know that made him such a target?

Allyson moaned softly in her sleep. Like a nervous new parent, R.T. rose and bent over her. He lifted a tress of hair so gently from her face, she never felt it.

Oh, Allyson. What a star-crossed pair we are.

Finally, when he slept, he dreamed that he and Allyson and Daniel were huddled together under an army-surplus blanket at a football game in freezing weather. They were laughing. Rather than relinquish the warmth to buy something to eat, they robbed Daniel of his last Hershey bar and took turns biting off their third. Allyson picked the almonds from her portion and poked them into his own mouth. She didn't like almonds, she said, but it was okay. He loved them, and he loved her.

Chapter 9

Like new in-laws on their best behavior, Allyson and R.T. tried to make the best of a bad situation. In the shivering, snowbound days that followed, they went to ridiculous lengths to avoid talking about the distant past and the recent past and everything in the middle. They worked out ingenious rituals to avoid touching each other or causing an inconvenience. Courtesy became sacred.

Like a recovering alcoholic who's suddenly confronted by a drink at every turn, Allyson began to see R.T. everywhere, in everything. The cabin was soon dwarfed by his bigness and his shoulders and his arms that could span a window as he stared at the snow, his head that had to duck doorways and his footsteps that echoed nimbly in her mind.

It was his back that broke her heart. Memories of its smooth, sunbrowned planes were blurred by the scars now marring its tanned breadth—irregular craters of violence, puckered and whitened by healing.

"It's nothing," he brushed her off when he was putting on a shirt and she was pretending to examine his dog tags while studying the scars instead. "Some men had a lot worse. It's nothing."

So she learned to cope with his showering and his shaving, his dropped sock here, his drying boots there, his clothes that he cared for as meticulously as a tailor would. He had a spellbinding way of dumping the contents of his pockets into the fruit bowl at the end of the day. He would roll his belt into a cylinder and tuck it beside his wallet.

In the darkness late at night, he would ask from his uncomfortable makeshift bed, "Are you asleep?"

"No," she would whisper, bewitched.

"Are you warm?"

"I'm fine."

When he slept, his breaths would fill the small room, but sometimes he tossed and mumbled and would jerk up with a start. There was a part of R.T. Smith she would never know, and she wanted to go to him at such times and cradle him in her arms and kiss away the dreams, whatever they were.

But she didn't dare lower her barriers. She would never get them erected again. So she hugged herself tightly in the darkness and tried to keep him from infiltrating her life down to the bedrock. What would she do when he was no longer there and she had to return to her lonely life?

The day she borrowed one of R.T.'s disposable razors, R.T. stepped from the bathroom, stripped to his waist, and waited in the doorway until she looked up from making the bed.

His jaws were covered with foam that smelled of mint. Droplets of water trembled from his mustache, and his wet hair spiked in six directions at once. His jeans were unzipped so far below half-mast, one deep breath would have proved a disaster.

Allyson's eyes widened at the rosette of blood spreading in the foam.

He pointed at her nose with the offending implement. "Darling, would you do me an enormous favor?"

She regarded him narrowly before replying, "What?"

"Cease and desist from shaving your legs with my razors."

"I didn't."

"You did."

"I only used the one."

"And I just maimed myself with it."

Recoiling, she clutched her robe tightly beneath her chin then angled him a more coquettish smirk. "I'm so very sorry, Major Smith," she cooed, and inched her hands into the air. "I give you permission to shoot me."

His grin placed another crack in her fortress, and when he walked over and pecked her upon the lips, leaving tufts of foam upon her face, her resolve languished dangerously.

"That's the thing I appreciate about you, Allyson," he said. "You know who's king."

Later, when she was dusting and he was outside jogging around Connie's parking lot like a Spartan, his legs churning like pistons and his nostrils spewing vapor, she spied his wallet in the fruit bowl.

She was wearing her silk blouse and a pair of R.T.'s sweatpants while her pantyhose and underwear dried in the bathroom. At first she gave the wallet no thought, but, Evelike, she returned. It was so innocent, lying there.

No!

Putting it out of her mind, she turned up the volume of the radio. The more she dusted, however, the more the wallet drew her until finally she tucked the towel beneath her arm, hitched up the sweatpants that threatened to droop to her knees and lifted out the wallet.

She flipped through his ID, keeping a furtive lookout through the frosted window. She came across a slightly out-of-focus snapshot—a bearded R.T. and Steve Grosvenor and a man with flaming red hair and freckles.

Their arms were draped across each other's shoulders. They wore limp, sweat-stained fatigues. Surrounding them were black children, their smiles large and white and adoring. Was the strange man Archie?

She burrowed deeper and unearthed another finger-worn photograph. It was barely holding together between the cracks, and she shivered to see herself dressed in a pink suit with a corsage pinned to the lapel. She hardly remembered her going-away outfit, and she had no idea what had happened to it. Daniel had been in the other half of that picture.

Incredulous, she shook her head while, behind her, the door opened. As if the wallet burned her hands, she dropped it.

Wind blew snow into the room as R.T. entered. Clumps of snow fell from his boots.

With a panic, Allyson swished the towel over the table and over the fruit bowl and across the back of the chair where the black cat awakened and stretched and opened his mouth in a great contented yawn.

"Kitz," she said breathlessly, and then added with a lame, flickering smile to R.T., "I was dusting."

A satyr's grin cocked one side of his mouth as droplets slid down his cheeks. Shaking himself, he walked mildly to the fireplace where he shed his damp jacket and pulled off his wet boots. In sock feet, he warmed his backside and surveyed the room.

"Looks good," he said, and admired the way she had rearranged the chairs and the table. "You're hired."

Allyson's senses were whipped raw. "Thank you."

"I'm surprised to see someone who can outdust Archie."

He laughed, but he didn't miss seeing the guilty catch in her breath, the devil! Or the distracted way she cleared her throat and compulsively folded the towel three times, then put it awkwardly away in the bureau.

Chuckling, he moved behind her and lifted a lock of hair from her ear and murmured electrifyingly into it, "Archie's the one with red hair, darlin'."

Heat scalded Allyson as he walked to the bureau and removed the dusting towel from the drawer, where she'd laid it upon her clean clothes. He *was* a devil! She wanted to melt beneath the rug and when he passed, she was sure she caught a whiff of brimstone.

They weren't the only ones caught by the blizzard. Two truck drivers from Vancouver had been trapped, in transit, and a chain-saw representative, along with Iris Kurble, who said she was a natural-foods expert on her way back from Eureka. Two GIs from the tracking station had been on the way to Fairbanks for R and R, so they stayed, too.

The worse the weather became, the better the Bear Cave looked. The more the wind howled, the more vital the telephone became. By the fourth day of confinement, the Bear Cave was a combination of Tavern on the Green, Arnaud's and London's own Connaught. The pay phone was a national shrine.

With their hair moussed and their skirts tight, Piper and Trish and Eileen, the "waitresses," divided their time between plastering themselves upon the pool tables, waiting tables in the café, to teasing Herb and drumming up business for Connie.

Herb, Allyson thought, was experiencing a cooking extravaganza. Each day Connie's chalk board happily featured dishes like Alaskan Sausage and Herb's Bacon and Hamburger Soufflé. Allyson and Iris Kurble ordered a lot of Campbell's soup.

"You always do that," Allyson said to R.T. on Friday after Trish had taken their order, poured their breakfast coffee, arranged the flatware, pursed her scarlet mouth adorably at R.T. and sauntered over to the two GIs to begin the whole provocative process over again.

In R.T.'s opinion, Connie's girls weren't half bad with their bangles and spangles and second-skin sweaters. Trish was proud of her endowments and displayed them to an even better advantage with her uplift bras and short skirts. Her face was pretty enough, but her makeup made him want to throw her in the shower, and the hair she teased and spritzed was straight out of a bottle.

Rather obvious, compared to Allyson's style, he thought. Allyson's chic was so downplayed, you couldn't get enough of it. She didn't wiggle, and she didn't flaunt. Yet, she could slip into a pair of slacks and a sweater, run a brush through her hair and walk into a room, and every man's eyes, and woman's too, would invariably follow her.

Look all you want to, he wanted to tell people every time it happened. *But if I can't touch, you sure as hell can't.*

Now, he glanced down at his spoon of sugar poised midway between dispenser and cup, then back up to Allyson. "Say what?"

Allyson's hands were laced and her chin rested prettily upon them. She was wearing a borrowed plaid shirt of Connie's, this one tucked into her jeans, whose legs she had tucked into her boots. She was as fresh as a daisy thrusting up through the snow. He, on the other hand, was down to his last pair of grungy cammie pants and a woolly pully.

Her hair was clipped with a barrette at her nape, and the sunny wisps caught the light from the wagon-wheel chandelier. The Western kerchief about her neck was new to him, too. She wore no jewelry, and her skin, awakened by the cold, bloomed prettily with color.

He followed the direction of her stare as Trish walked past. Grinning, he said, "They don't charge for looking," and continued to stir his coffee.

"I wasn't talking about Trish." Allyson took a quick sip of coffee, then made a gagging face at her cup. "I was referring to all that sugar."

R.T. tugged his cap lower onto his brow, it being a mark of ill breeding at the Bear Cave to eat without headgear. "This isn't going to be one of those lecture-R.T.-about-the-perils-of-diabetes days, is it?"

"Sugar's not good for you."

"And neither is Trish, hmm?" He enjoyed the way Allyson kept stealing sidelong glances at the woman who was putting quarters into the jukebox and bumping and grinding her hips with every click.

"That woman..." Allyson began as it dawned on her that she had just violated their unspoken pact by becoming personal.

"What were you saying, dear?" he teased.

"Nothing." She lifted her chin another notch and gave her head a haughty toss.

He wickedly resumed his perusal of Trish.

Herb had turned the fires high today. The room was stifling. All the tables were filled. Bill Hare and Nick Mackenzie, the two truck drivers, ordered Herb's Alaskan Sausage. Private Guy Jennings and Pfc. Chuck Paddock were playing a game of pool while they waited for their bacon and eggs. The two men played constantly. Chuck now owed Guy somewhere in the neighborhood of forty-five thousand dollars.

Iris Kurble was sharing a table with the chain-saw representative, and they were both so shy, they looked as if they were suffering from frostbite.

"But you really enjoy it, don't you?" Allyson said.

"Sugar?"

"Trish!"

R.T. leaned back in his chair and pushed the sleeves of his sweater midway to his elbows. "I'd say the word *enjoy* is a little exaggerated."

"Then why do your eyes glaze over every time she walks by?"

Did he detect a choice glint of jealousy in Allyson's green eyes? R.T. let his chair slam to the floor with a sharp crack and leaned across the table until the stubble of his hair was all but touching hers.

"Look *deeep* into my eyes, Allyson."

She paused in the buttering of her toast, frowning.

"What do you see in these eyes?" he quizzed.

She didn't flinch. "Lust."

Laughing, R.T. swiveled around to ogle Trish more thoroughly. "Well, you know me, Al," he drawled lazily, "I'm a dyed-in-the-wool fanny man. What can I say?"

No man, fanny or otherwise, could have failed to appreciate the way Trish was draping her anatomy over the pool table and writhing like a cat wanting to be scratched. Iris Kurble's mouth was hanging open, and Nick Mackenzie was nudging Bill to turn around to see the show.

Trish removed Guy's cap and settled it upon her bleached hair. Thrusting out her bosom and clicking her spiked heel shoes, she gave him a salute. When everyone in the café laughed—Allyson excluded—Trish played to her audience and stole Guy's pool cue. With a wiggle, she bent over and took careful aim and struck one of the balls. Then she turned around and looked straight at R.T.

"Major-pie!" she called, and gave the side of her hip a tantalizing slap. "Chalk one up for me!"

R.T. gamely lifted his cup in a toast. Beneath the current of laughter, he heard the rat-tat-tat of Allyson's fingernails on the table.

"You're drooling, Major-pie," Allyson murmured between her teeth.

"Hmm?" R.T. wouldn't have stopped playing his role for anything. "Sorry. Did you say something, dear?"

Her smile would have cut through steel. "You think that's good, do you? Hmm? *Major-pie?*"

It took all R.T.'s strength to keep from grinning. "Well, babe—" he scratched his jaw and pretended to ponder "—it sure as hell ain't bad."

Sweeping her gaze around the café, Allyson rose. There was something about her manner that attracted attention, though R.T. couldn't have put a finger on it.

"Excuse me a minute, would you, Major-pie, dear?" she purred sweetly.

He would have given up his rank before trying to stop her from gliding over to the cash register where Connie was hammering tacks into a sign that said Friday Is Western Day.

"Pardon me, Connie," Allyson said politely, and smiled, "but would you mind lending me your hat for a minute?"

Connie's Western hat was not an imitation but a genuine Stetson she'd bought years ago in Flagstaff, Arizona. When she heard the question, she relayed her own question to R.T. Had the poor, grieving mother finally snapped?

R.T.'s reply was a shrug. Who knew what grief could do to the human spirit?

"You can borrow mine, Mrs. Wyatt," Nick generously offered from across the room.

"Thank you, Nick," Allyson said as her smile grew more lethal, "but Connie's will do nicely."

Connie removed her hat, and Allyson fit it upon the back of her own head. By now the room was spellbound. Even Herb had poked his head out the kitchen door.

With the tantalizing slowness of a stripteaser preparing to take the stage, Allyson pulled her shirt from her pants and tied it about her middle. Not once did she look at R.T. as she bared her midriff above a smooth, trim waist and molded jeans. Now she looked more like a cowgirl in a beer commercial than the demure mother whose son was supposedly ailing away in Seattle.

She walked up to Chuck who was leaning on his pool cue. Coolly acknowledging Trish, she nodded politely to Guy.

"You wouldn't mind me borrowing that for a minute, would you, soldier?" she said, pointing to Chuck's stick.

Chuck's Adam's apple bobbed excitedly. "Oh, no, ma'am. Be my guest."

The Bellamy Brothers had finished singing on the jukebox, and no one was inclined to put in another quarter. Every eye in the place was riveted upon Allyson's fantastic rear as she moved to the pool table and bent over to study it. Chuck looked at Guy, and Guy looked at R.T. R.T. was remembering those wonderful winter evenings when he'd taught Allyson to shoot pool. What he didn't understand was how that sweet, innocent girl had become this vamp who was turning a pool shot into foreplay.

"What d'you think, Chuckie-pie," Allyson drawled as she made an erotic production of chalking her stick.

"Oh, Lord, Mrs. Wyatt," Chuck said nervously as he studied the table, "you'd have to be Tom Cruise to make that shot."

"Just call me Fast Al," she said, and blew on the stick. She bent over the table, and every man in the room leaned forward. "Number three into the side."

With a stroke as gentle as a baby's kiss, she sliced the three ball into a side pocket. The cue ball rolled to a gentle stop at the far end of the table. She walked around as if she were moving across a stage. She squatted down to eye level and Bill Hare and Nick Mackenzie came out of their chairs.

"Number six into the corner," she said.

In four shots, she cleaned the table and then called the pocket on the eight ball. When it sank, everyone split eardrums with whistles and cheers, right down to Trish and the chain-saw representative.

R.T. tipped back his head in silent, private laughter. *Touché, Allyson, touché.*

With almost prim fastidiousness Allyson then returned Chuck's stick and walked to the tree where the coats were hanging. After returning Connie's hat, she wiped her hands on the back of her jeans, leaving two white, resiny handprints.

R.T. didn't know whether the handprints were a final touch or not, he only knew that the sight of them was like a fist that struck him square in his belly. If he hadn't already been in love with her, he guessed the hook would have been set, then and there.

Turning, she held up her hand in a wave. "See ya, Major-pie," she called, picked up her coat and walked to the door.

At noon, the snow stopped falling. The hush was like the reprieve that comes when a sick child suddenly stops coughing and drifts into a sweet, restful slumber.

Everyone at the Bear Cave ran outside and didn't care one whit that the cold bit their cheeks and their nostrils smoked and their laughter was a frigid puff of mist. *We've been liberated!*

To celebrate, Connie brought out bottles of carbonated white wine that she called champagne. Herb announced that he would spend the afternoon cleaning off the gasoline medians. He was back in business and lunch would be in brown paper bags.

Allyson was eager to tell Kaye that within hours air travel should be restored. Even the moose, when it grinned, seemed more sincere.

She toasted him with her Diet Coke as Kaye reported, "Michael has a cold."

Allyson choked on her drink. "Oh, dear. Are you giving him vitamin C?"

"He's taking everything, Allyson, including a healthy portion of my menopausal nerves. Poor darling, he woke up last night with a bad dream about his father and refused to settle down. He'd seen Daniel's name in the paper. You know how he reads everything. Keeping a secret from that child is hopeless."

Allyson considered talking to Michael but didn't want to remind him to miss her. "You're all right, though?"

"Actually, no. I made a colossal fool of myself by calling Richard Wyatt in the middle of the night. With the best of intentions, Allyson, I swear. I thought it would help Michael if he could talk to his grandfather, then Richard told me he was worried sick himself, that he didn't have any idea where Daniel was. The Department of Justice had just been over there, and you know how frail Richard is. Anyway, Richard is frantic and Michael has a cold. Ask me another question."

It took Allyson the total of two seconds to realize that there were some secrets which should not be kept. She told her mother everything.

"I haven't seen Daniel yet," she said in conclusion, "what with the blizzard, but tell Michael that his father is perfectly all right. He was in a car wreck. And call Richard, poor man. In fact, when I see Daniel, I'm going to insist that he call them both."

"Joan and Grant," Kaye said, "have offered to get me out of the house for a few hours, bless their hearts. Margo's going to keep Michael tonight. You know how Michael dotes on Margo. She's the only one who can beat him at Nintendo. We're going to the opera. *The Rites of Spring*. You know how I adore *The Rites of Spring*."

Allyson didn't have the heart to tell her mother that there was only *one* rite of spring. And she was about to ask if Global Defense was off the hook since Grant was going to the opera, but Kaye proceeded to rattle on about how the decision came down that, yes, there was enough evidence against Global to justify a trial, and, yes, the jury was presently being selected. Grant was being charged with misconduct.

"It's Richard Nixon all over again," Kaye said. "They're trying poor Grant's case in the media. If the company isn't absolutely ruined by the time the trial's over, it'll be so damaged that no government contract will ever come its way again. It's important to put up a good front right now. That's why we're going to the opera."

By the time R.T. appeared at the telephone, a basket on his arm that was covered with a red-and-white cloth, Allyson was drooping. She pointed to the receiver with a hangdog face, and he teased her by pointing to the bottle beneath the checkered cloth.

"Enjoy the opera, Mother," Allyson said, and poked through the basket, which held an array of sandwiches and fruit and plastic containers of potato salad and coleslaw, typical picnic fare. "Tell Grant I'll see him in a couple of days."

Along with my resignation, she thought guiltily, and wished, with hindsight's perspective, that she'd submitted it the day Bolten disappeared. Now her quitting truly would reek of a rat's desertion.

"Tell him yourself, darling," Kaye said. "He's standing right here."

Allyson dropped the checkered cloth in surprise and touched R.T.'s sleeve without realizing it. "Grant? There?"

"Just a minute. I'll put him on."

The moose, Allyson noted in distraction, wasn't smiling any longer; he was leering. Outside, Herb had started some kind of fearful snow-clearing apparatus. Her nails were burying into the toughness of R.T.'s cuff and when his fingers sought hers, she grasped them tightly.

"Grant!" she exclaimed when he came on the line. "What a surprise!"

Holding her hand, R.T. snagged a nearby chair with his boot and pushed her gently down into it. He placed the basket on the floor and waited above her, his foot braced on a rung and his fingertips stroking her shoulder.

"Shame, shame on you," Grant teasingly scolded. "Kaye just told me about Daniel. Why didn't you tell me yourself? Is Daniel getting good care at this hospital?"

Allyson felt as if she had innocently tested the water of a pool only to discover quicksand. Daniel had ordered her to tell no one, and she'd not only told Kaye, now Grant knew. Why didn't she just drag out Herb's flashing sign and tell the whole world?

"It's not a hospital, Grant," she said, and stared blindly at R.T.'s belt buckle with its Marine insignia. "It's a tracking station. And I'm sure he's all right. It's a military place."

"That's perfect. The military's big on health and safety."

"I haven't even gotten to talk to him. His car's still stuck in some gully somewhere..."

"Well, what's a new Porsche good for? Cheer up, it'll be insured to the hilt."

"Grant, I really did want to tell you before, but Daniel was so nervous..."

"I understand, but I'm not sure the Justice Department will."

Was she imagining things, or was the quicksand up to her knees now? She idly plucked a piece of debris from the knee of R.T.'s pants.

"Grant, I may not know exactly what's going on, but one thing I'm certain of, Daniel would never do or say anything to hurt Global Defense. To begin with, he doesn't know anything. I don't know why the Justice Department's going on and on about it."

Grant laughed. "The Feds have never been known for their street smarts, darling."

R.T. was straining to hear, and Allyson shared the earpiece with him.

"Are the airports open up there?" Grant quizzed.

"They will be soon," she answered. "Right now, the roads are still closed."

"Well, keep us posted, sweetie. Oh, you'll be pleased to know that the Bolten file's been rebuilt. Fifty-six man-hours and every account on record back to eighty-two. Hen's teeth, but your people did it."

"I'm sure the government's thrilled."

"That's something of an understatement. Take care, now. If Daniel needs anything, and I mean *anything*, let me know."

The quicksand was closing over her head, Allyson was certain, but she didn't understand why she felt that way. Sighing as she hung up, she said, "You'll be the first to know, Grant."

She had to lean back in order to focus R.T.'s frown. "That was Grant," she said unhappily.

R.T. was worrying the edge of his chipped tooth with his tongue, and Allyson suffered a need to hide herself inside his fatigue jacket and pull it over her head and remain there the rest of her days.

"I can't wait to meet this man," he said.

"You two would probably hit it off," she mumbled. "You couldn't be more different."

"Thank goodness for that."

Allyson was on her hands and knees, spreading a quilt before the heater of the Honeymoon Cottage in a display of her derriere that R.T. found painfully erotic.

Since her conversation with Grant Melbourne, R.T. had been in a state of inner anguish. Their time together was coming to an end and he wanted to shout that he hadn't said the things he'd meant to say. He hadn't changed anything; he hadn't made her see that his returning to a life without her was hardly worth the trouble.

For days he had been haunted by scenarios to keep from losing what little he had of her. One plan was as futile as the next. Even his more bizarre fantasies no longer comforted him. Of his being awakened in the night by her; of being seduced by her insatiable mouth and hands and whispers and then entering her quickly and believing the lie that only he could make her happy. Of him taking her to the farm and walking across the fields, hand in hand in the moonlight; of her laughter as she tipped her face for his kiss. Of her rocking their child. Of her sitting on the back steps in the summertime, wearing the whisper of a nightgown and brushing her hair.

They were ashes in the reality of this moment, and he thought of the word *marriage*. What an irony. He had medals to prove his bravery, but he wasn't courageous enough to ask *that* question, not with their history, not the son of Reavis and Eva Smith down on his knee, proposing marriage to the daughter of Kaye and Orin Randolph.

Nor could he picture Allyson consenting to be his lover. And even if she would agree, he couldn't settle for that.

So what did that leave them? Hopelessness. They would pick up their lives where they'd left off and soon this interlude would be a memory that they recalled only on sad, rainy nights.

"This Grant Melbourne," he said as he lifted the champagne from the basket and idly broke the seal with his thumbnail.

He pulled the cork, and the wine spewed mockingly from the neck. She looked up, and he clasped the glasses by their stems, filled them and placed hers before the bend of her knee where she knelt.

"You haven't told Melbourne you're quitting your job, have you?" he asked.

The food basket was balanced upon her lap. She clasped the handle in a death grip, and was unaware that Connie's shirt was drawn tautly across her bosom. The sunlight angling through the window, bright from the snow, had turned her hair to Rapunzel gold. She was so beautiful, the side of her neck so incandescently perfect, he felt a painful burr in his heart.

She made a sound that wasn't a yes or a no.

"When are you going to do it?" he persisted. "When you go out the door to start this new job of yours?"

She placed the basket in the center of the quilt and sat pleating the hem with her fingers. She stared at her hands with an involvement so total, he wanted to shake her. He emptied the fruit upon the bed and dusted the bowl with the elbow of his sweater, tore open a package of chips with his teeth and emptied it.

Munching one, he nudged the bowl closer to her. As if countering his move, she pushed Connie's basket toward him.

"I wouldn't do that to Grant," she said. "Grant's been good to me."

Suddenly everything about her made R.T. furious: her beautiful hair and drugging fragrance, the line of her cheek, her loneliness, her show of poise that he was certain wasn't what she was really feeling, her ability to break his heart.

"How good is good?" he asked quietly, lethally.

His tone made her look up. "I don't think I want to have this conversation, R.T."

"I don't see why you're getting so uptight about it, darlin'," he drawled, and stretched himself out so he could trace the grain of denim across her knee with a corn chip. "You told him more in five minutes than you've told me in five days."

The corn chip came to a meaningful stop at the crease of her jeans, and they considered each other without the masks, as if they were experiencing a countdown to an explosion that would annihilate them both.

"You obviously know Grant Melbourne quite intimately," he said. "Want a chip?"

With a flashing toss of hair, she snatched the chip and threw it at his head. "How dare you say that? I've known Grant Melbourne all my life!"

"And you trust him?"

"Of course, I trust him. Don't be ridiculous." Sniffing, she snatched an apple from the basket, took a dribbling bite and licked juice from her fingers.

"It just seems to me, my little porcupine—" with his knuckle, R.T. blotted a runnel of juice before it could reach her chin "—that if anyone has anything to gain by Daniel not testifying before the grand jury, Grant's your man."

"What?" Her face screwed up in confusion and she stopped chewing.

Smiling disagreeably, R.T. held out her glass of wine and picked up his own. "Let's see," he mused, and clinked their glasses together. "What'll we drink to? Grant? Your new job?"

She plunked her glass resentfully on the quilt. "Grant Melbourne is one of the nicest, sweetest, most understanding men I know, R.T. Smith! He's gotten a lousy deal from his father—"

With a pointed finger, R.T. was tempted to give his treatise on lousy deals from fathers, but he placed their glasses on the table instead.

"Gee, that breaks my heart, Allyson. That's the saddest story I ever heard."

With a sniff, she crunched morosely on her apple again. "You can be so tacky when you want to be, R.T."

"And you can be so evasive. How good has Grant been to you?"

Her chin lifted and a foxy smile reached her lips. "Are you jealous, Major?"

"Yeah, maybe."

"Well, it's a little late in the game for that. This is me, remember?"

"It was just a question. I wasn't aware you were so hung up on the guy."

"I'm not hung up on Grant Melbourne, dad-gummit!"

"Then why don't you move in with me?"

Even as he was speaking, R.T. tried to stop the words. In all his most frustrating scenarios, he had not imagined himself laying his heart so open to pain.

But they were said now, and nothing could erase them. With a look that defied his analysis, she scrambled to her feet. She didn't fling his words back into his face as he expected, but stalked to the bathroom and tossed the apple core into the wastebasket. She rinsed her hands and walked back into the room, pointing her finger and opening her mouth, but then dropping down to sit, hunched like a betrayed Indian princess.

R.T. cursed his stupidity and he tried unsuccessfully to shut Pandora's box. "Where's your new job?" he asked in a lame attempt to make conversation, any conversation.

She stared at a spot on the quilt, her eyes out of focus and her hair swirling about her jaws.

He leaned gently forward. "I didn't hear you."

Her hands were fretting. R.T. vaguely remembered another time when they had done that, but he couldn't recall where. He touched her fingers and they instantly grew still.

When she confronted him, her eyes were the color of the sea. She drew in her breath to speak, and he had the distinct premonition that all his scenarios didn't matter. His life was about to change, and there was nothing he could do about it.

"Atlanta," she said.

Chapter 10

Rising, R.T. stared down at Allyson like a monarch who has just learned of a rebellious faction within his kingdom.

"Atlanta?" The word was unwieldy and didn't wish to be said. "As in Ray Charles?"

"It's a once-in-a-lifetime opportunity," she defended from where she knelt upon the quilt. "I'll be working for Earl Kolpechy in broadcast graphics. He didn't have to give me the job, others were more qualified. I'll be leaving in two weeks, R.T. Less by the time we get back. I would have been a fool—"

"Oh, yes—" he cut her off with a savage slice of his hand "—a fool."

R.T. felt the same helplessness as when he'd chewed his nails and watched the ambulance taking his mother away. Now Allyson was going away, out of reach, out of his world. At the exact moment when he had exposed his need, she said she was leaving.

He wanted to roar. He wanted to rage. He wanted to destroy something. But he forced himself to lie with a diplomacy that instinct warned him was the only way.

"Of course," he said with stiff formality. "You would have been a fool not to have taken the job. I understand completely."

"You understand nothing," she mumbled from behind a veil of sun-shot hair.

"Maybe it's you who doesn't."

Confusion pulled at her eyebrows.

What did he have to lose now? R.T. asked himself. The spear was already thrust through his heart.

"Maybe you ought to ask yourself, darling," he said, facing her point-blank, "why you chose Atlanta. Twenty-five hundred miles from Seattle. That's a hell of a lot of miles. Ever wonder why?"

With the bravado of a wronged champion, she flung her head back with a snap. "Twenty-six hundred, to be exact."

"Oh?" R.T.'s smile froze on his face. "That's even better. Twenty-six hundred miles. Not particularly conducive to dropping by for dinner, is it?"

Or moving in? he asked himself wretchedly.

Her eyes were emeralds—hard and glistening. All the tenacity that he had admired in her during the past seemed to culminate in this one moment. Let it go, he warned himself. Let *her* go. But how could he? She was his life.

"It isn't as if you were in a habit of having me over for dinner, R.T.," she said.

That was true. "So geography is to blame for that?"

"Not geography." She held up both hands, then dropped them. "It's . . . it's . . ."

"What?"

He was striding back and forth through the room now, more like the old R.T. than he knew—all his defenses sticking out a mile, the wild boy who was used to taking life by the throat and strangling it until it yielded.

He stopped at her side and she thought, looking up from where she bent, that he could have been some medieval warrior with his spread legs and muscle-banded thighs and hard belly. She would hardly have been surprised if he'd dragged her to her feet by the hair of her head.

"You can't answer me, can you?" he demanded, blue eyes shooting sparks.

"All right!" she cried, and lunged to her feet and whirled to place distance between them. "But I don't know how you have the nerve to ask me that now. After all these years. I've hated you, R.T. I've loved you, yes, but I've hated you. And then I've hated myself for hating you. I'm tired of all the hate, can't you see? I'm tired of looking at happy people and grieving because I'm not one of them. And now I have a chance to start over...."

She threaded her hands through her hair. The silence was an accuser—pointed fingers and rattling scales of justice. R.T. swiped a hand over his own face, and the gesture was so heartbreaking, Allyson flinched.

"So you need a twenty-six-hundred-mile solution for what happened back then?" he said.

He didn't have to make this so difficult. It wouldn't have hurt him to show some sympathy.

"You say I don't understand," she accused. "Well, I do. I know why you did what you did. I admired your loyalty to Daniel even when I despised it, really, I did. That part was fine and good, but—" Memories briefly halted her words. "But I have a few years left, R.T. I'm not getting any younger, and staying in Seattle, year after year..."

She waved away her words, unable to finish. But the truth was there. Exposed at last. Hanging between them like Poe's pendulum, swinging toward one, then the other with its bright killing edge. Allyson didn't know what to think when he looked from her to the room and down at his hands.

His words came with unexpected tenderness. "You don't have to run twenty-six hundred miles to get away from me," he said, and unhappily flexed his fingers. "I'll stay out of your life if that's what you want, but..." He heaved a sigh. "You don't have to go away."

When she didn't reply—how could she?—he moved to the window and looked outside, his shoulders rounded as if he were suffering some terrible internal hurt.

"I shouldn't have said that." He bent his head low. "You have every right to go. But—" he faced her unexpectedly, his expression haggard and beaten "—if you go, go knowing that I love you, Allyson. I always have."

Somewhere in the world, Allyson thought as she pressed her fingers to her lips and wondered how her life had veered so far off course, somewhere things were normal. Babies were being born and the dead were being laid peacefully to rest. Life was going on in its usual fashion. But here, in this room, the world had stopped turning. They couldn't go back, and they didn't dare go forward.

"You waited fourteen years to tell me that?" she whispered in disbelief.

He resumed staring at the snow. Muscles played across his back. He stuffed his hands into his pockets and his fists were outlined beneath the poplin.

He said, "Did you expect me to come running over and ask Daniel for a few minutes of your time?"

"Daniel and I have been divorced for over six years, R.T. Did you never hear of the telephone?"

Sharply, before she could move, he spun on his heel and struck his wineglass from where he'd placed it on the table. It crashed against the fireplace into an explosion of a hundred sparkling pieces.

"Oh!" She gasped at the ruins, then at her own ruins.

"And now you're afraid that we might find something in all these ashes!" he accused as he stepped toward her. "You're so afraid, you can't even be honest about what you're doing. I wonder if you know, Allyson—" he began slowly to stalk her "—why you've never taken a lover. You say you're tired of living with the past, yet in all those years, you never found someone. Have you never asked yourself why that's so?"

But it wasn't like that! she wanted to cry. It was true that she'd thought about him and remembered, even when she'd become bitter, but she hadn't waited. That she had decided to leave Seattle was proof of that. This argument was proof!

Retreating by inches, she extended her hands, fearing where this would end. "You're not being fair, R.T. You're twist—"

"Fair?" His laughter was spine chilling. "Why don't we just have a little talk about fair? I once broke your heart, I admit that. I might as well, right? So now, when I hand you my heart on a platter, you tell yourself you have the right to grind it up in little pieces because it's only fair that you get your turn at me. Is that about on target? Hmm?"

"R.T...." She inched backward until she bumped the wall at her back. "Please understand."

"No."

He was a conquistador staking his claim, assaulting her, stripping her of facades. Positioning himself before her, he clasped her face and tipped it beneath his and drew his thumb electrifyingly across her lips.

His breath kissed her eyebrows, her cheeks. "Ask me to stop, sweetheart, ask me to drop dead, but don't ask me to understand."

The sob that rose into Allyson's throat refused to be swallowed. He did love her, she knew that, and she loved him, but what came afterward? Did he think he was the only one afraid to be hurt again?

"I won't even ask if you want me," he whispered as he pulled her irrevocably into his embrace. "I know you want me. I can feel you inside me like a knife."

A moment of hesitation...of questions without answers...of caution that could find no reason for not evaporating. Why? Why not? Could they hurt any worse than they did at this moment?

Their embrace, when it finally came, had a painful sting to it, a ferocity, a released voltage that encompassed both with an eternity and a space so brief, it was nothing more than a wink of heaven's eye. They were not two bodies then, but one. Their straining arms closed fiercely and held as they were consumed by history and the inevitable tides that had brought them together again.

Then Allyson could not breathe. In her fury, she could not stop kissing him and being kissed. Their desire flashed out of control and he thrust her desperately against the wall. His hot tongue plundered hers and his breath branded her as she tried to tear his clothes from his back.

He caught her so hard against him, her feet left the floor.
"Not a day has passed . . ." he moaned, shifting his mouth
hungrily upon hers.

"The night . . ."

"I know . . ." His teeth closed upon the lobe of her ear.

"Ohh!" Her head swung back as her nails dug into his
arms.

Being dressed only heightened their need to a frenzied
despair. From somewhere far away Allyson heard the buttons of Connie's shirt being ripped from their threads. Neither could bear the seconds to negotiate zippers and buttons.
He shoved her hands away and stripped her jeans to her
knees.

Allyson kicked at the willful things until her legs flashed
free and she climbed him and locked a leg desperately
around his back, raining delirious kisses upon his eyes, his
cheeks, his lips, her hands dipping into his pants to find the
shaft of him.

"Easy," he whispered. "Easy."

But there wasn't a second to lose. Time was the one thing
she did not have, and when he didn't move quickly enough,
she jerked her own panties aside and took him into her
hand, tipping herself so her bones became his bones.

"Help me," she begged as she pressed her face into the
curve of his neck in surrender, her open mouth sweeping the
tightened cords, her teeth scraping and her moans sound-
ing as if she were being torn asunder. "Oh, help me."

Madness engulfed them as she impaled herself with a
willing cry. She held him so closely, she could feel the scars
on his back as sweat sleeked off them. When he filled her,
she said his name over and over.

Did he say her name, too? She didn't know. She knew
only the rightness as he rocked with her, anchoring her to
the wall, rising up into her like a spire so that she took him
deeper and deeper and cradled his head to her breasts because he belonged to her, at this moment, in a way that he
would never belong to anyone for all eternity.

Then he gripped her hard as the end threatened. She
couldn't bear the parting.

"I can't . . ." he tried to say through the delirium that strangled him. "I'm sorry, I'm sorry."

She had known she could not hold him forever. Loving him more in that moment than she had ever loved anything, she clung with the instincts born in those who love. It truly didn't matter—none of it, not even the years and the wasted dreams. They were as close now as two people could be as he shuddered and his mouth searched for hers in the pain of his long-denied release.

The ultimate irony, then—the reality that should have been no more surprising than the paths their lives had chosen to take. Outside, Steve Grosvenor pulled up with an innocent crunch of tires upon the snow.

"Hey, Skipper," he bellowed, and blared the horn in a signal that their long wait was over. "The road to the tracking station's bein' cleared. Let's give it a try."

Caught in the act of sex. There was nothing in the human condition more defeating.

R.T.'s distress was not that he had been denied the moments of sweetness that came after, but that nothing had changed. With his two strong hands and a heart full of love, he hadn't changed anything—not Allyson's ingrained allegiance to Daniel nor her need to place two thousand six hundred miles between herself and him.

And Allyson, feeling him withdraw with a tenderness that made her want to weep, was not surprised that they were returned, rudely, to the same time-worn reality. In her woman's wisdom, she had always known that sex didn't solve anything. Sex created terrible problems, and part of her hated R.T. Smith because that was true, and she hated herself more.

"It's all right," he whispered when her lips trembled. "Are you okay?"

Allyson's breath uncoiled like silk. No, she wasn't okay. Could he not look and know she wasn't okay? He would be typically male now and think her distress was because she hadn't floated off into some silvery orgasmic bliss when the truth was, he was right: she *was* running from him to Atlanta, and she would keep on running.

He made quick work of repairing his clothes. He then saw to her own, helping her into her jeans and refusing to allow her the luxury of self-consciousness. When she was buttoned and zipped, he drew her hair aside and reverently cradled the curve of her cheek.

"The hazards of adulthood, my love," he said, and let his smile stroke her with adoration. "I would say I love you, but I said it before, and look what happened."

Before she could compare his love to what she was feeling, he strode to the door and jerked it open.

Cold washed into the room like truth.

"We're coming," he shouted to Steve, and deliberately neglected to invite him in. "I have to change."

"Take your time," Steve shouted back, which meant, Allyson was certain, I know everything that's going on in there.

Not trusting herself, she escaped to the bathroom. As R.T. changed, she shakily stuffed her panties with tissues. She brushed her hair and thought she looked motley and horrible. She splashed her face with water to return its color.

Looking up from the towel, she found R.T. resplendently uniformed in the doorway, a hand braced upon each facing as if he were presenting himself for crucifixion. How dazzling he was, how handsome, how much of what she loved. She saw his medals and insignia, his crisp tie and stiff collar and knew that never again would they generate that delirious oblivion they had once possessed. Their first shared love had been the best of them both.

No husband ever studied a wife more closely. "I'm trying to read your mind, Allyson Wyatt."

"If I don't understand what's going on in there—" she placed the towel neatly on its rack "—you certainly won't be able to."

"You're sorry it happened."

"It's not like it hasn't happened before, is it?"

"Hell, honey—" his self-mockery sent her pushing past him into the bedroom "—once every fourteen years ain't a bad average, is it?"

She fetched her coat and shrugged into it, found her fur hat and stood distractedly fluffing it, reminding him of another motel room. "We don't exactly do much talking first, do we?"

A moment passed before the point of her remark found its target.

R.T. laughed briefly as she mauled the fur. "You're worried about safety?"

The look she shot him was one for which no words existed. "I worry about everything, R.T. I'm not using anything for birth control, for one thing. I told you there hasn't been a man in my life, and then there's the matter of—"

She moved her hand distractedly, and R.T. buttoned her coat as if she were a treasured child. He arranged her hat and her hair and when he was done, he turned so their reflection found them in the bathroom mirror. He drew her back against his chest and wrapped his arms about her waist so he could balance his chin upon her fur hat.

Outside, Steve was revving the engine.

He grinned. "You're afraid of getting pregnant."

"It's not out of the realm of possibility, no."

"If you have a baby, Allyson—" he moved his lips to her ear and whispered softly so that the tease was almost missing "—I'll do the right thing by you."

Allyson's temper yawned. "That's not what I meant."

"We could make a beautiful baby."

"R.T. . . . ." She attempted to pull away, but he held her fast.

"I used to dream about it, you know—what our baby would be."

"R.T.—"

Sighing, he released her. "All right. If you're worried about safety, I'm as safe as they come. The military sees to that. I wouldn't gamble with your life, Allyson. I love your life. I want to be *in* your life. In fact, I don't think I've ever wanted so many things as I do at this moment."

The Jeep engine was impatient.

Then why don't you ask me to marry you? Allyson wanted to blurt. *Why don't you give me something to sacrifice myself upon? Talk me into it while I'm weak and full of you.*

But Steve was waiting. And Daniel was waiting.

"Hold it," R.T. said before she moved completely away. He blotted a smudge of mascara from below her eye, then stepped back to give her a swift inspection. "Perfect."

Allyson gave herself a final once-over in the mirror. What was happening in her life? It had lost its sharp clarity.

"Daniel will know," she predicted grimly. "He'll take one look at my face and know."

Olsen Tracking Station consisted of three observatories—white-domed buildings that housed supersensitive radio telescopes capable of tracking an object the size of a golf ball three thousand miles away. The compound was surrounded by a chain-link fence, whether to keep the military in or civilians out was unclear. Like a sore thumb, a sentry box had been thrust up through the snow at the gate.

Though the storm had stopped and the sun seemed to have sprinkled the whole world with sequins, the wind still cut like a scythe. Breathing was painful. Everyone was wearing sunglasses to keep from going snow blind.

Leaving Steve to trail along behind, R.T. followed Allyson inside. His shock of seeing Daniel upon a stark hospital cot, his head bandaged and his right arm in a sling, was unexpected. Nor was he prepared for the pain of watching Allyson's horror as she moved to the side of her ex-husband.

"Oh, Daniel," she murmured as she went to him, peeling off her hat and coat and gloves, and placing them upon the only chair in the room. "What has happened to you?"

Michael's photograph had showed the strong likeness the boy had to his father. Daniel's blond beauty had not dissipated, had only become slightly more weighty with the years. His genius had somehow prevented the hardness that came with life, and he sent R.T. a grateful boy's smile over Allyson's head.

"It's a lot worse than it looks," he said shyly. "Hey, R.T., I'm glad to see you, man. What have you sprouted over that top lip, huh? A mouth toupee?"

Tucking his hat beneath his arm, R.T. clasped Daniel's hand, and then they dispensed with macho images and hugged each other, eyes misting as they slipped, for a time, into another place of their lives, to an innocence that could be remembered but not recaptured.

"Some place you've got here," R.T. said, as he looked around at the stark ugly walls, the acoustic tiles on the ceiling, the functional medicine cabinets.

"Yeah." Daniel smiled awkwardly at Allyson.

"Yes, well..." R.T. coughed into a fist. "How's it going?"

"Fine, fine." Daniel allowed Allyson to inspect his bandages. "How've you been doing?"

"Better than you."

Daniel laughed. They all laughed, and R.T. picked up Allyson's coat from where it had slithered to the floor. He draped it neatly over the back of the chair and folded her scarf and placed it with a man's tidiness into her fur hat. He drew the chair close to the bed and straddled it.

Daniel asked Allyson all the routine father's questions about Michael, and despite his claim to be doing well, he was nervous and jittery, R.T. thought. His eyes never stopped moving. Though he talked to Allyson, his gaze kept returning to R.T. and flitting away.

Presently, R.T. followed their track and saw the surveillance camera mounted to his left near the ceiling in one corner of the room. He casually reconnoitered the room and guessed there would be another, though he didn't see it.

With a curl of his lip, he nodded, and the urgency melted from Daniel's shoulders.

Steve Grosvenor tapped lightly upon the door and poked his blond head inside, inviting another round of introductions. Alerting Steve that the room was bugged was easy, and when Allyson finally caught on, the conversation grew as interesting as a pair of old socks.

Daniel kept thanking them for coming. "It was a terrible imposition, I know."

"What're friends for?" R.T. countered, and Allyson inanely agreed by saying that friends were supposed to impose on each other.

When that subject became too awkward to handle, she shut her mouth and found herself a place to sit on the end of the bed. Steve placed himself beneath the monitor and leaned against the wall.

"Tell us what you can," R.T. said to Daniel, meaning, *We'll interpret until we get it right.*

Daniel explained the shooting of the Chevron station, making so much of it being a case of mistaken identity that everyone was certain it wasn't. When he said he had come up for a vacation, when they knew positively that he had not, they gradually caught on that what was said was exactly the opposite of what had happened.

"I had a birthday last month," Allyson said, testing Daniel's cryptic code.

Grinning, Daniel said he hoped it was a good one.

"How old are you?" R.T. inquired, and Allyson told him she was the same age as he and they all knew it.

"I'd forgotten," he said.

The nurse interrupted with medication, Daniel asked for a glass of water. When Allyson fetched it he said, "Did you find that file you were looking for, Allyson?"

"Yes," she lied as the nurse left the room. "It turns out it wasn't important at all. I told R.T. all about it."

"I know you were upset about nothing." Daniel took a mouthful of water and tossed back his head to swallow. "You get upset too easily, Allyson."

"I'm sure I do."

Laughing, Daniel patted the mattress beside him. "Allyson, d'you remember when we all went over to Eddy Conaveris's that night when his parents had gone to Las Vegas?"

She smiled. "And you hacked into that dating service on Eddy's old IBM workhorse?"

Daniel agreed with a series of lying nods.

Still straddling the chair, R.T. crossed his arms upon Allyson's coat. Her perfume enfolded him. "I remember," he said, and warmed to his performance for the benefit of the camera. "You could've put someone else's name into that service though, bud. I must've gotten two hundred damn calls from overweight women."

The truth was, Eddy Conaveris wouldn't have known an IBM computer if it had flown past him with wings. And Eddy didn't live with his parents; he lived with his brother and sister-in-law and their three children. The old computer was Daniel's, and unless R.T. missed his guess, Daniel was telling Allyson it had something to do with the disappearance of her Bolten file.

A sheen of sweat had broken out on Daniel's forehead and his hair, dampened, had turned to cornsilk. Moving to wring out a cloth with fresh water, Allyson bathed his face while R.T. picked up her gloves from the floor where they had dropped. He paired them and placed them neatly into her pocket.

A paper rustled and fell upon his knee. Opening it, he saw his own phone number and initials scribbled down and traced and retraced until the paper was nearly worn thought. Smiling, he slipped it into his pocket.

"I know this is a drag," Daniel was saying, "but that medicine's knocking me dead cold. What's the word on when you're going to fly me out of here?"

Steve came away from the wall. "The sun's shining. We could go right now."

Even as he spoke, Daniel's eyes drooped to a medicated half-mast. "Why don't we say first thing tomorrow?"

Steve moved closer to the bed. "It's fine with me if it's okay with everyone else."

Allyson and R.T. consulted each other and nodded. "Sure. First thing after breakfast."

Daniel extended a hand to the pilot. "It's been good meeting you, Steve. Thanks for flying Allyson up and taking care of my friends."

Grinning, Steve flipped a salute from his patch. "No sweat. Any friend of R.T.'s is a friend of mine. Look, you guys say goodbye. I'll be out in the hall."

Nodding, his face lax from the drug, Daniel took Allyson's hand and placed a kiss upon it. "I'll be all right, babe. Thanks for coming. If you talk to Michael tonight, tell him for me that I love him."

The curve of Allyson's back when she leaned over to kiss Daniel on the cheek made R.T.'s heart twist with a desperation that he only partially understood. Over her head, Daniel was seeking R.T.'s eyes with an urgency that was unmistakable.

As Allyson straightened, R.T. touched her shoulder. "Go on with Steve, why don't you? I'll say goodbye and be there in a minute."

Her eyebrows were skeptical, yet she picked up her things and moved obligingly to the door. "A minute?" she said as she looked back.

"A minute."

As she left, R.T. stood at the foot of Daniel's bed and felt a twinge of damnation much as if he were waiting before the principal's desk to give an accounting for what he'd spray painted on the Cardinal Heights water tower.

Daniel shifted onto his side, and R.T. walked around and stood beside him. They were poised at some crucial nexus, he and Daniel. The past code that had existed—the yuppie friend and the rebel, the groom and the best man, the computer expert and the Marine—no longer held. This was man to man.

"R.T. . . . ." Daniel's voice was slurred around his words. "I want to apologize, man. If there'd been anyone else I trusted enough, anyone I could've turned to—"

R.T. extended his hand and Daniel clung to it, his color that of the sheet and his grip no stronger than a child's.

"I would never have forgiven you, Dan," R.T. said.

"How does she seem to you?" Daniel asked.

"Allyson? She's strong, you know that."

"I should never have married her."

"Dan, don't say—"

Daniel waved away the reminder as if they were far past that. "This Grosvenor? Is he any good?"

R.T. grinned. "Well, I only saw him walk on water once, but he claims he does it all the time."

Laughing, Daniel closed his eyes.

Thinking that he had drifted off to sleep, R.T. was preparing to leave when Daniel opened his eyes and whispered, "Come closer."

Puzzled, R.T. bent nearer. Like a young boy, Daniel laid his arm across R.T.'s back. He said huskily, "I don't have much time."

As old guilt rose in R.T., it took all his will to bear the honesty in Daniel's eyes.

"I know about you and Allyson."

"Oh, God." R.T. began pulling away, feeling like David must have felt for loving Bathsheba.

"No, no." Daniel was insistent. "Don't say that."

"Dan—"

Daniel was turning his head from side to side. "It's all right, man. If I couldn't have her, there's no one I'd rather she love than you. I know what it cost you to let her go."

There was no shame like that of having wronged a friend. R.T. wanted to hide his face. He wanted to weep. But Daniel was fighting medication just to remain conscious. He lifted his head and blinked his eyes until he could focus.

"Give me your hand, R.T.," he said.

R.T. was surprised when Daniel laced their fingers together and made a tight fist.

"If anything happens," Daniel whispered, "if something should happen and I don't make it, she's *your* responsibility."

His friend's trust buried itself deep into R.T.'s belly like a fist. "I'm not listening to this, Dan. Not another word."

"You have to take care of her, man. And Michael, too. I'm entrusting the two things I love best to you. Promise me."

"That's the medicine talking. Of course you're going to make it."

Daniel's grip was amazingly strong. He told R.T. about the bullets fired into his bed, about his fear, his regret. "You owe me, R.T. Promise, dammit. I can be at peace if you promise."

Don't put me in this position! Don't you see what you're doing? R.T. wanted to tell Daniel that he would do everything, that it would be his privilege. But to be sworn to it was the one thing Allyson would not accept. She would not see his own love as love but as the obligation of a vow he'd sworn to Daniel.

R.T. bent his forehead to a clenched fist and squeezed his eyes tightly shut. He whispered, "Whatever Allyson and I felt was a long time ago, Dan. We were kids. She has her own life now. She's stronger than you think. She's not letting her mother or me or anyone else tell her what to do. She can take care of herself, and that's God's truth."

Daniel's fingers were a vise. "You didn't promise. Promise . . . !"

With his heart gripped in an iron fist and his breath threatening to stop, R.T. bent low until his head came to rest against Daniel's.

"I swear, on the friendship we've had for each other, I'll take care of them. You have my oath. Rest now, Dan. Go to sleep."

Slumping upon the pillow as his breathing leveled into that of peaceful, dreamless slumber, Daniel's face became that of a trusting boy. As he straightened, R.T. drew the back of his hand along the jaw of the face that had always been so quick to laugh with him, so happy to share.

Trembling, R.T. touched his own face. The room, as he stood and looked around it, offered no solution. He could again hear the screams of the women as they clawed at his clothes and clung to his legs in the rain, pleading for him to find their children. *Help me, help me.*

The shame, when he walked out the door, was worse than any he'd ever known.

Slowly, as the door shut quietly behind R.T., Daniel Wyatt opened his eyes. With a small contented sigh, he unclenched his fist and leaned across the bed to drop the nurse's tiny white pill into the wastebasket beside the cot. Then he lay back, satisfied and at peace. Smiling, he went to sleep.

Chapter 11

"I said, what did you and Daniel talk about for so long?" Allyson repeated in a tone so resembling a grappling hook, R.T. wondered if he hadn't made a mistake in wanting to step beyond the perimeter of bachelorhood.

She was gathering her clothes from the closet. In one giant swoop, she collected them, trekked across the cabin floor, tripped over the hem of her coat and left a trail of clattering hangers as she dumped everything onto the bed where the cat lay curled in an oblivious ball, sleeping.

The cat clawed his way from beneath the avalanche and headed for higher ground. Good thinking, R.T. decided.

Their lovemaking had not been discussed. It was as if leaving it stranded on an island of silence imbued it with an insanity that need not be coped with immediately.

But it really solved nothing. The plan was that they would pack tonight. In the morning they would collect Daniel from the infirmary. From there, Steve would pilot them back to Seattle. And then?

R.T. wished he knew. The weather, for once, was cooperating. Allyson was the one who was flitting around, more nervous than the cat, as if she couldn't wait another second to put Operation Atlanta into action.

"Daniel's not thinking too clearly," R.T. hedged, and plucked the cat from where the beast had found sanctuary in his own wooly pully.

"You and he talked a long time," she argued as she folded and sorted.

R.T. wished she would drop the matter. He didn't want to lie, and he couldn't bring himself to tell her the truth. "We hadn't seen each other in a long time."

"What did Daniel say?"

"What do you think Daniel had to say?"

"How should I know?" She inspected a small tomato stain on her skirt. "Daniel tends to think in TSO."

R.T. rescued her silk blouse from the pile of clothes.

"I like this blouse," he said, and held it up to his chest and looked through the bathroom door to the mirror. He preened ridiculously. "Don't you think it's my color?"

She grabbed it from his hands. "Tootsie you are not."

"I think you should wear it to dinner."

"Oh, you do, do you?" Her chin dared him when she peered over her shoulder. "What's wrong with what I've got on?"

R.T. worried the chip of his tooth then worked himself up to the edge of his mustache.

"Ahh..." He grinned cannily. "You know, Allyson darlin', my old grandma has a saying—it's better to be alive than dead. Connie's shirt is beautiful on you. It shoots a great game of pool. I just like the green one. It's more... Scarlett O'Hara." He gave a hug yawn and patted his mouth. "If you know what I mean."

To R.T.'s amazement, she laughed. With a sweeping shift of strategy, she sauntered to where he stood stuffing clothes into his duffle.

"You know what I like best about you, R.T.?" She purringly looped her arms around his neck, grinding against him in a way that would have aroused a dead man.

His lip curled. "Is this multiple choice or fill in the blanks?"

"It's your sensitivity, R.T."

He locked his arms about her back with a warning that she was walking very close to the fire. "Scarlett O'Hara never did that."

"But Scarlett didn't know you, did she?" She brushed his lips with a coy flick of her tongue. "Besides, Scarlett is dead. And so are you going to be if you don't tell me what you and Daniel talked about! *Dead as in door nail!*"

She attempted to twirl away, but Connie's shirt had twisted and her breasts were spilling half out of her bra, their satin, nippled curves setting his teeth on edge.

"I should warn you," he said, drawing her arms behind her back so their bodies molded together like pieces of a puzzle, "there are things a Marine knows to do at times like this. We can turn torture into a thing of beauty, Allyson love, so don't mess with me."

"Mess with you?" Her challenge was sultry and breathy, and R.T. could feel the quick throb of her heart beneath his, the sharp catch of her breath. Part of her was enjoying the danger of the game, but part of her was playing it with a death grip.

"I'm not scared of you," she said with a flutter of lashes.

"Oh, you should be, lady." He laughed huskily. "You should be."

But her coyness had disappeared and his own amusement was disintegrating. One tiny jest had taken them on a long journey, and they both knew it.

"Do you know I could eat you up?" He sleeked the curves of her hips, cupping them and pulling her upward, closer to the desire he wanted her to feel. "I could lick you from the top of your head to your little toes. I could lock us in this room and not come out for three days."

Her tongue crept out to moisten her lips, and her eyes were large with need. "I have to know what Daniel said, R.T." she said honestly. "Please."

Deep in his truest heart, R.T. knew he would curse himself a thousand times if he told her. He could lose any chance he might have with her. But perhaps it wasn't there to lose, and he was as incapable of dishonoring her with a lie as he was of laying a birthright at her feet.

Aching for what might have been, he took her face in his hands. "He was worried about you, darling," he said, and tenderly kissed her eyebrows, the line of worry between them. "He made me promise that if anything happened to him, I would take care of you and Michael. I told him I would. And I will."

She pushed away and held up her palms as if he had sneaked up on her from behind, a predator from the past.

"No," she whispered as misunderstanding caught them in its deadly sights. "You're not going to do it to me again, R.T. I won't let you. I don't have to learn the same lesson over and over. No, no, no."

Was his life never to be anything but offering himself at his woman's feet? What did it take to be worthy of her, for God's sake?

A knock sounded at the door. Never more grateful for an interruption in his life, R.T. spun on his heel and jerked the door open to glare at Trish, who was shivering and dancing upon the sawdusted porch.

Her face collapsed when she saw his expression.

"Telephone, Major," she said lamely. "And it sounded important."

R.T. grabbed up his jacket, made a final, bleak survey of Allyson and the room, then said, "I'll be back."

But he lied. He didn't come back. After thirty nerve-racking minutes, after Allyson had looked at her reflection in the bathroom mirror for the dozenth time and swore she was a fool, swore that she was above such stupid stunts, swore that R.T. was *not* living in Daniel's shadow but that she was craving to punish him anyway, he still had not come back.

"Well," she said to the woman who stared back at her from the glass, "are you going to get yourself in gear and go get him? If I were R.T., I wouldn't want to come back, either. Not if I got myself analyzed by a maniac every time

I opened my mouth, not to mention having to look at drying underwear.''

She snatched two pairs of hand-laundered panties from the towel rack and threw them onto her pile of clothes to be packed. Then she fished out her skirt and put it on, along with the green silk blouse. She brushed her hair until it shone and teased it a bit and put on fresh makeup. She brushed mascara on her lashes and blusher on her cheeks and fluffed tiny ringlets about her face so that she was pretty and unstudied. As a final touch, she dabbed perfume behind her ears and her knees and gave herself a critical scrutiny before she fetched her coat.

She looked at her watch. Forty-five flaming minutes!

"Who are you trying to kid? Haven't you ever heard that a leopard doesn't change its spots? The best thing about R.T. Smith is that he never changes. He came here to help his friend Daniel, because he can't change. To him, you're what you always were—a gratuity. For pity's sake, Allyson, do grow up."

Hot, stinging tears welled. "And don't you dare cry. Get your fanny over there and hold up your head as if you don't give a damn. And then you go home and pack up your junk and get yourself to Atlanta as fast as you can. Now, do it!"

With shaking fingers, she raked the curls from her hair and caught it in a seal-sleek ponytail. Tearing off the green blouse, she jerked an old sweater over her head and shimmied into her jeans. She pulled on her boots and dragged a pair of leg warmers over their tops until she looked as if she were suffering from some hideous disease.

Dragging on her coat, she scooped the cat from the bed, snatched open the door, threw the cat outside to the snow and slammed the door as hard as possible. Then she chugged across the barren wasteland at the end of the world and cursed herself. And R.T.

The front door of the Bear Cave was stubborn and half frozen. With the wind pulling at her hair, Allyson pushed it, but it wouldn't open. Dangerously near tears, she placed her shoulder against it and shoved with all her might.

The door swept open and she went staggering into the café, catching herself heavily upon the counter and almost going down on her knees from the force of the impact.

She looked up to see if anyone had seen her disgraceful entrance.

"Happy birthday!" everyone shouted, applauding.

With an astounding amount of ingenuity, Connie and Herb and the girls had transformed the Bear Cave into an impromptu banquet hall.

As Allyson caught herself upon the cash register, she peered up at newspaper streamers festooning the ceiling, sweeping from the corners of the room to the now-still paddle fan. There, they collected into a graceful centerpiece containing everything from artificial flowers and fruit to the girls' sparkling rhinestone chains. A banner made of food wrapping stretched across one wall, announcing in bold red letters Happy 33rd, Allyson! Butterflies fashioned out of paper plates dropped from the ceiling. Charlie Daniels was singing that the South was going to do it again, and the moose was having the time of his life.

"She's here!" squealed the girls.

Nick and Bill and Guy and Chuck, Iris Kurble and the chain-saw representative looked up as Connie and the girls rushed forward, en masse, and hugged her.

Torn between her astonishment and the knowledge that only one person could have arranged this, Allyson searched for R.T. He was standing at the end of the bar, talking to Herb. He had braced a boot on the foot rail of the bar and grinned wanly.

You finally made it, I see.

How did you do this without my knowing? she telegraphed him.

I'm a con man, don't you remember? His eyebrows were as unhappy as the smile that kept disappearing beneath his mustache.

"Well, all right, guys and gals!" Connie was booming in her bullhorn voice. "The guest of honor has finally arrived." Then to R.T., with a wag of her finger, she said,

"And you said she'd come in here spittin' fire. Shame, shame, Major. She's a darlin'."

I see you didn't wear the blouse.

I almost didn't come, blouse or no blouse.

I'm glad you did.

Are you? Really?

"All right, then, let's do it!" Connie roared, and lifted her hands in a conductor's pose. "One . . . two . . . three . . . altogether now . . ."

"Happy Birthday" had been sung more melodically but never more earnestly. Allyson suffered her spotlight like a trouper, smiling for a few seconds, then laughing back at the girls and folding her arms, dropping her hands to her sides then lacing her fingers in a smiling pose of resignation.

As the song neared its end, Herb scurried from the kitchen, balancing a cake on a tray held high above his head. In the center had been placed a Fourth of July sparkler.

"We didn't have any candles, Ms. Wyatt," he apologized.

"Oh, this is fine." Allyson laughed. "Just fine, Herb."

The girls were passing out chicken salad sandwiches and another round of beer. Everyone was encouraged to "liven things up a little in this Cave." Someone put Hank Williams, Jr. on the jukebox, and as the cake was cut, all the men crowded round and asked Allyson to dance.

The gathering, Allyson thought, would have appalled Kaye Randolph, and if she, Allyson, were back in Seattle and had been invited, she would have probably declined Connie and her girls and Herb and his culinary disasters and the fellow travelers who had come in from the cold.

But here, in this place, she felt as if she'd been paid a high compliment. They were, briefly and bizarrely, family. So she gave them back the only thing at her disposal, her warmth and wit and laughing comradeship.

From afar, R.T. watched as she gamely laughed at the men's jokes and protested at compliments that were becoming a bit tipsy. Allyson smiled at him. He smiled back. Both of them wanted to talk, but never had the time been worse.

Shortly before midnight, the party broke up and people wandered out in twos and threes, calling good-nights and wishing many happy returns. Trish and Eileen disappeared to a place Allyson was sure she didn't want to know about, a man on each arm.

The lights behind the bar cast a warm, moody glow of mirrored amber and sparkling crystalline liquids. Cleanup was left for tomorrow with its clearing weather and improving roads. The guests who had been family for the last days would pass into history and leave only a smudge upon the tapestry of their lives.

Allyson found herself alone with the moose and R.T. and the sociable sputter of the Budweiser sign. The colors of the old-fashioned jukebox smeared, reminiscent of another age when men in uniform danced the Lindy, with their pompadoured ladies wearing seamed stockings and spectator pumps.

Allyson found a garbage sack beneath Connie's counter and wandered through the silent room, scooping up paper plates and napkins and empty bottles and dropping them inside with a whispery crunch.

R.T. hadn't asked her to dance, but she didn't take it as a slight; never, in all the years she'd known him, had she ever seen him on a dance floor.

After she knotted the sack and put it away, the silence grew tangible. She studied R.T. from a distance—the tall, brooding man in relief against the rainbow of the jukebox. Her breath stopped and started like a bad engine. His hands were tucked beneath his belt and his pants bloused over the tops of his boots. His sweater hugged his hips.

Making her start, he inserted several coins into the jukebox and they rolled down the gullet of the machine where they clicked. Presently, music filled the empty spaces of the café, but not the rowdy country-western tunes that had graced her party, but an old Glenn Miller tune with saxophones and a melancholy clarinet.

As inevitably as a compass needle swings north, she moved toward him until she was so near she could have touched his back. He didn't turn at her sound and the song played out. When it began again, he came around and smiled briefly, then folded her into his arms.

Oh! How right it was to lean against him and feel the texture of his moves and draw in the spicy eloquence of his scent. With a lyrical grace that amazed her, he danced her around the small space until she felt as if she were luminous and floating, buoyant, her hair swirling about their heads like a wreath.

It was over much too soon, and the only music left was the fizzing sputter of Connie's sign. They remained in each other's arms, moving occasionally and asking nothing of the shadowy warmth except that it wrap them in safety.

"What're you thinking?" she whispered as her cheek pressed his sweater.

"I don't know." A sound vaguely like a chuckle was muffled by his sigh. "The past maybe, how perfect your back is beneath my hand, the smell of your hair, the nights I dreamed of you, I don't know."

She spread her hand upon the side of his hip and marveled at the strength of man, a resiliency of bone and muscle whose power had never been equalled in all the world's great history.

"We're at the end of the world," she mused dreamily. "We're the last two people alive. The life we left isn't real."

He drew in her scent and tightened his arms about her. "But our time together is ending."

"I know."

"And we have to go back."

"I know."

Eventually he released her, and Allyson felt an overwhelming loss as he stepped back. He gazed about the room, at the makeshift chandelier and party frills. His ear bent toward his shoulder as if he were listening to wise voices inside his head.

He said presently, "You know, it's always been my belief that the character of a man is determined by what he's willing to lay on the line."

Allyson was struck by the things about R.T. Smith she did not know, the complexity of him.

"When I was a boy," he reflected, as if to himself, "I wanted to live the way everyone else did more than anything. I copied you and Daniel and hoped your genteel edge would rub off, but I came to realize that I would never be what you two were. I could never run fast enough to catch up. I could never work hard enough...."

His shoulders lifted, then dropped. He stared in resignation at his boots. "Let me tell you, that was one hard truth."

Allyson's heart ached with an empathy that had been entombed there too long. "That so-called edge may not have been right for you, R.T. I'm not so sure it's right for anyone."

"Oh, but it does have its advantages, babe." Looking up, he smiled briefly and unhappily. "It does have advantages."

His profile was hardy and angular as he considered the minuses of his past. He touched his temple.

She started to go to him, but he said, "There were times when I got so tired of being pushed and shoved and stepped on, I wanted to just scream out, 'When will it be enough?' I watched you tonight, and you were so pretty and everyone loved you. I wanted to be a part of all that, someone on the inside who could make you laugh. But I wasn't and I never can be. I was prepared to argue with you tonight about moving to Atlanta, about a lot of things, to try to prove some point, but . . ."

His breath came in a long sigh, and Allyson's eyes brimmed. She crossed her arms hard over her breasts, for they ached, *she* ached. Going to him, she leaned her cheek upon his shoulder and circled him with her arms.

He pressed his face into her hair. "God, I don't know one reason in the world why you should marry me," he groaned.

Oh, R.T.! Standing on tiptoe, Allyson sought the side of his neck with her lips, where the muscles were corded and taut. She skimmed his collarbone and placed her mouth against his ear. He sighed as if he had wanted her to do exactly that.

"I want to hope again, I really do," she whispered as she wrapped her arms tighter and tighter around him. "Love me tonight and make me forget the mistakes we've made. Make me believe we can start over, R.T. Make me believe that the past can't hurt us anymore.''

Perhaps it was a pipe dream—that flimsy escape from the past. But their mouths clung with a sweet desperation. His hands cradled the back of her head, and Allyson met his tongue with hers and slipped her hands beneath his belt, closing her fingers on the flesh of his buttocks, the smooth and scarred flesh.

Daniel's ghost rattled its chains in the distance, yet R.T. took her back to their room and shut the door.

"I love you more now than I did then," she confessed as she rose on her toes and kissed him. "I'm capable of more. I can accept more."

In the solitude they stood together for long, throbbing moments, searching each other in the shadows. Ever so slowly, she moved over the contours of his body and thrilled to his heat, his stirring. As he unbuttoned her shirt and freed her breasts, she let her head tip upon its neck's axis. Her hair swung free, and his kisses melted upon her throat, making her shiver as she thought, This is all the sensation I can bear. There is no more.

But then he slipped his fingers beneath the lace of her panties and found her. She clung to his shoulders and heard her own voice cry out, but it was only the strange illusion inside her head.

"Did you mean it?" he was whispering as his breath roughened with pleasure. "About wanting to believe?"

"I'm not sure I know how."

He laid her back upon the bed and slid his leg across her waist. "Do you think about tomorrow?"

"Tomorrow, I see us losing each other."

"Why?"

Allyson struggled to open her eyes, but she was drugged with the headiness of him. She didn't know why. She didn't know anything except that she must arch upward and let him know how badly she wanted him.

He made love to her with a desperation that was both heartbreaking and deliriously exciting. There was no time for delicate inquiries, only demands and hungry taking before destiny had its way with them. So Allyson made herself brazenly available, straddling him and lifting her arms and offering her breasts and her warm, hollowed crevices.

As he rose up in her like steel, she gasped with the sensation that startled her. In her mind's eye she saw them—she saw the sheen of sweat play upon his skin as he struggled with his perilous agony of enduring. She tried to take control of her own sexuality, but he knew her secrets now and he took pleasure in opening her—parting the petals of her flower—satisfying her in ways she had not imagined with his hands and his fingers and his kisses and his hot, sleeking tongue.

"Do you love me?" he demanded as he gathered her for a final conquest.

"Yes."

"Say it."

She could hardly speak. "I love you."

"Promise you won't see us losing each other tomorrow."

"I promise." Allyson felt as if she were turning to silver. She was melting. She was being poured—yes, yes!

Only then did he enter her, with a searching, intensely sensuous probing. She clung to him, rocking as the waves swelled and submerged him. He strained against her and gasped through clenched teeth, his head tilted back and his eyes closed.

She wept when it was done, for she had lied. The future was black in her mind and she could not see them together. How could they do it? How could two lives as complex as theirs converge into one?

Sobs battered at the doors of her heart.

"Shh, my love," he whispered as he held her and blotted the tears with his fingers. "It's all right. Everything's going to be all right."

Though she did not understand, this time she did not protest.

Chapter 12

Cluttering Allyson's awakening were voices—a stream of watery exchanges.

"Sergeant Wallach's report..."

"...name?"

"Tate. Anchorage..."

"...the military..."

"...in the area. Mrs. Wyatt. The Bear Cave...half hour?"

She stirred, loathe to leave the bliss of her dream. R.T. had been in the dream, his love by turns worshipful, then demanding, then teasing, then a zenith of bright flames. Now she couldn't remember where sleep ended and began for he would draw her into the hollowed urgency of his body, slipping between her legs as if seeking a sheath until he was magically inside. Had she dreamed him, looming above her? A blaze of vibrant maleness soaring from a mat of dark curls until they were once again immersed in their own fragrances and liquids and her heart stopped and she died and came to life again?

It was no dream. Hers was a tenderness no woman could mistake.

She peeped from beneath the edge of the blanket like a criminal. Everywhere their clothes lay strewn. The bed was a shambles, the sheets and blankets at odds with the mattress, and the room was chilled. The door was open. Sunshine, cold and glistening, was scattering diamonds on the snow and framing R.T.'s height.

Barefoot and shirtless, his shoulders were a contrast of hammered copper against the snow. He was an unbuckled prince summoned by a messenger, and when he shut the door and turned, half-zippered fatigues shifting loosely about his flanks, Allyson didn't move for fear he would see she'd been watching and their desire would erupt again.

She wasn't ready to talk. The question was posed now: Could marriage be the answer for them? Why not? They weren't children. They knew the pitfalls that were peculiarly theirs. They knew where the mines were buried and how to circumvent them. They had made mistakes, but they had learned. Did she want to risk marriage again?

He walked into the bathroom, and she heard him brush his teeth, heard the rush of water as the toilet flushed. There were things she would never again be able to pretend with this man.

Ostrichlike, she turned her face into the pillow where his scent still clung. She drew it deep into her lungs.

The mattress gave as he lowered himself to the edge. She didn't move. Then, as if awakening she stirred and opened her eyes, letting in a pinprick of light. He smiled and leaned across her legs, his chest much broader in the light of day, vastly more naked with its whorls of black hair.

"Someone was at the door?" she quickly asked, not wishing to betray that she wanted him again, tenderness or no tenderness. "Or did I dream that?"

He pondered the tops of her bare shoulders and surprised her by leaning down to press his lips not to her cheek or to her throat, but to the top of her wrist, his breath sweet and strong.

Straightening, he drew in a breath until his ribs were corrugated against his skin. "Someone *was* at the door."

The distress in his tone made her pull herself up onto an elbow, taking care to keep the blanket over her sloping breasts. "I heard my name, didn't I?"

"A detective is here. Tate, he said his name was. He's investigating the shooting. He's also run a check on Daniel and found out that the federal government wants to question him. He would have been here sooner, he said, but he couldn't get in by plane until today."

There was in his eyes a familiar icy light, and his body was as tense as a strung bow. His face was too exposed.

Allyson ran her tongue across her lips that were sensitive and chafed. "Tell me all of it."

"Daniel is missing from the infirmary."

At first glance, a person might mistake Detective Steiger Tate for a clergyman. A shock of white hair rose brusquely out of his forehead and lent him the look of piety, but his rascally grin made one know immediately that he knew every trick in the book and that keeping secrets from him was hopeless.

Steiger Tate was not so far removed from his youth that he failed to discern the relationship between the tall Marine major and the well-bred blonde when they entered the Bear Cave Café. The officer, he decided, would be straightforward. The woman would have to be approached in a more circuitous fashion, as one would solve a riddle. But that was all right. He thrived on riddles.

The café was noisy with the clatter of serving, though it quietened for a fraction of a second when the couple walked in. Daniel Wyatt's ex-wife was wearing an excellent coat and boots and a white fur hat that hadn't come cheaply.

She hugged a bag that was slung across her shoulder, her manner toward Major Smith one of long-standing intimacy. Protectiveness was on Major Smith's face when he held her coat and watched her hair settle gracefully upon her shoulders. He removed his cap and tucked it with military precision beneath his arm. Yes, indeed, a handsome couple. Tate could remember worshipping a woman as the officer revered Allyson Wyatt.

But that had been a long time ago. Rising, Tate waved them to his table.

"I'm Steiger Tate, Mrs. Wyatt," he introduced himself when they approached and he invited them to sit. "What would you like?"

Allyson hadn't expected to like the detective. He had to have guessed that she and R.T. were lovers, and she resented that. But his smile made a person smile back, even if she didn't want to.

"I try to always have some of Herb's hash browns and sausage whenever I get up," he was saying, his face round and pink as a baby's. "It's kind of a tradition."

"You see a lot of crime around these parts, do you, Detective?" R.T. inquired with a testy edge that drew a look of censure from Allyson.

The lawman seemed oblivious to R.T.'s moodiness and mopped the yolks of his eggs with the last crust and washed everything down with black coffee. Sighing, he wiped his mouth and leaned back, prepared to let everything digest.

"Not much crime," he said in a friendly way, "but whenever we get it, it's usually a doozy. I hear your birthday outperformed the blizzard, Mrs. Wyatt. Congratulations. May I say you don't look anywhere near thirty? You must have been a child bride."

"And you, sir," she pointed a teasingly chiding finger, "have kissed the Blarney Stone somewhere along the way."

After the ordering was done and the food brought by Eileen, who spent so long a time arranging napkins and eavesdropping that R.T. informed her they didn't need anything else, Allyson cut straight to the heart of the matter. "I'm aware that Daniel has disappeared, Detective Tate." She carefully placed her cup into its saucer. "Surely you don't believe we had anything to do with it?"

Steiger Tate made an inquiry with his eyebrows about the appropriateness of having a cigar. When Allyson shrugged, he peeled the cellophane from one while R.T. removed a cigarette from his pack and sat thumping it on a thumbnail. Like a judge peeved with a difficult jury, he turned the cylinder from one end to another, over and over.

"Why don't you tell me everything, Mrs. Wyatt?" the detective said. "Beginning with the reason you came to Nakatak."

With sagging enthusiasm, Allyson recounted what she knew, starting with the disappearance of the Bolten file and Daniel's phone call. The detective removed a pair of half glasses from his pocket and anchored them to his nose. He looked much more like Dr. Watson than Sherlock Holmes as he took copious notes, interrupting her to check a point now and then.

"Well, now," he approved when she was finished, "this will help me enormously." He leaned back to puff his cigar and ponder the ash at its end. "Let me just clarify a few points and make sure I understand your husband's particular genius."

"Ex-husband."

"Of course. I understand how Mr. Wyatt could come and go in your computer system if he had a mind to, but why would the Department of Justice want to question him in their Ill Wind case against Global Defense?"

"Their what?"

"Their Ill Wind case. That's what they call it. Why didn't they question you instead, Mrs. Wyatt? You work with the Global files very day."

"They *did* question me," Allyson replied, "but you have to understand that Daniel has a history there, too. He designed the main frame that Satellite Communications is using. When SCI outgrew that system, Daniel helped me design the new system that Global is using now."

The detective absent-mindedly doodled on his pad. "Then, what you're telling me is that your ex-husband was privy to information that no one else has."

"It's possible."

R.T. was teetering so precariously on the back legs of his chair, Allyson thought one good breath could tip him over. He mentioned to Tate about Daniel's nervousness at being monitored in the infirmary.

Steiger Tate turned to a fresh page in his notebook. "And this person named Eddy? Mr. Wyatt has taken this man into his confidence, you believe?"

"Eddy Conaveris never had any IBM," Allyson said. "Eddy wasn't into that kind of thing. Frankly, detective, we've been very straightforward with you, and now, if you don't mind—"

"May I be as straightforward with you, Mrs. Wyatt?"

Allyson was puzzled.

"When you look at me," he prompted congenially, "what do you see?"

Not understanding, she turned up a palm.

"I'll tell you what you see," Tate explained. "A small-town cop who's over fifty years old and on a dead-end street, Mrs. Wyatt. And now I find myself, for the first time, on a case that has the federal boys' tongues hanging out. I'd like to take this case all the way. Maybe that's dreaming on my part. Maybe I'm just tired of young men in three-piece suits taking the top cut, but I'd consider it a personal favor if you told me everything you know or even what you guess, what you think. Every detail, no matter how small."

Allyson sought R.T.'s reaction and found a thunder-cloud of folded arms and brooding eyebrows. His mouth was a tight line beneath his mustache, and she was reminded of the young hellion at war with authority.

"Daniel is the one with the IBM, Detective Tate." She awkwardly fiddled with the clasp on her bag. "This is a personal opinion, you understand, but I got the feeling yesterday that Daniel took the Bolten file—I've always thought this—and he put in the IBM. It must have something important to do with the case. I can explore that once I get back to my own computer, but that's not what disturbs me the most right now. Where *is* Daniel? Who could come onto a military base and take him out like that? The man was running. He came up here, got himself shot at, and now he's gone again. He may even be dead. Whoever is after Daniel has long arms, and that scares me."

Detective Tate drew his hand over his hair as if generating electricity. He didn't answer her question but faced R.T.

instead. "How much do you know about Steven Grosvenor, Major Smith?"

The front legs of R.T.'s chair struck the floor with a crack like a rifle shot. "Enough to trust him more than I trust you, sir." His scowl was quelling as he leaned over the table. "We were buddies. Does that answer your question?"

"Mr. Grosvenor made a predawn departure from the airstrip, Major," Tate said.

"What?" R.T. exclaimed as Allyson swiveled around in confusion.

The detective laced his fingers across his stomach as if he had just made a very good move in chess.

"It's my opinion that Mr. Grosvenor flew Daniel Wyatt out of Nakatak sometime around dawn," he conjectured. "If this is the case, you wouldn't happen to have any idea of where he would take the man?"

Allyson was still trying to digest the news about Steve Grosvenor. The rascal! How could he?

"Daniel did ask me about Steve," R.T. recollected as he studied the cigarette in his fingers.

"Oh?"

"When I went back to talk to him."

Steiger Tate peered over the rim of his glasses. "What is it, Major? What's on your mind?"

"Grant Melbourne," R.T. said, then slipped the cigarette between his lips and flicked the wheel on his lighter, cupping the flame and inhaling deeply.

Allyson snatched the cigarette from between R.T.'s lips and ground it into the ashtray. "R.T., you have a mental block where Grant Melbourne is concerned."

The detective cut her off with a click of his pen. "Go on, Major."

R.T. plucked a shred of tobacco from his lip. "I don't have any argument with Allyson's trust of Grant Melbourne, particularly. Up to now I've always believed that whoever was after Daniel was on the contracting end of things, some middleman with hungry pockets who wasn't afraid of screwing the government. It never occurred to me that Grant Melbourne could be the one with his backside in the fire."

"Wait a minute!" Allyson protested.

"How did you come up with this?" Tate was scribbling furiously.

R.T. poked unhappily among the ruins of his cigarette. "I haven't the faintest idea."

"You're crazy, R.T." Allyson's poise was as shredded as the tobacco in the ash tray. "That's . . . just crazy. Grant wouldn't do that."

"Mrs. Wyatt," Tate interrupted, "you spoke with Mr. Melbourne on the phone . . ." He paused to retrace his steps through the notes. "Yes, here it is—shortly before you visited the infirmary."

Allyson repeated everything she could remember about her conversation with Grant, then said sharply to R.T., "What could possibly be wrong with any of that?"

Pondering, R.T. slumped low on his spine, his legs stretched out before him and crossed at the tops of his boots. "Tell me again what Melbourne said when you told him Daniel had wrecked his car."

"He said that Daniel shouldn't worry, that it was insured." Allyson shrugged.

"Not exactly." He shook his head. "When you told me before, it was different."

Nearing her wits' end, Allyson rummaged in her bag for a lipstick. Finding it, she started to draw it across her mouth but stabbed at him with its pink tip. "He said 'What's a new Porsche good for? It'll be insured to the hilt.' What could possibly . . . be . . ."

Suddenly Allyson covered her mouth, her eyes widening.

"How did Melbourne know that Daniel had a new Porsche?" he said. "Daniel told us he'd only had it a couple of days."

It wasn't possible. Grant wouldn't; he couldn't. But it made sense, didn't it? That strange conversation the morning Bolten had turned up missing? All of it made sense, and if it were true, Grant was behind the attempts made on Daniel's life.

Aghast, she whispered, "Now he knows that I've talked to Daniel."

A muscle flexed dangerously in R.T.'s jaw as he came around. His hands, when they clutched the edge of the table, were eagle's talons. Frightening shadows filled his face. He was afraid for her, Allyson knew.

Steiger Tate said, "Mrs. Wyatt, you must realize this could make you a target too. Even more so if the grand jury wants to question you, as I expect they will once you return to Seattle."

Like a sleepwalker, she put the cap on her lipstick and came to her feet. Was it only last night that she and R.T. had whispered about hoping? Whispered about tomorrow? This *was* tomorrow!

She groped for her bag, and without warning, its contents clattered to the floor, spilling in all directions. On the verge of weeping, she blinked at the clutter, then dropped to the floor and began collecting her things.

R.T. brought his face down on a level with hers and scooped up her comb and brush, her nail clippers.

"If Grant's done this thing," she choked out from behind her hair, which draped between them, "I have to go to the authorities, R.T."

"Listen to me." Dumping her items into her bag, he took her hard by the shoulders, forced her to look at him. "You have to do one thing and one thing only, Allyson. This is not negotiable. This is not something you can think about. You put as much distance as possible between Grant Melbourne and yourself and keep your mouth shut."

"Would you?" she challenged bitterly.

"You're not me."

"Yes, well . . ."

"Mrs. Wyatt . . ." Tate peered over the edge of the table. "What would you tell the authorities?"

Looking up, her skirt a pool of rust upon the floor, Allyson started to say she could tell the authorities a hell of a lot. But could she? Really?

She came to her feet, miserable. "Don't worry. I'll find something."

Rising to his full height, R.T. squinted thoughtfully into the distance, his thumbs hooked lightly over his belt. Presently, he said with a sigh, "I never thought I'd say this, much less believe it, but now I'm pretty damn grateful for that twenty-six hundred miles."

Thinking she must have misunderstood, surely, Allyson blinked at him with baffled lashes. "What's *that* supposed to mean?"

"That the sooner you put those miles between you and Global Defense, the better I'll like it."

Confounded, she leaned toward him. "You're not—"

"Atlanta, Allyson." Swiveling, he punctuated his words with sharp jabs of a finger. "Exactly as you planned and as quickly as you can. It's the best move you could make."

They had to appear ludicrous, Allyson thought, facing each other down in the Bear Cave Café. Did R.T. honestly think she could walk away from this?

Her protest was vehement as she hoisted her bag to her shoulder. "Forget Atlanta. I can't go now. I won't. And I can't believe that you'd say that. I may be the only one who *can* find the evidence against Grant, especially if Daniel hides and refuses to come out. I couldn't face myself if I crawled off to Atlanta and hid."

He started toward her with the frustration of a military man accustomed to obedience without question. "You're not listening."

"*You're* the one who isn't listening!"

Under his breath, he swore bitterly, and Allyson was certain he called her an idiot. They had unknowingly switched sides, she and R.T. In one of life's choice treacheries, they were adversaries again. And, as usual, the catalyst was Daniel.

He was extracting his wallet and slapping bills onto the table. With classic male chauvinism, he grumbled, "We'll talk about this later."

Allyson was sure they would. They would talk and argue and come away with more bitterness than they'd known before. Around the café, people were craning to see what the ruckus was all about. Steiger Tate was settling up with Eileen for his own bill.

Allyson hurried to fetch her coat and when R.T. moved behind her, she shrugged into it before he could assist. She rushed to the door, but he beat her to that and bridged its opening with a meaningful shove.

"So, you think you'll play Sherlock Homes now?" he said as the cold sunshine struck their faces. "Like some heroine on *Movie of the Week*?"

She was experiencing a wave of terrible exhaustion. "I'm not thinking anything, R.T., except what I have to do."

"D'you think Daniel imagined six bullets in his mattress?" He followed hard on his heels. "What will you do if those bullets turn up in yours? Or Michael's?"

Allyson refused to look back at him. "You're overreacting."

Angry, he twirled her around in the path. The sun was blinding at his back, making him taller, stronger. "You're enough to turn a man's hair gray, Allyson Wyatt."

Why were they fighting? Why wasn't he holding her, reassuring her he would help? Why couldn't he be glad she was staying in Seattle? Things could be the way they used to be.

She threw back her head in a warning. "The government will take care of me," she said coldly. "It was different with Daniel. I won't be a hostile witness. They'll want me to learn everything I can and testify."

He looked as if he could gladly strangle her. "You're talking about some witness-relocation thing? Christ, Allyson, listen to yourself. It's crazy."

She brought her foot to the slushy tarmac in a stamp. "Only hours ago you were blaming me because I was going to Atlanta. Now, you're blaming me because I'm not. You were the one who said—"

"I changed my mind, dammit!"

In his haggard anger, Allyson saw the death of their fragile dreams. He was ruthlessly crushing them before they could take their first gasping breath. Around them, cus-

tomers with new faces were pulling up in the parking lot and
bustling through the door. Their time-out-of-time was history now. They were back in the real world.

And it was a cold world. She was suddenly freezing.

Disheartened, hugging herself, she stuffed her hands into
her pockets, bent her head. "Please don't fight me on this.
Don't you remember? You sent me away, and I went. I did
what you said, but now—"

"Allyson, sweetheart . . ."

"I'm not that helpless girl anymore."

"No. You're a woman, and I want you to keep on being
one."

She sought his face in dismay. "But this is my time to
make things right, once and for all." She clutched the front
of his fatigue jacket.

"That's what you said when you asked me to fly you up
here. You said if you came, you could make things right.
How long are you going to keep making things right, Allyson?"

"As long as Grant doesn't have an idea that we suspect
him, I'll be fine."

"Sweetheart . . ."

The roar of the Jeep drowned out his reply. It skidded to
a messy stop, and Steve Grosvenor tumbled out and
tromped through the slush.

"Hey, big dog," he called, and flashed Allyson a grin.
"How's about us flyin' out of here today?"

Neither R.T. nor Allyson said a word.

Steve looked behind him as if searching for a reason for
their glumness. Failing that, he ambled nearer. "Want some
M & M's?"

R.T. gave him a look that would have made a chain saw
back up with respect. But Allyson, after all her lectures
about sugar, tossed virtue to the wind.

She took both bags of candy-coated peanuts without
bothering to thank him. Like a dyed-in-the-wool sugar junkie, she ripped one open with her teeth and popped a whole
handful into her mouth at one time.

"I'll get my things," she said, the words garbled by a full mouth as she trudged morosely toward Honeymoon Cottage.

Steve Grosvenor coughed lightly and nervously adjusted his eye patch. "What's the matter with her?"

"Shut up, Steve," R.T. growled, and moved away with matching dourness.

"You got it." Steve blew out his breath. Women. They'd do it to you every time.

Part Three

Chapter 13

Long pennons of tan dust streamed from behind the Beast, staining the broad underbelly of the November sky as they hung briefly above the road then drifted moodily to the gravel again.

R.T. was speeding toward the farm he'd bought the hard way, with a Marine's tough-fisted dollar—one hundred prime acres that were nestled in low hills with strands of pine and oak and a cold, trout-laden stream ribboning the grassland. The day was cold, yet he drove with the window down, needing the consolation of his land because it, like his career, had been carved out of nothing.

Being with Allyson the last few days had taught him something about family. Family offered a man salvation, but though he had constructed himself one of mismatched pieces, he was still a lost man.

When he had fenced this land, sweating under the hot sun, he'd thought he was staking out his territory for the future. With every stroke of the sledgehammer, he had made an investment for Allyson in his mind. For a few stolen moments, when he'd been part of her, body and soul, he had thought that future was within his grasp.

Then a domino had toppled. One circumstance had fallen
catastrophically against another until it seemed the only way
to save her from Grant Melbourne was to lose her. Again!

Their quarrel at Sea-Tac airport had been as defeating as
that other one years before. Her stubbornness about returning to work had made him want to hit her.

With a skid of tires and spraying gravel, he brought the
Beast to a skidding halt. Dust wrapped him in a choking
cloud as he climbed onto the running board and gazed as far
as he could see—at the winter wheat where two dozen sleek
Herefords grazed, at the broad fence that provided boundaries for six expensive Thoroughbred mares.

Looking up, the horses sent their excited whinnies ringing across the fields. R.T. slammed a palm against the door
and placed his fingers between his teeth in a signal to race.

"Come on, you infernal, flea-bitten nags," he grumbled.

Climbing into the truck, he slammed the accelerator to the
floor, and for the last mile the mares stretched themselves
out—streaks of pounding, driving muscle that thrilled R.T.
to watch. He wished Allyson could see their hooves throw-
ing clods of rich earth behind, their manes streaming.

At the fence, they pulled up short, and R.T. skidded to his
own stop before a rambling two-story farmhouse. His eye
made a practiced sweep over the house and the hills beyond. The truth was as cold as the wind that whipped his
cheeks and bit his ears.

God in heaven, what had he been thinking to hope that
Allyson would find beauty here? Before him stood a farmhouse that rambled—in an orderly fashion, yes, but the
clapboards had never been painted and the new repairs he'd
made shone like sore thumbs. The upstairs windows were
gaunt, having never seen a curtain. The upstairs wasn't even
furnished yet—not by Liddy, whose knees wouldn't allow
her to climb the stairs, nor by a man bound to a wheelchair
nor a blind youth nor a man who was away from home for
too long at a stretch. Even if Grant Melbourne was put behind bars tomorrow and Allyson didn't go twenty-six
hundred miles away, what had he been thinking?

A frolicking pup careened and skidded around the corner and came to a wiggling, excited stop at R.T.'s boots.

"Hey, Manny," R.T. mumbled as he once again saw himself in the rejected canine. "It takes one to know one, doesn't it, pal?"

Archie Swan knew something was wrong when R.T. walked into the house and gave his usual shout of "Anybody home?" Archie had a philosophy about life: when a man had no legs and spent his life depending upon two spoked wheels for mobility, he had to keep himself free of barnacles. That had its ups and downs, but it made a man capable of spotting a fraud a mile off.

Wheeling his chair to the doorway of the front hall, he watched Liddy emerge from her room. "Sparkey, you're back," she said to R.T., and opened her arms.

"Hi, Gran," R.T. said as he hugged her and found Archie over her head. "How's my favorite girl? Did you miss me?"

"Pooh, I'm no girl." Her scold was loving. "Behave yourself. And put me down. I'm an old woman."

"Old my foot." With laughter that was too forced, R.T. placed her upon the floor, then reared back in pretended shock. "Why, before I know it, I'll have to buy you one of those bright red compact cars to tool around town in."

Her smile had become lost somewhere in the past ten years. "You'd forget."

"Me forget you? I could as soon forget the gout."

Liddy dutifully placed his fatigue jacket upon a hook in the hall. "Well, you're back, Sparkey, that's for sure."

Chuckling, Archie returned to the kitchen, and R.T. gave Liddy another hug before he ducked through the door and into the kitchen. "Gran, you really gotta quit callin' me Sparkey."

She followed him and hesitated in the doorway, her eyes as blue as his own. "You're my Sparkey boy."

Turning, moving patiently back to her, R.T. opened her now-soft palms and placed kisses there. "I know, Gran."

But Archie saw in the sluggishness of R.T.'s step a need for Liddy to be the rock she had once been.

Liddy studied the tall, brooding man and with a lucid clarity that surprised both men, retrieved her hands and said, "You have a lot of love goin' to waste inside you, R.T. A lot of love."

With his mouth hanging open, R.T. didn't move until Liddy had disappeared into her room. When he turned, he shrugged sheepishly at Archie. He gazed about at the walls that were papered in a cozy, old-fashioned print and at the cracking linoleum that no one manufactured anymore. He leaned over Archie's shoulder as the man stirred a concoction on the stove. "Yum-yum," he said dryly. "My favorite, peas."

"You hate peas," Archie reminded with a cackle that passed for his laugh.

"Do I?"

"Of course you do."

Stretching his elbows to his back until the cartilage popped, R.T. walked to the cookie jar.

"Now, these—" he lifted out a handful "—I do like." He bit into one. "What happened while I was gone?"

"The winter wheat came up." Archie directed R.T.'s attention to a stack of mail as he steered his chair to the sink and talked over his shoulder. "White Pockets is about bust with that foal of hers. One of the doors blew off the barn and Kahn's been accepted by Juilliard. But I guess he told you that when you called from Alaska. For a day or two, I thought I'd go through the ceiling. The kid practices night and day. Drives me crazy. And one of your orchids has a blight."

Grinning, R.T. glanced through the mail as he chewed. Most of them were bills that would deplete his bank account to a state of terminal anemia. Holding the last two cookies between his teeth, he slumped to a chair and proceeded to pull off his boots and nudge them beneath a kitchen chair.

"I think we've raised ourselves a hell of a kid, Arch," he mumbled around the cookies. "Where is he?"

"In the gym." Archie wiped his hands on a towel. "How was your trip? Your man, Wyatt? How'd it go?"

"As far as I can see, everything's okay. Grosvenor flew him out without anyone knowing. He wasn't inclined to talk about it, so I didn't pry. Where Daniel is now is anyone's guess. But it wouldn't surprise me to hear from him. 'Course, everything else has turned to crap. Other than that . . ."

"That's it?"

Scowling, and angling a look around the door to make sure Liddy wasn't within earshot, R.T. swallowed another bite of cookie and asked, "Is that supposed to translate, 'How did you and Allyson hit it off?'"

Archie's rusty eyebrows lifted in amusement. "No, but now that you mention it . . ."

R.T. wolfed down the last cookie. "I'll be in the gym or the greenhouse. Call me when dinner's ready."

The gym was little more than a bedroom that R.T. had converted for Archie and Kahn. It was no surprise to hear Strauss's "Death and Transfiguration" pouring through the joints and walls as R.T. walked closer.

Inside was a set of weights, some gymnastic bars and an upright piano that was pushed against the wall. As were so many handicapped people, Kahn had been compensated by God in other ways. Upon his natural slimness, he had contoured a miraculously adept physique. He was stripped to his waist now, and golden muscles strained as he gripped the bar and swung his legs straight above his head, toes pointed.

Holding the pose for a moment, he completed the backward portion of the arc with a series of snaps and landed upon the mat with a light, balletic thud. He had to be, R.T. thought, one of the most beautiful young men he'd ever seen.

"R.T.," Kahn called with an eerie accuracy as he picked up a towel, wiped his face with it and draped it about his neck.

"Hi, sport shoes," R.T. said, and cuffed him affectionately.

"What d'you think about Juilliard?" Kahn asked breathlessly as he moved his hand briefly over R.T.'s face.

"I think it's damn wonderful."

Smiling, Kahn sniffed. "You found Archie's cookies, I see." Then he cocked his head and got a curious expression on his face. "What happened to you?"

"What're you talking about? Nothing happened to me. I've been gone."

"No, you're different."

"Oh?"

"Yes, you're…happy. But then, part of you is very sad."

Sometimes the kid saw too damn much. "And you, twinkle toes, are crazy."

When Kahn smiled, the world lit up. "I know."

"But you're great, too."

Kahn laughed. "I know."

Stripping the towel from around the boy's neck, R.T. popped the boy lightly on the behind. "Did you take care of the greenhouse while I was gone?"

With an uncanny sureness, Kahn walked to the double doors at the side of the gym that had originally opened onto a small stoop outside of the house. The added-on room was an enclosed area of smoked glass and sky lights.

R.T. closed the doors behind them. The temperature was controlled to satisfy the assorted array of hothouse flowers that R.T. grew for no good reason except that he enjoyed them.

"Your Lepanthes," Kahn said, moving unerringly to the species, "it's got a blight."

But R.T. hardly noticed. His life had a blight, and its name was Grant Melbourne. Damn Daniel for hightailing it without telling what he knew!

Leaving Kahn and the blighted Lepanthes, he returned to the kitchen where he rummaged through a drawer until he unearthed a scrap of paper beneath the pliers and screw drivers and garbage-sack twist ties. On it was a phone number.

Without a word to Archie, he dialed. When a man's voice came on the line, he said, "Do you know who this is?"

"Yes," the man said.

"I need a favor."

Cocoran Gifford was with naval intelligence, an old friend. "You got it," he said.

"There's a guy out here in Seattle who's kicking up a lot of dust. Could you find out what you can and get back to me?"

"No sweat. What's the name?"

"Melbourne. Grant Melbourne of Global Defense."

"Ah, yes. Gimme a couple of days."

"I'll owe you one."

When R.T. hung up and found Archie's rusty eyebrows on alert, he shrugged. "Precautions," he said tightly.

"Sure," Archie agreed, and grinned. "Dinner's ready."

"I don't like chicken," Michael announced from where he was perched like a sparrow on a high kitchen stool in his grandmother's kitchen.

Though the two-story house on Randolph Avenue was old, it had been kept in excellent repair. Every ten years or so, the kitchen was remodeled, and it was presently in its butcher-block-and-copper-pots stage.

Delicious smells perfumed the whole house as Margo transferred Kaye's curried chicken from its baking dish to a silver serving dish. Some of Allyson's fondest memories were connected to the maid, Margo. Now Margo was placing everything on the wheeled cart—julienne green beans with slivered almonds, and brussel sprouts that bobbed in a thin sauce. Her stout white apron crackled like paper when she walked toward the formal dining room.

Kaye looked up from her butcher-block island where she was chopping for the salad—a melody of snips and cuts. She pointed an excellent German knife at her grandson, whom she adored.

"Terrible child," she teased. "Allyson, did you hear what he said? You mean to tell me, Michael, that you don't like grandmother's curried chicken?"

Michael solemnly shook his head.

Kaye braced her knife handle on the counter with a *thud*. "Well, what do you like?"

"Hamburger and french fries."

"My child, the connoisseur," Allyson said as she grabbed her son about his waist and pretended to gobble his neck. *Aghrrrr*, she could hear R.T. say. *I turn into Dr. Jeckyll and devour innocent young virgins.*

Not wishing to become immersed in those defeating recollections, Allyson removed napery and third-generation sterling silver from the hutch and trailed into the dining room behind Margo.

"Grant is fit to be tied," Kaye said, having talked about little else ever since Allyson arrived. "He needed Daniel to come forward now. We were all counting on you to bring Daniel back."

"Well…" Allyson shrugged, unable to tell Kaye that her days since returning from Nakatak had been spent having a nervous breakdown in her office by day and poring over the massive printouts of the Bolten file by night.

Grant had poked his head through her doors only once and, with a laugh that made her wonder if she and R.T. hadn't imagined the whole thing, called, "Welcome back, beautiful."

Once she hooked her computer into Daniel's computer and entered the name Eddy, her printer had begun spitting out Bolten's original records that went back five years. She had found nothing to justify Daniel's predicament.

She cocked her head and asked her mother, "Was that the doorbell?"

Snip, snip, snip. Kaye glanced up. "You're awfully nervous tonight, Allyson. Ever since you came back, you've been as skittish as a mouse smelling a cat. What's the matter with you?"

R.T. was the matter with her!

A soft chime drifted distinctly from the front of the house. Though she was certain it wouldn't be R.T.—he had been made unwelcome in this house too many times—Allyson automatically glanced down at her appearance, the correctness of her smooth wool slacks and wine-colored

Laura Ashley sweater, her black stockings and matching flat-heeled shoes.

"I'll get it," she said quickly.

"It'll be Greg," Kaye called after her. "Poor darling, he's working himself silly for this new show."

"Poor Greg," Allyson repeated with an irreverent wag of her head. "Poor everyone, Mother. If you only knew."

She swept open the door and stared point-blank at Detective Steiger Tate.

Facing Tate was like stumbling upon a skeleton in the closet. Or Fibber McGee's notorious storage where she must slam the door to keep her life from spilling out on the floor. When he perceived her thoughts, he took hold of the storm glass.

"I went to your apartment, Mrs. Wyatt," he explained politely. "Your landlady said I might find you here."

Allyson rolled her eyes. "Doreen Penn, she knows all and tells all. Very well," she sighed dejectedly, "come in."

Kaye was walking from the dining room, and Allyson intoned, "It's not Greg, Mother."

"Oh, I've come at dinnertime." The detective smiled apologetically at Kaye and removed his hat. "I can wait in the living room until you're finished, ma'am." Then, to Allyson he said, as one conspirator to another, "I really must talk with you about Grant Melbourne, Mrs. Wyatt."

"Grant? What on earth about?" Kaye demanded with a comically apt flourish of her knife.

Allyson introduced the man to Kaye, and a smile found the detective's face. He placed his hat upon a nearby table, unaware that his hair was sprigging out as if an electrical current had shot through it. No one offered to help him with his coat, and he removed it and placed it across the back of a chair.

Kaye glared at the coat and brandished the knife.

"My visit is nothing that would warrant a stabbing, Mrs.—"

"Randolph," Kaye supplied, and stared sheepishly down at the knife. Lowering it, she hissed to Allyson under her breath, "What's going on here?"

*   *   *

Dinner was not a pleasant experience. They couldn't allow Steiger Tate to remain in the living room, so he sat at Greg's place. Between the detective's questions regarding Grant's culpability in the Department of Justice's Ill Wind investigation and Allyson's stilted, evasive answers, Kaye got the impression that she was being put upon. Not only did Greg's absence upset her terribly, she resented every word that came from the detective's mouth.

After dinner, when they retired to the living room and the man brought out a cigar, she snapped, "You can't smoke that thing in my house."

The detective obligingly returned it to his suit coat.

Allyson was so nervous, she finally announced that she and Detective Tate could continue this discussion at her apartment.

"Actually, I've learned what I came for," he said, and extended his card. "Here's where I can be reached. And I want to express my appreciation again for the help you and Major Smith were in Nakatak, Mrs. Wyatt. It was invaluable, truly invaluable. We'll be talking again soon, I'm sure."

After he had gone, Allyson stood in the foyer for a time before she gathered the courage to return to the living room. There, she found her mother standing beneath the oil painting of Orin Randolph's father that was mounted over the fireplace. Numbly, she began gathering coffee cups.

Just as she thought—and prayed!—that perhaps Kaye had missed making the connection of R.T. to Tate's remark, her mother said, "Correct me if I'm wrong, Allyson. That man wasn't talking about—"

"The same, Mother," Allyson said with a jaw as rigid as steel. "And I don't want to talk about it."

"Well, my dear, I certainly do."

The shrill of the telephone blessedly interrupted them, and Kaye swept across the room. "I'll get it, Margo," she called, and added to Allyson as she covered the mouthpiece, "It'll be Greg, groveling. Where have you been, young man?"

A moment of strained silence followed. Allyson stood holding coffee cups as Kaye turned and extended the receiver.

"Some man from the Justice Department," she said, blanched with shock. "He says his name is Thurgood Lord. He wants to know if you can be in his office tomorrow morning at eleven o'clock."

A person just couldn't win, Allyson thought.

At eleven o'clock the next morning, Allyson met her mother in the lobby of the Justice Building downtown. Kaye had insisted on coming, and Allyson was secretly grateful for the support. The morning's headlines had blared across the newsprint: Grand Jury to Begin Hearing Troubles of Global Defense.

"The only good thing about you moving to Atlanta next week," Kaye said as the elevator whisked them up to the third floor, "is that you won't be connected to Global Defense anymore. Really, Allyson, the scandal. Orin would be horrified."

Having once dreaded explaining to Kaye that she was moving, Allyson now wondered how to inform her mother that she wasn't moving. After three attempts to reach Earl Kolpechy, she still hadn't spoken with him. He was in Paris. When he discovered her change of plans, he would probably target her for annihilation himself and save Grant the trouble!

The elevator shuddered to a stop. Kaye's high heels clicked upon the gleaming tile of the corridor. Her survey of Allyson when she twisted back was unsettling.

"I really don't understand you, Allyson."

Kaye was referring to R.T., but Allyson pretended to misunderstand. She glanced down at herself. "You mean because I'm wearing a suit?"

She'd worn her pink Chanel suit and a pink hat that covered all her hair. In her bag, she even had a pair of gloves tucked away, and her high-heeled shoes matched her suit. She looked like a yuppie, she thought, and didn't have the

faintest idea why she'd gone to the trouble for a federal
agent.

"You know who I'm talking about," Kaye said as if the
name left a sour taste in her mouth. "That . . . Smith man."

Allyson's stop outside Thurgood Lord's office was exasperated. She faced her mother as she should have faced Kaye
fourteen years before when she'd let herself be talked into
marrying Daniel.

"Mother, his name is R.T. You were wrong about him
back then, and you're wrong about him now. Your fancy
social register leaves a lot to be desired, you know. It's big-
oted. If Daddy were alive, he'd agree. R.T. happens to be
worth ten of any man I know."

"Allyson!" Kaye bridled. "The man's father is a criminal! He's like one of those . . . Colombian drug lords."

"R.T.'s his own man, Mother. He always was. And he has
more principle, more honor . . ."

Kaye's mouth snapped shut, and Allyson sighed with fu-
tility.

"Now, come along," she said, and looped her arm in
Kaye's. "Let's go meet the feds."

Thurgood Lord had decorated his office with remarkable taste. The interior walls were covered with a pastel mu-
ral, and the furniture was arranged in casual leather
groupings. In one corner beside a ficus tree was a white
marble sculpture of a naked girl.

"They allow things like that here?" Kaye asked.

Allyson laughed. "It's art, Mother."

"It looks more like pornography to me. I don't know if I
trust this Agent Lord, Allyson, if this is an example of his
taste."

"I wouldn't worry too much about it." Allyson grinned.
"I doubt he'll trust you, either."

Kaye drew her mink coat about her as if to keep from
being defiled by bad taste. When the receptionist indicated
that Agent Lord was presently with someone, Allyson
moved directly to the magazines, and Kaye sat as far away
from the naked statue as possible while she watched the office door.

"Don't look now," she said after a moment when Ally-son had picked out the least boring read on the racks and was settling upon a leather sectional, "but coming out of that office is one of the most striking men I've ever seen in my life. He's staring straight at us. Dear me."

In her day, Kaye Randolph had been an eye-catching beauty, but she rarely looked at men with sexual interest. Men her own age were either spoiled or soft, and the younger ones were far too materialistic and effeminate.

The man coming out of the office was younger than she by two decades, but he possessed an undeniable worldliness and appeal. He was adjusting a button on the jacket of smart dress blues of the U. S. Marines. A braided hat was tucked properly beneath his arm. He had turned back to speak to the federal agent and his profile was caught in silhouette. It was vaguely familiar.

Allyson followed her mother's direction. "Good Lord," she said, and dropped the magazine to the floor with a distracted ruffle of pages. Her face turned the color of her Chanel suit as she came forward in her chair.

The deep timbre of the man's voice jarred something loose inside Kaye's head. She made a doubletake from Allyson's astonished face to the stranger's. His steps were sure and quick as he approached, and a dazzling smile spread beneath his mustache, his teeth large and white, one of them chipped.

You weren't invited here, young man. You may leave this house anytime you're ready.

Does Allyson know you're kicking me out, Mrs. Randolph?

Don't be impertinent. This house doesn't belong to Allyson. It belongs to me. And while we're at it, R.T. Smith, why don't you just leave Allyson and Daniel alone. You don't fit in here. You never did and you never will.

I'm sorry, Mrs. Randolph. I was just going. Please excuse me. I'm leaving now.

To Kaye's shock, R.T. Smith came to a stop, not in front of Allyson, but directly before her. Instantly on the defensive, she tried to think of something to send the man reeling back, but R.T. inclined his head with the honest courtesy he would have afforded someone very high in rank.

"Mrs. Randolph," he said, and graciously took her hand, though she hadn't offered it. "How nice to see you again. I would have recognized you anywhere. Don't you intend to age like the rest of us?"

Nonplussed, Kaye opened her mouth, but a response eluded her. "R.T.," she finally managed to choke out, and retrieved her hand, hugging her mink tightly to hide her embarrassment. "You're the last person I expected to see."

His eyebrows, when he raised them, were silkily self-mocking. "Aww, you know the old saying about bad pennies."

Allyson thought they had both lost their minds. She had never known anyone to incapacitate Kaye Randolph, but the woman was actually blushing.

"Ahh, on the contrary, R.T., you look as if you have achieved a great deal with your life." Kaye fluttered her fingers at his medals.

He gave the medals a dismissive wave. "They're nothing, really. Allyson . . ." His manner transformed from one of courtesy to the intimate disapproval that only a long involvement could generate. "You didn't say you were going to be here."

His inspection moved up and down her at will, pausing here and there to appreciate her suit and her hat, her legs.

Wishing she could be as bold, Allyson sounded like a child caught stealing. "I didn't know myself."

Kaye looked at her daughter in amazement. Allyson looked at R.T. R.T. looked at Kaye, and all three of them tried to smile but managed little more than pained grimaces.

"Well!" R.T. said finally. "Why stand when we can sit? You two ladies may be young as chickens, but I'm getting old. Allyson, when's your appointment?"

As he spoke, he waited to take Kaye's fur coat, and as Kaye slipped out of it, she laid her hand repentantly, uncertainly upon his arm. "R.T., I just wanted to say—"

His cocked smile disarmed her completely. "Kaye," he protested gently, and covered her hand with his, "it isn't necessary."

"What's not necessary?" Allyson pruriently asked.

"Why, you've become a charming gentleman, R.T.," Kaye said.

Allyson might as well have been conversing with herself. "What are you two talking about?"

"Who would've thought it, huh?" R.T.'s laughter was rich with good humor.

"About what happened back then, I mean..."

"What happened back when?" Allyson whispered in a mocking shriek.

They took their seats and Kaye, who was astonishingly self-conscious, crossed her legs and uncrossed them, her perfectly eyebrows puckered. "You mean, you never told her?"

"Never told me what?" Allyson demanded.

Spanning her forehead with her hand, Kaye shook her head in consternation. "Oh, R.T."

"There was nothing to tell," R.T. told her quickly. "And I don't have the foggiest notion what you're talking about, Kaye."

Which only made his lie as obvious as a flash flood.

Sighing, Kaye looked up, her eyes misty with unshed tears. "You're wasted in the military, R.T. You should be in the diplomatic corps."

Leaning forward, Allyson said through gritted teeth, "Will someone please tell me what's going on?"

R.T.'s laughter was lavish. "Allyson, Thurgood Lord's going to call you in a minute. It seems our friend Steiger Tate has preceded us and been called a few uncharitable names. Whatever he knows, he's not about to share with Lord. Kaye, while Allyson talks to the good agent, why don't I buy you a cup of coffee downstairs? You can tell me what Greg's doing these days."

"What a boring subject," Kaye said, laughing. "And you surely have more important things to do than babysit me."

With graceful masculinity, he crossed his ankle over his knee and saw to his uniform creases. "And after you're finished, Allyson, I know this really good Italian restaurant. If I walk in with you two ladies, I'll impress the heck out of the maitre 'd.''

That was it—no inquiries about how she was doing, about her days at the office, about her opinions of their interlude in Alaska, romantic or otherwise. He was too busy charming the pants off her mother!

Before she could open her mouth to say she was finding it increasingly hard to believe Grant was guilty of even a parking violation, Thurgood Lord's receptionist stepped from her cubicle. "Agent Lord will see you now, Mrs. Wyatt."

Allyson popped from her seat like an overwound spring.

She walked irritably to the office door, and when she realized that R.T. was following, she said from the side of her mouth, "You fraud. You nearly gave me a heart attack. What is going on between you and my mother?"

His smile was guileless. "If you want to know that, ask her."

"I'm asking you."

He grinned. "Asking me what? For a date?"

"I don't go out with conspirators."

"Oh, I'm not talking about getting caught in a blizzard in Alaska. I'm talking about a regular date. Dinner and a movie and a Visa card bill to knock my socks off."

Thurgood Lord was waiting in his office doorway. Out of sight of Kaye, R.T. was less inclined to disguise his hunger to sate himself with her. While the agent looked on, he detained her with a light touch upon her cuff.

"You look . . ." His smile was that of a hot-blooded bad boy, but it slowly dwindled. "God, I've missed you."

And she had missed him, more than she could admit. She reached out to touch his hand, but drew back. "You won't tell Kaye about Grant, will you? I mean . . . what we suspect. She thinks I'm still going to Atlanta."

R.T.'s gentleness was replaced by sternness. Thurgood Lord was extending his arm in an invitation to enter. Allyson didn't want to leave R.T. this way.

To his back, she whispered, "R.T.!"

Turning as he fit his hat upon his head, he paused. "What?"

"Do you have a cigarette?"

One side of his mouth curled. "Never touch the things, myself. Nasty habit. Disgusting. Kaye and I'll be waiting out here when you finish."

Chapter 14

When the attendant drove the Beast down the ramp of the four-tiered parking garage and came to a screeching, rubber-streaking halt, Allyson gazed at the relic R.T. was driving and began to giggle in a way that made her wonder if she hadn't been around Connie Clements too long.

The parking attendant was a shuffling youth with braids exploding from his head and the name Fred stitched to his red windbreaker. He climbed out of the ramshackle truck and looked at R.T. as if to say, *Any man who drives somethin' like this is just askin' for it.*

"You find my truck amusing?" R.T. frowned at Fred, then frowned at Allyson and resumed frowning at Fred.

"I'm sorry," Allyson gasped, and smothered her laughter with the gloves that matched her pink suit. "I don't mean to be rude, but—"

"Yes, you do." R.T. gave a droll, wounded sigh.

"I can't help it." Allyson drifted off into peals of laughter, then faced R.T. with exaggerated gravity. "It's just that you spend seventy-five dollars impressing me with the most delicious food I've ever put in my mouth, R.T. You charm my poor mother until she's absolutely eating out of your hand. Do you know she said to me as we were leaving that I should bring you over to the house? 'He's absolutely gorgeous.' Those were her exact words.''

Allyson coughed discreetly into her pink-gloved fist. "And then you drive..." When she could talk again, she asked of the parking attendant, "Exactly what is this he's driving, Fred?"

Fred wasn't about to nibble on that one.

"Ahhh..." He located a spot of scalp between his braids and scratched. "Whatever it is, ma'am, it runs like one bad mother—"

"Yes, well..." R.T. fished his wallet from a hip pocket. "This truck is my history." He proceeded to flip broodingly through the section of folding money and drew out a bill with a motion so slow that Fred's eyes bugged. "History is important. Right, Fred?"

"Oh, yes sir," Fred wisely agreed.

"It shouldn't be taken lightly."

"Affirmative, sir."

"How much for the parking, Fred?"

"Two dollars and fifty cents, sir."

While Fred eyed the paper airplane that R.T. fashioned out of the bill, Allyson stepped to the front fender of the truck and traced the rusting path of a dent. She had once placed a dent in this truck herself, in front of Nordstrom's.

Turning, she found R.T. studying the way her hips filled the straight skirt. Her chide was a pout of lips. "If you're quite finished with that, do you remember how this dent got here?"

R.T. dragged his eyes to the dent as if he'd never noticed it before. He moved closer, bending low and squinting. "Fred?"

"Yessir." Apprehension edged Fred's voice as he, too, inched nearer.

"Did you put this dent in my truck?"

"Oh, no sir."

"Are you sure, Fred?"

"Absolutely sure, sir. Absolutely."

Straightening, R.T. said with a perfectly straight face, "Maybe the dent fairy did it."

Glowering, Allyson aimed a finger at R.T.'s nose. "That's right, R.T. Dig a pit for yourself, but don't ask me to pull you out."

R.T. not only failed to reply, he perused her so long and so thoroughly, Allyson caught a flyaway breath and thought he couldn't have made her more skittish if he scooped her off her feet and kissed her blind. All through lunch he'd riveted her with looks like that, smiling at Kaye but awakening sensations of sublime arousal in her.

Fred was uneasily shifting his weight from foot to foot. "Ahh," he tactfully cleared his throat. "Are you gonna take this . . . vehicle out of here today, Major?"

R.T. glanced down at the folded bill in his hand. He straightened to a commanding height. "Would you like a tip, Fred?"

With a grin the boy stepped to the Beast and blew condensation on the sideview mirror and polished it with the elbow of his windbreaker.

"Good thinking," R.T. said, and slapped the bill into the boy's outstretched palm.

Michael's school was on the other side of town. Not until R.T. had driven for some time through the slushy streets, not asking directions once, did Allyson realize that he would, of course, know where the school was.

She could picture him parked in the truck that no one would ever look at twice. What had gone through his mind as he watched her pick up her son at the gate all those years? Had he seen her frowsy? Sick? Exhausted? What emotion would drive a man to do such a thing? How could he now be so hard-nosed about Atlanta?

By the time R.T. swerved into the curb before the school—a sprawling brick building that resembled a home more than a school, with its shrubs and manicured lawns and fenced playground—Allyson was grateful that the last bell had rung. Bright-coated children were tumbling across the grass, racing for cars, and there was the predictable scuffling and clamoring and shrill cries. Someone was lowering the flag. Teachers were everywhere, holding their skirts against the wind, their hair flying as they made sure each child was met by the proper authority.

"There he is!" Allyson said, and pointed to Michael as she opened the truck door.

Michael appeared lost as he lingered around the fence and waited for her, swallowed by his heavy coat and cap and mittens. He clutched his backpack and searched unhappily for the familiar red Mercedes.

Hurrying through the gate, Allyson signaled the supervisor that she was taking Michael home. Michael grinned with relief. Stooping, she hugged him with a fierceness that made him protest.

"Mom," he wheezed, "stop squeezin' so hard. You're gonna make me barf."

Laughing, Allyson removed his cap and lovingly combed his silky blond hair with her fingers. "Why do you think God gave mommies such strong arms?"

As she buttoned his jacket and retied a shoestring, he giggled down at her. "For whacking the daylights out of little kids."

"Brat."

With a final tweak of the shoestring, she gave a playful swat to his behind and rose. But she was instantly confronted by R.T.'s height, and she saw that Michael was confronted by the same thing, only more so.

"Hello, Michael," R.T. said, smiling down, a heart-warming tenderness on his face.

Michael was much too polite to refuse to reply to an adult, but Allyson could sense his confusion. There had never been a man in her life except Daniel. The child in Michael considered Daniel and her together in some strange, pseudo-married fashion.

Please be gentle with my son, R.T., she wanted to plead. *He doesn't understand about things like this.*

"Hi," Michael said breathlessly as he stared, awestruck, at the uniform.

"Michael, this man's name is R.T.," Allyson explained. "He's a good friend of your father. He's also my friend from a long time ago. We used to chum around, your father and R.T. and me. But when we were young."

"Young as me?" Michael quizzed with a mathematician's tunnel-visioned logic.

"Not quite," R.T. said, chuckling. "Allyson and I had lunch with your grandmother, Michael. That's why you missed the Mercedes."

"Oh. You takin' Mom and me home?"

"Is it okay?"

"I guess so."

That over, Allyson prepared herself for an agonizing period of awkwardness. R.T. wasn't a father. His companions were tough and hard. And even if they weren't, Michael was more difficult than most children. His intuitions were much more easily alerted and disappointed. Quick to detect a fraud, he sometimes had difficulty relating even to Daniel.

Yet now he walked easily between the two of them without comment, and R.T. surprisingly didn't make the mistake of trying too hard. He didn't attempt to engage Michael in silly conversation, nor did he try to horse around with Allyson.

"What kind of a cap is that?" Michael presently asked as they were reaching the gate.

Without hesitation, R.T. said, "A Marine hat. Would you like to wear it?"

"Sure."

Michael allowed R.T. to pluck off his small headgear and replace it with the large cap that promptly fell over his ears and covered his eyes and half his nose.

Michael comically rolled his eyes beneath the brim. "It's a little too big," he said gravely.

"Slightly," R.T. mildly agreed, and made no attempt to help. "Watch your step. Here's the truck. Do you drive, Michael?"

Alarmed, Allyson sought R.T.'s face with a signal that he was going too far with this getting-acquainted ritual.

But Michael was shaking his head and trying to see from beneath the brim of the hat. "I'm only six."

R.T. gave the matter thorough consideration. "Well, I don't know..." He scratched his mustache. "Correct me if I'm wrong, but I think six is a good age to learn to steer. I believe I was about six when I learned. This truck has a standard shift. Do you know how that works?"

Michael could have been pondering the future of mankind for all the thought he gave the matter. Presently, he removed the hat and climbed into the truck.

"Nope," he said. "I don't know."

"Then I'll shift the gears and you can work the steering wheel."

"But I don't have a license."

"That's a valid point." R.T. nodded thoughtfully. "But there're adults in the front seat. I think it'll be all right."

To Michael's mind, the truck was the most beautiful machine on four wheels. Allyson found herself torn between her pride for Michael's unfamiliar maturity and her own preempted maternity. In many ways, her son provided a companionship as satisfying as that of any adult. They had lived alone since his birth, yet he climbed into R.T.'s lap with an exhilaration that he rarely displayed with anyone, not even with her.

She felt oddly betrayed.

Over Michael's head, R.T. found her. *He's beautiful. You've done a good job, Allyson.*

Don't take him from me. What'll I do if you take him from me?

Love is very large. It takes nothing away.

R.T. showed Michael how to start the truck. With a military man's penchant for precise detail, he explained to Michael the workings of a standard gear shift. When Michael understood after only one telling and repeated it almost verbatim, proceeding to inform R.T. that he also understood the theory of combustible engines, as well as steam engines and atomic and nuclear power, R.T. cut Allyson a sidelong look of astonishment.

"Daddy taught me," Michael said, and steered the truck with all the concentration of a diamond cutter about to cut the Hope.

"Your father's a smart guy," R.T. said.

"My father doesn't live with us."

"Oh."

By the time the truck was parked before Doreen's brownstone, Allyson thought that a plain, straightforward nervous breakdown would do quite nicely. She had never seen Michael so elated, so full of energy and so disappointed to be home. His excitement magnified her own failures ten times over.

"Can we do it again?" he wheedled as they piled out of the truck and gathered up belongings. "Can we, can we?"

They reached the steps, and Allyson could almost feel Doreen's eyes behind the drapery. Now she would be blessed with an inquisition from her friend.

From the door, Allyson turned to view the sun bright at R.T.'s back. The long rays glanced off his brass buttons and glinted upon the toes of his polished boots. She wished that everyone who had brushed him aside as "that bad boy" could see him now. How proud she was of him!

He stooped and brought his face down to a level with Michael's. Her son was wearing the military cap again, and R.T. removed it, settling it upon his own head.

"Are you going to drive some more?" Michael said.

R.T. looked at Michael a long time. "Do you know the Old Man's rule, Mike?"

Clutching his backpack, Michael chewed his lip. "Who's the Old Man?"

"The Old Man—" R.T. smiled affectionately "—well, Michael, the Old Man can be a lot of people. But whoever he is, he's always the boss. No matter who a person is or what he does, there's always an Old Man around somewhere. Sometimes it's even a mom, and you always have to check with the Old Man before you do anything."

"You have an Old Man?"

"Absolutely. Not only do I have to do what the Old Man says, I can't complain about it. I have to say 'yes, sir' and 'no, sir' and snap a salute. That's called respect. That's how you always tell when a person is grown up or not, by their respect for the Old Man.''

Astonished, Michael confronted his mother. "Do you have a boss, Mom?"

Nothing had prepared her for this, Allyson thought. A woman could do pretty well where she was personally concerned, but when it came to her child, she was naked, she was raw and she was capable of the best and the worst. Now her life was unexpectedly right before her eyes—the two things she loved most, a small boy and a big Marine. It was the sweetest, most painful moment she could have imagined.

"Yes, Michael," she said in a twisted voice. "I most certainly have an Old Man. And I think, if you ask R.T. with respect, he might come up and have something to drink. Some Pepsi..."

As clearly as the sun, she could see R.T. at the wheel of his truck all those years ago, trying to find pocket change for the fast-foods clerk. His love made her tremble with fear of how vulnerable she was.

"I'd love to," R.T. said with a tenderness that robbed her of speech.

When Doreen Penn popped out of her apartment and gave Allyson her the mail in person, Allyson wasn't surprised and she braced herself for a battery of questions. As Michael and R.T. were chattering happily on their way to the stairs, the landlady didn't disappoint her.

"My word, child," she whispered with wonder creasing her sweet, round face, "where have you been keeping that splendid hunk of a man?"

Allyson shrugged with calculated blandness. "He's my skeleton in the closet, Doreen. What can I say?"

The woman's eyes grew as large as plates. "What a closet!"

Allyson laughed, leaving Doreen to her own suppositions and rummaging for her key as she climbed the stairs. "You'll have to excuse the place," she told R.T. as she unlocked the door and moved past him. "It's a mess with all the packing."

"Ohh," Michael whimpered when he walked in and froze with shock.

Immediately behind him, Allyson gasped, horrified.

The apartment, R.T. saw as he peered over their heads, was small and compact. It had been systematically demolished—packing boxes torn to pieces, their contents dumped everywhere, furniture slashed and gutted, carpets torn up and rugs ripped and thrown back, cabinets emptied, books jerked from their bindings, broken glass scattered from wall to wall. One of Michael's toy trucks had been jammed through the screen of Allyson's computer.

Rage boiled inside R.T. Too stunned to move, Allyson stood wringing her hands. Michael was wandering through the living room, searching for his small belongings with tears drizzling down his cheeks.

Allyson made a sound that wasn't quite human, and she strode through the wreckage, her eyes taking on a feral glow, her bosom rising and falling sharply. Her hands were convulsive upon the strap of her bag, and she was the color of a corpse.

R.T. gave himself mental orders as if he were snapping commands to his men. First things first: survival, not feelings. Grief could come later. Now he must secure the perimeter; Allyson and Michael must be taken to safety. That Melbourne could get so close to them made him murderously afraid.

He searched for the telephone and found its connection ripped out of the wall.

"Allyson?" He took her by the shoulders, but he didn't think she knew who touched her. "I've got to go downstairs. Come with me."

"No, no." Distraught, she flung his hands away with amazing strength. She raked her fingers heartbreakingly through her hair and mumbled, "I'm going to bring him down. I'm going to bury Grant Melbourne for this. I'm going to put him in the ground. I'm going to make him wish he'd never been born."

If she had not been disenchanted with Melbourne before, this had done the trick. But R.T. would rather she recognize her danger than the need for vengeance. He caught her close in his arms, and she wriggled, hysterical in her struggle. "Stop it," he ordered her, and clamped his hands painfully upon her arms. "Get ahold of yourself. You have no proof of who was here, Allyson. You have to think of Michael now, honey. Michael." He shook her. "Think of Michael."

She sagged against him, knowing it was true. Her eyes, when they found his, were ravaged. "Then what do I do, R.T.? Keeping taking this kind of thing? Is this the way it's going to be now until they find what they want? Until somebody is killed?"

With an iron grip on his feelings, R.T. forced himself not to sympathize. "Your first duty is to be calm. Your second is to leave Seattle. Let others deal with Melbourne. Do what I tell you. Listen to me."

Grateful to have someone who possessed the physical strength and character to do what she could not, Allyson sought Michael and found him squatting upon the floor, his wrecked Nintendo clutched to his chest.

She dropped to her knees and sought R.T. with her eyes. *Help me.*

R.T. wanted to put his fist through a wall. He strode toward the boy. "Mike?"

Peering upward, his lips quivering in an attempt not to cry, Michael lifted his arms. R.T. swept him up in a fierce hug, bending his dark head to the smaller fair one. "It's okay, son. We'll fix everything."

As Allyson watched Michael's frail arms wrap around R.T.'s neck so tightly, she knew that there were parts of her son she could never truly touch. Michael needed a father. Michael needed this man. How could she leave Seattle and take Michael away? But she must, and the irony of her life was staggering.

"My God!" Doreen Penn whispered from the doorway as she entered the room and stood hugging herself. "What happened?"

Allyson clapped her hand over her mouth, eyes streaming.

"I'll call the police," Doreen said.

"No!" R.T. told her sharply, then gentled his explanation. "We don't know what we're dealing with here yet, Mrs. Penn. I wonder, could you make us something hot to drink while we decide?"

"Of course." Doreen was in her maternal element now. She closed Allyson in her strong, stout arms. "Come downstairs, dear. You can use my telephone."

In the downstairs apartment, while Allyson held Michael with fearful desperation, Doreen fixed everyone hot chocolate and coffee. R.T. telephone Steiger Tate, then he called Archie at the farm. Next, he called a man named Jesse Hurlburton, told him to locate Jack O'Banyon and Sam McDivitt and gave him the address of Doreen's brownstone.

After his men arrived and shyly introduced themselves, shaking Allyson's hand and exchanging furtive grins behind R.T.'s back, Steiger Tate descended upon them and made an official inspection of the apartment. For the next two hours the men placed everything from the apartment into crates, boxes and garbage sacks. When they were finished, not one trace of Allyson remained at Doreen's brownstone.

"I want these things placed where they can't be vandalized," R.T. directed Jess Hurlburton. "And make sure no one sees you do it."

"Yes, sir," Jesse said, and relayed a smile to Allyson. "What about her car?"

"That, too."

After the three men told her how sorry they were that this had happened, R.T. explained to Steiger Tate that he was taking Allyson with him to the farm. The detective made safety a priority, and R.T. explained that Sam McDivitt was going with them, to make sure that no one got this close again. No one could do that better than McDivitt.

"But first," R.T. said with a quick, unhappy look at Allyson, "we're going to go by Richard Wyatt's house and pick up a computer. Allyson's isn't working anymore."

He understood, Allyson thought, her gratitude welling as she slipped her arm around his waist. He understood that she must do *something*, even if it failed.

"Thank you," she said.

"You're not alone." His reassurance was a kiss upon her head. "I'm here."

Yes, he was here. And even through the maze of her past protests, she could see the wisdom of taking Michael to Atlanta. But for how long? A few weeks? A few months? God forbid, a few years? Did safety and security have a time schedule?

He didn't offer to relocate in Atlanta himself, she noticed—not that she expected him to, for his roots were here, his family was here. But he could have said, It's only temporary. You'll be back before you know it, and then we'll spend the rest of our lives together.

His hand remained on her shoulder, generating heat between them. Was it possible that R.T. was, even now, doing what he did best? Fulfilling a vow of honor to Daniel? Oh, he could say he loved her and had always loved her because it was true. He could make love *to* her, but in the end it was Daniel, always Daniel.

She had never been so unhappy. She should have pulled her heart out of reach when she still had the chance. Now it was much, much too late.

Chapter 15

While Sam McDivitt stood watch from an upstairs window, Allyson slept six hours straight and then crept down the farmhouse stairs at the crack of dawn. She followed her nose to the kitchen where Archie Swan was moving about in his wheelchair, brewing coffee.

After having fished a decent sweater from a garbage sack, and a pair of jeans and penny loafers, her toilette had to be satisfied with a shower and shampoo and a dab of lipstick.

Just as she was about to announce herself, all clean and country fresh, Archie said without glancing over his shoulder, "It's a heck of a lot warmer in here than it is out there, Mrs. Wyatt."

"Caught." She laughed as he popped a wheelie with his chair and spun it around. "How did you know it was I?"

"No one has a step like yours." Archie's chuckle rumbled around in his chest before it got out. "R.T. clumps around like Andre the Giant, and a butterfly makes more noise than Kahn. Liddy doesn't walk, she scoots. And McDivitt? The man doesn't walk, he infiltrates. Who else could it have been but you?"

"Good point, Sherlock." She gave her head a friendly toss. "But if you don't stop calling me Mrs. Wyatt, I'm going to start calling you Archibald. Where is everyone?"

Which meant, Where was R.T.? The rest she knew, that the sun was burning away the last patches of snow, that the horses were nibbling winter wheat, that the cattle were lowing as they waited at the barn door for hay and that in the driveway out front, a grid of tracks had been left from pickups moving her things.

Upstairs, Michael was curled in a snoozing ball, safe and sound, thanks to R.T.

"Why aren't you sleeping in like everyone else?" Archie said, and motioned for her to hold out her cup so he could pour coffee. "Easy, oops."

Allyson cuddled her cup and looked around a kitchen that was the warm, friendly kind that a woman sees herself taking care of a family in. R.T.'s reticence when he'd given her a quick tour the night before was puzzling. How could he not know what he had in this farm or how much he'd accomplished? How could he not know how much she wished he would say, *Forget Atlanta. Marry me and be queen of this house.*

"I can't stop thinking about what happened," she admitted.

Archie plowed into his shirt pocket and found a packet of tobacco and papers. He proceeded to roll himself a cigarette, cupping the paper just right, tapping tobacco, rolling, licking, pinching and striking a match on the side of his chair.

He saw her watching and grinned. "I tell the big guy I do it to save money, and it bugs him to death. One thing you'll learn about the Skipper is that he fancies himself the provider of the realm. T'tell the truth, I just like to roll my own, always have. What's gonna happen to you and Michael now, Allyson? Got any plans?"

Allyson took the chair across from him, her coffee positioned before her like a crystal ball. She explained about her job in Atlanta and how R.T. was adamant that she stick to her plan, though she fought every inch against it. She indicated the upstairs where Michael was sleeping.

"Now, it's gotten very, very serious, Archie. For the first time, I'm really afraid."

"It's probably best that you go. You'll be safe down there."

But she wouldn't be happy there.

Archie palmed his cigarette. "It's been a long time since the Skipper's been this upset, let me tell you."

Allyson nervously worried the beginnings of a hangnail.

"Normally I stay out of people's affairs," he said. "But there's something about the Skipper you ought to know."

Without a shred of self-sympathy, he told her about the schoolhouse in Angola and about the timber that fell across his legs.

"For weeks after they took my legs, I wanted to die," he said. "For months. But R.T. hounded me, the son-of-a-bitch. He drove me crazy, coming to the hospital and badgering me till I cursed him. Finally I stopped wanting to die and wanted to kill him." He laughed against the backwash of smoke that wreathed his head. "After that I started getting well. When I was ready to leave the hospital, he brought me here." He gestured to the house around them. "You probably think this place looks bad now? It was the sorriest place I'd ever seen."

"Oh, no!" Allyson shook her head. "This house...I thought when we came in last night...about how much fun it would be to really fix it up. My goodness, Archie, the bedrooms upstairs are phenomenal, and R.T.'s made such a good beginning. And the floors! Do you realize how beautifully they would refinish? These high walls and the papers they make today—I can just see them all creamy and light, such lovely things. They're—"

Embarrassed to find herself rambling, Allyson jumped up and poured herself more coffee that she didn't want. "I think it's genetic," she mumbled. "We must be born this way."

Archie didn't return her laugh, for he saw with a friend's perfect clarity why R.T. had fallen in love with Allyson Randolph Wyatt.

He stubbed his smoke and said, "Don't hurt him, Allyson. Skip's got his heart stickin' out a mile. Just don't hurt him."

Before Allyson could reply, the back door slammed. With a blast of male virility, clumping boots and mud-spattered jeans, R.T. loomed large in the doorway, his cheeks whipped red by the wind and his jaw stubbled with beard. The brim of his cap dripped water, and the width of his shoulders was accentuated by a quilted vest zipped over a plaid shirt.

His stance was alarmingly capable, and his smile splashed her with its own kind of sun.

Allyson shakily placed her cup on the counter and prepared for a battle of words.

He covered the distance between them and pulled off leather gloves as he came. "And here I was sayin' that the morning couldn't get any prettier," he drawled as he stuffed them into a hip pocket and circled her waist, reeling her full against him.

Allyson's senses trembled at the smell of cold in his hair and his clothes, the vigorous hardness of him.

"You stink of horses," she gasped, and tried to remind him that Archie was seated at the table.

But he kissed her hard and thoroughly, then set her firmly upon her feet. He said to Archie, "You'll be happy to know that White Pockets is a proud new mother, Arch. A sassy little filly."

"How about that?" Archie laughed.

"Yeah." Grinning, R.T. traced Allyson's right cheekbone with a fingertip. "A sassy little filly."

It was in Allyson's mind that if she could find Daniel's hidden information in his computer, she could even yet get them all off the hook, could remain in Seattle and then have a serious talk with R.T. about the future.

Over the years, Daniel had added rank after rank of add-ons onto his computer so that the IBM's memory virtually had no limits. Allyson found almost everything imaginable stored inside. Following her hunch, she entered the code Eddy.

The appearance of the original Bolten file was no surprise, but working her way through it made the search for the proverbial needle in a haystack only too real.

Her job, naturally, had ended abruptly with the trashing of her apartment. She had typed up a phonily sincere letter of resignation, explaining to Grant that she'd been vandalized and was moving away. She mailed it and waited for the explosion. It didn't come.

While R.T. caught up on farm work that had been neglected during his last tour, and despite Steiger Tate's almost-constant presence underfoot—"Just checking in to see what you've turned up"—plus Jess Hurlburton staked out upstairs with an M-16, and the appearance of men from the Justice Department, so that the farm became a sort of operational base, Allyson's days were surprisingly tranquil.

There were moments when she wondered if she hadn't imagined Daniel's wound and the threat of violence. She pored over profit-and-loss statements, payrolls, notes of corporate meetings, correspondence. The problems of their love affair were put on hold.

Late at night, however, when the day wound down and the house was wrapped with cold, when Steiger Tate had gone back to his hotel and the men from Justice had returned to the city, R.T. would stretch himself before the fireplace as she pored over one last printout.

Sometimes he would lower himself to where she sat cross-legged before the fire and would wrap himself around her from behind. He would breathe in the fragrance of her hair.

"Everything will be all right," he would whisper. "You'll see."

"Sure it will," she would say.

Michael did not return to school. It was too dangerous, and R.T. reminded her that the boy would be transferring to a new school in Atlanta, anyway. A few days' absence wouldn't hurt.

Michael and Kahn had become inseparable in a way that reminded Allyson of Daniel's friendship with R.T. Michael had finally found someone who could challenge his mental quirks, and Kahn had discovered the infinite patience of a child who adored being his eyes.

Grant Melbourne had conducted a lot of business through the Bolten Company. Many of the contracts acquired by Global Defense had been subcontracted to Bolten. Allyson doublechecked each name she came across.

It was four evenings later that she leaned back in her chair and exclaimed, "I've found the glitch!"

Liddy had deserted her crocheting and gone to bed, but Steiger Tate remained, swathed in a cloud of cigar smoke on the opposite side of the living room. R.T. was stretched full-length on the sofa, a computer printout tenting his face. Kahn and Michael were playing chess upon the rug, and Jess Hurlburton, who had spelled McDivitt, was posted beside the front window.

"What glitch?" R.T. said, and plowed from under the crackling paper.

Steiger Tate dragged his exhausted body across the room and looked over her shoulder. Allyson pointed to a man's name on the screen. "Do you see this Duane Hickson?"

Joining the detective, R.T. read aloud the name at the bottom of a contract between the U. S. Department of Defense and Grant Melbourne's company, "Duane Hickson."

"Now, look," Allyson instructed, and called up another document that recorded payroll checks issued by Global Defense in the month of September 1988. She scrolled to the entry that showed a check issued to Duane Hickson in the amount of one hundred twenty-five thousand dollars.

"This is a consultation fee?" she asked. "Some consultations."

Tate crowded R.T. so that the tall man bumped Allyson into the console.

"Easy, Tate," R.T. grumbled.

"Sorry," the man said. "Who's Duane Hickson?"

Allyson grinned. "All right, you guys. Neither of you has ever seen this next document, okay? Daniel could get into a lot of trouble."

"You mean, more than he's already in?" R.T. quipped wryly.

"This," Allyson said as she booted up another document, "is from when Daniel once hacked into the Pentagon's system. There's no telling how long it's been here. I really just lucked onto it. Look . . ."

She ran a search through a registry of army personnel and brought her cursor to a stop at one Colonel Duane Hickson, Ret., Contracts.

"Son-of-a-gun," R.T. said with a low whistle of amazement. "The creep's been taking kickbacks from Melbourne!"

Steiger Tate was so impressed, he grabbed Allyson's head and placed a smacking kiss on its crown. "Mrs. Wyatt, God love ya! Thurgood, eat your heart out."

Twirling about to add her own delight, Allyson crumbled with the realization of what her discovery meant. Her job here was finished. If finding Duane Hickson meant what she thought it meant, there was nothing to prevent her from going to Atlanta. If she hurried, she could even arrive under the wire in time for her first day at work for Earl Kolpechy.

She turned off the computer. "Well," she said numbly, "that's all I have to offer. If you two gentlemen will excuse me..." Rising, she moved to the stairs with the heaviness of an old woman. "I'm very tired. I think I'll go upstairs."

"Allyson . . ." R.T. was following her.

Commitment's strange elixir of love and hate swelled in Allyson's throat. She loved R.T., but he was wearing her out with his male complexities. He wasn't saying the words her heart needed to hear.

"It's all right, R.T.," she said without looking at him. "I'll see you in the morning."

The saddest part was, he let her go without a word.

* * *

But at half past midnight, when Allyson stared at the dark ceiling of R.T.'s upstairs bedroom that had been neatly textured and left to wait for further instructions, she finally accepted that she was a fool.

She had worked a miracle tonight, dammit! She had placed in the hands of the law a key that could unlock many doors. Daniel, wherever he was, would be safe now. Grant would, in all likelihood, get whatever was coming to him.

And she was suffering because of a man. R.T.'s love notwithstanding, she was convinced that he was thinking more of Daniel than of her. Why else could he leave things so unsatisfying? No plans, no hope? It was no good. Better a clean, permanent break than this!

Taking care not to awaken Michael as her gown swirled about flashing bare legs, she slipped into a robe and a pair of heavy wool socks. Like some restless lunar moth, she flitted across the cold hallway to R.T.'s room.

The door creaked shrilly beneath her fingertips, and she froze as Jess Hurlburton opened another door at the end of the hall and peered out. Wide-eyed, she crossed her arms over her breasts.

His appraisal seemed to see straight through the cotton gown. Giving a friendly nod, he disappeared.

Allyson pressed her heart to keep it from leaping out of her chest and opened R.T.'s door enough that she could enter. If she didn't act now, while she was angry, she would wind up in tears and be right back where she'd started.

Warily, on tiptoe, she entered. "R.T.?"

His bed was unmade and empty and she experienced a faint betrayal. *Go back to bed where you belong.* Moments later, she was making her way down the hall, to the amusement of Jess, she was certain. The old house creaked complaints as she moved through it, as if it were cold and ailing with gout. All the rooms on the lower floor were dark, and R.T. wasn't watching television in the living room. Had he gone outside?

She proceeded to the workout room, and its emptiness echoed her steps. Pushing open the door to the greenhouse where a grow light burned twenty-four hours a day, she thought she saw a man.

The paranoia of the last days made her think immediately of an intruder. Alarm pebbled her skin. R.T. wouldn't be crouched against the wall in his own house, at the farthest part of the room, hunkered down among the gym mats and flower pots and seedling racks.

But the longer she squinted, the more convinced she became that it was R.T. His head was buried deeply in hands and he rocked back and forth. Despair radiated to her through the violet haze, in the grieving creak of his boot leather as he came forward and rocked back, forward and back.

Her own reasons for coming here were forgotten. *Oh, R.T. My darling, what has happened to you?*

She ventured closer, seeing now the open sides of his plaid shirt that grazed the floor. She could fathom the straining ropes of his neck and his curl-dusted chest, the lean folds of his abdomen where they creased.

And then, with such vicious speed that she had no time to cry out, he was on his feet and clutching her in a grip so deadly, her bones could have snapped with one flex of his arm.

"It's me!" she choked.

"Allyson?"

She steadied herself shakily upon his chest. "I came looking for you."

"I—I'm sorry." He shook his head as if to clear it. He looked around, and she thought he was surprised to find he was in his own house.

He mumbled, "You shouldn't be here. What's the matter?"

That should have been *her* question and she craned to read unspoken messages in his eyes. But he kept his head turned, and when he tried to touch him, he circled her wrists and drew them away.

"Go back to bed, Allyson." His voice was thorny with emotion. "Go back to bed and go to sleep."

"I can't sleep." She couldn't leave him like this.

"This . . ." His indrawn breath was tattered with distress. "This isn't a good time for me."

"Then come sit with me. What's wrong? You're shaking, R.T. You're soaking wet. Let me make you something to drink. What's happened? Is it Daniel?"

Trembling gripped him, and she knew intuitively that his trouble was connected to what Archie had told her. There were in R.T. Smith scars that didn't show like the scars on his back, scars that were layered between those and the old scars of a frightened, unwanted boy.

Slowly, lovingly, she folded him into her arms. "Come," she said, "sit with me. We don't have to talk. Just...sit and let me hold you."

She drew him to one of the mats as she would have guided Michael. There, she pulled him down and for long moments, she simply smoothed his hand in silence. At times she caressed his knee or sleeked his eyebrows and straightened his collar, touching him in lots of inconsequential little ways but always touching—reminding him that she was here.

After a time, she glimpsed wetness upon his cheeks, and she knelt before him and kissed away his tears as he had often kissed hers. She stroked his rebellious hair, which she adored, and drew his face into the curve of her neck.

"It's okay to be sad, R.T.," she whispered as she held him close. "You can be sad with me."

Presently, he wrapped his arms around her and held her so tightly, she was part of his body.

"They were just children," he mumbled around the grief in his throat. "I shouldn't have been there. None of us should have been there. And then their blood was all over me, and they looked up at me when I carried them. Sometimes they didn't even cry. They just looked at me—babies with those eyes, those eyes, those eyes . . ."

So, that was it! R.T.'s private hell. Allyson's own grief mingled with his and she drew him lower upon the cushions, cradling his head to her breast, rocking, rocking.

"Let them go, R.T.," she soothed. "You can't hold what cannot be held. They wouldn't ask you to. You can't ask it of yourself. Let them go, my darling."

"They pinned medals on me. When I came back to this country, people who wouldn't have spit on me before suddenly wanted me to come to parties. They thought I was some freaking hero all because I had the blood of dying children on me."

For a long time they lay upon the mat, until Allyson lost track. She wondered if they slept. Later, he stirred, and she, stiff and cramped, opened her eyes.

"I'm still here," she said.

"I know."

Sighing, calm now, he shifted until his cheek rested upon the bowl of her belly, his breath hot through the cotton gown. He drew in her scent, holding it until it was a part of him. Longing was born swiftly between them, and he grew rampant and hard. Her own quickening was painful in her breasts.

He pushed onto his hands and gazed down. "Why did you really come?"

She shook her head. "I was here. I am here."

He lifted her hair from her face, and his frown propelled her to some deeper honesty. She slithered from beneath him and crawled onto her knees.

"I came to make you want me," she admitted.

He didn't buy that. "I mean, why—*really* why?"

She didn't want to expose that much of herself, but the reason had plagued her for days. She took a fortifying breath. "I wanted to make you want me so much, you couldn't bear to let me go away."

As he viewed the woman kneeling opposite him, her loveliness shimmering beneath the veils of her hair, R.T. felt the hot heat of desire. He was so painfully hard, he feared he could not move. His brain was on fire with need of her, and she was using her sex as a weapon.

"Don't make this more difficult than it already is," he begged in a voice that had corroded. "You know I'm not here all the time. I can protect you when I'm here, but what would happen when I go? You and Michael would be more exposed than you are in the city. You said it yourself—

whoever wants Daniel has long arms. You can't stay. In your heart, you know that.''

Her eyes were so wide, their whites shone all around the emerald irises. "I understand perfectly," she said, wanting to wound him, whether it was fair or not.

R.T. deflected a look off the ceiling. "You understand nothing."

"Then I came to make you suffer."

"Consider your mission a success, my darling."

R.T. expected her to fly away in a burst of fury. He did not expect her to rise to her feet and move toward him, her hips swaying and her look that of a sorceress. With moves that were primal and erotic, she shed her robe and drew her gown over her head. Wearing only the whimsy of her socks, she licked her lips and shook out her hair, lifting her hands to push it back.

When her breasts thrust forward, R.T.'s throat tightened until he could not swallow. Slowly she drew her fingertips along the pale flesh inside her thighs and sleeked her sides, touching her breasts and letting her head go back.

"Take me," she slurred as she gyrated sultrily and tangled her fingers in the tufts of curls at the juncture of her thighs. "Take me and get done with it."

R.T. steeled himself to resist. "You go too fast."

Aflame, Allyson wished she could break him. She wished she could bring him to his knees—this determined Marine. Boldly, she licked the pad of a finger and found the button of nerves sucked so sensuously within velvet folds.

"You're playing with fire, woman," he warned.

"Then burn me."

When he snagged her with an arm, Allyson caught a quick breath and threw a leg about his waist, pressing herself to the hard ridge straining against his jeans, lifting herself to be taken.

But he refused. "You started this," he growled. "I'll finish it."

He set his own pace and followed his own will. Allyson writhed as he licked her and laved her and kissed her and suckled her as if in punishment. And when he was through,

he began again until insanity was beating at her skull. She
kicked at him then, and he pinned her down. She struck at
him, but he made love to her. They could have been at war,
and when he, aching, entered her at last, she threw back her
head and fought her way on top, as if in a triumph.

He laughed, and bending, she sank her teeth into his
shoulder. His laughter turned to pain as she goaded him and
he slammed her to her back. More and more she taunted
him, until with every thrust he seemed to hurl them both
into some deeper, more violent ending. At last, when she
was weak, and dripping and whimpering and whispering his
name, purring her surrender, he held her tightly against him.
Afterward, when Allyson had lost all track of time and her
scent was mingled with his and his sweat was dewy upon her,
he dressed her as if she were a child. Then he dressed himself and swept her up in his arms.

But he did not take her to his bed. Gently, so gently that
Michael never stirred, he laid her beside the boy.

Bending, he placed his lips upon her ear and whispered,
"I'm trying as hard as I can to do what's best. The decision
is in your hands. You'll know when the time is right to come
to me. When that day comes, I won't say no to you. I did
that once. Not ever again."

Chapter 16

Allyson thought she hated R.T. a little for putting the decision into her lap. She had been there once before, and she had wound up making one of the worst decisions of her life and marrying Daniel.

Her desperation to find a solution grew. With a Daniel-esque expertise, she hacked brazenly into the IRS files, found Duane Hickson and got back out again. Hickson, it seemed, was presently living on El Campo Boulevard in Los Angeles. By the looks of his income tax return, he had not paid taxes on his last kickback from Global Defense.

Gotcha! she thought with a smile, and chalked up a point in her favor.

Steiger Tate returned from Los Angeles where he talked with Hickson. He lumbered up R.T.'s back steps, burst through the door, peeled off his overcoat, washed his hands at the sink and sat down at the kitchen table as if he'd lived there for years.

"Grant Melbourne isn't our man," he announced, and steepled his fingers as if about to pray.

Allyson was in the process of passing the mashed potatoes to Liddy, who was serving Michael's plate. The boy's appetite had increased markedly during his days at the farm, and a new bloom of health ruddied his cheeks. He had become R.T.'s shadow, and he was presently sitting proudly between him and Jesse Hurlburton, Jesse having relinquished his lookout upstairs long enough for a hot meal.

Archie was en route from the cabinet to the table, a pitcher of iced tea balanced precariously in his lap.

Forks lowered to plates at Tate's words. Looks deflected from face to face.

"You're kidding," Allyson finally managed to say, and pressed a napkin to her mouth while she sought R.T.'s eyes for reassurance.

R.T. sat at the opposite end of the table, a coffee cup poised numbly between the table and his mouth. His mouth flattened into a grim line.

"Now, now," Tate soothed as his tie licked the gravy. "Before everyone goes off the deep end, Hickson says that Grant has been a pawn of Joan Melbourne for years. Grant isn't our man, but Joan is definitely our woman."

"Oh-oh." Archie brought his wheelchair to a stop.

"The problem is," Tate added, "Hickson won't testify against Joan Melbourne. He swore he'd perjure himself and do time before he'd testify. He's terrified of the woman. I believe him."

Dressed in a black sweatshirt with its neck slashed and its sleeves hacked out, his pitch-dark hair and mustache making him look like a slightly reformed version of Lucifer, R.T. came to his feet with such urgency, dishes trembled upon the table.

"Hickson may not be so tough when he's facing a sentence for obstructing justice," he said.

The detective was blandly spooning sugar into his tea. "I've questioned a lot of people in my time, Major Smith, and you get a feel for these things. I think the colonel will stand his ground."

Muttering what Allyson guessed was an oath they were all better off not hearing, R.T. angrily kicked his chair away. Everyone flinched as it crashed against the wall. He strode to where the coats were hung and jerked his jacket off a hook. Shrugging savagely into it, he fished a pair of crumpled gloves from the pockets. Pulling them on, in a brittle voice he said, "I have to check on the horses."

"Can I come?" Michael chirped as he slid out of his chair.

The hardness softened momentarily around R.T.'s eyes as he grinned and ruffled the blond hair. "Ask your mother."

Allyson agreed that Michael could go, but she was making a dreadful mistake, she knew. Not even a seedling, after its roots had become entwined around another, could be easily transplanted.

Not until Steiger Tate had returned to his hotel and Jesse had resumed his watch upstairs and Liddy, Kahn, Michael and Archie had gone upstairs to bed, did R.T. toss another log on the fire and wonder what he could say to Allyson to relieve the tension that was mounting steadily between them.

She sat curled upon the living room rug, forlorn in her long, wraparound skirt and dark wine-colored blouse. She stared moodily at the late-night news as she stroked Manny's head, which rested trustfully upon her knee.

R.T. despised that he didn't have the money to leave Seattle. He would take his family and relocate to a place where Grant and Joan Melbourne wouldn't find Allyson. But a Marine's dollar refused to stretch that far. It would hardly feed and clothe the people who depended upon it, and his roots were sunk deeply into this farmland. How had his hope of a life with Allyson been reduced to a denominator of money?

With butterfly softness, he drew one of the pins from her hair. Freed tresses cascaded slowly down her back. She gave no evidence that she noticed, and he pushed her hair aside and placed a breathy kiss upon her nape.

"God, I love you," he whispered, and buried his face desperately in the sweet-smelling locks.

Her words, when they came, were maddeningly detached and practical.

"Maybe we could confront Joan, R.T.," she said. "Maybe we could tell her we have proof of what she's done.

In a public place, perhaps, where she couldn't be so cool. Maybe she would do something to give herself away. Maybe she would say something that would help us.''

R.T. felt as if he were walking on the oldest coals known to man. ''Come to my bed tonight, Allyson. Stay the night with me.''

She turned, and her blouse, a rich, silky affair with cut-glass buttons, shifted over her breasts, sculpting their sweet softness. R.T. ached to touch them, to rest his head there and close his eyes in a stolen moment of peace.

But her distance was so powerful, so forbidding, he didn't dare. She rose, her slim grace stifling any arguments he might have offered. She paused briefly to place her hand upon the side of his face.

''I love you too, R.T.,'' she said, her smile so perfect, he loathed it. ''But it's not enough, is it?''

Leaving him to his sullen alienation, she moved across the room and wearily climbed the stairs.

R.T. gazed at the dog that now sat on his haunches. Grateful for some understanding, even that of a dumb animal, he walked Manny to the door and let him out.

He stared a moment at the cold night. What would he do when Allyson left him? Would he, like a spoiled boy robbed of his favorite toy, lick his wounds and try to figure out where it had all gone wrong? He might, if he could rise above the old habits of his youth, try to perceive why his ego fed so ravenously upon the debts to Daniel that always seemed to him outstanding.

After banking the fire, he turned out the lights and walked to the stairs. But he dropped to the bottom step and buried his face in his hands, his chest wracked with helplessness. How had he managed to screw up his life so badly?

''There's something to be said for the surprise factor, you know,'' Steiger Tate said the next afternoon as he considered Allyson's idea and helped himself to one of R.T.'s cigars at the same time. ''You may just have stumbled onto something, Mrs. Wyatt. If we could come up with a plan to trick Joan Melbourne into giving herself away, I've got a feeling that Colonel Hickson might work with us. But it wouldn't be easy. Joan Melbourne has been dealing with the Justice Department for some time now. She picks and chooses where she goes and who she goes with.''

R.T. was outside with the horses. Allyson was still searching through documents in Daniel's computer. She was about to turn it off when a block appeared in the right-hand corner of the monitor.

She leaned back with a catch of breath that brought the detective's head sharply up.

''What?'' he said, and walked over.

Allyson stared in silence at the words that glowed green: ''FOUND YOU!''

''Maybe it's Mr. Wyatt,'' Tate suggested.

''And maybe Grant's gotten himself another hacker,'' Allyson retorted.

''Aren't you going to answer it?''

''What if I respond to this and it turns out to be Grant's man? He'll know that we're on to him. That would blow everything.''

''You have to do something, Mrs. Wyatt.''

With an oversize caution, Allyson carefully entered the response. ''Eddy?''

Immediately, the words appeared in the block. ''Conaveris in the flesh. Happy Birthday, Babe.''

The block disappeared as quickly as it had come, and Allyson looked at Steiger Tate, a sheepish half smile on her face.

Steiger Tate's confusion was plain. ''What th' hell was that all about?''

Shaking her head, Allyson rose from her chair and gave the terminal a pat. ''It means, detective,'' she said as she fetched her coat and gloves, ''that Daniel's alive and well. I've got to tell R.T.''

Each year the Greater Seattle Center for the Performing Arts held a huge fund-raising event, the organization being Joan Melbourne's favorite charity. This year, Joan was us-

ing the publicity to counter some of the rumbling that
Thurgood Lord and his men at Justice were kicking up.

The annual auction was held in the spacious foyer of the
new wing of the Museum of Science and History, a prestigious wing that Joan's money had helped build. The pro-
ceeds underwrote one of the arts. This year the ballet was the
lucky project.

The day the announcement appeared in the paper, Steiger
Tate announced to Allyson and R.T. that he had come up
with a plan.

"Nothing very elaborate," he said, "but you never know,
it might just work."

The next evening, Allyson and R.T. left their wraps at the
front door of the museum and walked through the mezza-
nine and into the wing where the auction was already in
progress.

"There she is," Allyson told R.T. "There's Joan."

The museum was three stories high. A spectacular spiral-
ing stairway reached from the ground floor to the third,
wide as a thoroughfare so people could travel up and down.
On the second story, a string quartet was playing Haydn. On
the third-floor balcony, which overlooked the entire wing,
Joan was giving a small party for her most intimate friends.
She looked remarkably like Jacqueline Kennedy in her
flowing, coral-colored silks.

R.T. said wryly of the stairway, "The highway to
heaven."

"That depends on which way you're going," Allyson
quipped dryly.

Ordinarily, Allyson wouldn't have attended Joan's fund-
raiser. Especially not now with her clothes having to be replaced, all her lovely Claibornes and Ellen Tracys and Jones
of New Yorks.

R.T. had insisted on buying her a new dress for the affair.

"No," she said. "I absolutely cannot allow it."

That evening he returning from the city with an irresistible box under his arm from Bouffant, one of the best shops

in Seattle. He placed it upon the kitchen table as casually as a sack of oranges.

Allyson was helping Archie with dinner, and she plopped a fist to the side of her hip. She angled R.T. a suspicious smirk.

"You can't buy me," she drawled.

He tweaked her nose. "I wouldn't dream of trying."

For a good half hour, she circled the box as if it were an enemy that must be approached downwind. When the telephone rang and R.T. answered it, she inched closer and toyed with the luscious lavender bow.

"Gifford!" R.T. exclaimed, and braced a shoulder against the wall. Allyson was only half listening as he murmured into the receiver, "Boy, you did good, Cocoran. That packs a pretty good punch."

Hanging up, he caught her just as she was giving the box a shake. Flushing, she returned it to the table and said with airy innocence, "Who was that?"

"A friend of mine in intelligence. Are you going to open that, Allyson, or shall I take it back?"

She had scooped up the box and ducked out of the kitchen, so now she was walking into the museum on R.T.'s arm wearing a gorgeous strapless Fernando Sanchez—black, shimmering, showing lots of décolletage and black-stockinged leg, her only jewelry being large button earrings of faux sapphires.

"If this neckline were any lower," she said from the side of her mouth as she kept a poised elegance pasted on her face, "I'd spill right out of this dress."

R.T. kept his eyes straight ahead, but he chuckled softly. "If you do, my love, I guarantee you'll raise more interest than anything they've got on the block tonight." He shot her a wicked look and ogled her cleavage. "There are men in this room who would kill for that."

"But not you, eh?" she retorted.

"Especially me."

She giggled prettily. "My mother was right. You should've gone into the diplomatic corps." From beneath her lashes, she slid him a head-to-toe inspection of her own. "You're not so bad yourself."

He digested her remark for a moment, then laughed. "Boy, that really hurt to say, didn't it?"

Allyson jutted her chin with more playfulness than she had felt in days. "I'm not really into pain, Major."

He was, Allyson had to admit, stunning in his dark military dress with its black tie and gold cummerbund. His snowy shirt was so stiff it crackled. Gold braid was on his cuffs and white hat, and he wore white gloves. His rank insignia was discreetly attached to his left lapel. No man in the place was so attractive or so virile, and she felt the daggered looks of a dozen women at her back.

High above them, Joan Melbourne had positioned her magnificent body against the thick Plexiglas railing on the balcony and was smiling down at her guests. Neither Allyson nor R.T. could keep from staring, she was so beautiful.

When she was joined by Grant, who was as resplendent as she, Allyson closed her fingers upon R.T's sleeve. "They've seen us," she said breathlessly. "The curtain's going up."

"Welcome to the party, bud," R.T. snarled softly as they prepared to ascend the broad stair.

Allyson hesitated. "Maybe they'll both topple over the railing and save us all a lot of trouble."

"I wouldn't count on it."

"What if Joan won't nibble at the bait? Then I'll have exposed myself for nothing."

"Do you have a better plan?"

"No."

"Then go with it."

For several moments, Allyson and R.T. moved slowly back and forth on the lower level. Every few seconds, Allyson deliberately looked up at Joan and Grant, then jerked her head away as if she didn't wish to be caught observing.

"Do you think they're getting nervous yet?" she whispered. "They have to get nervous."

"Give 'em time, babe."

"I think you should make the phone call now."

R.T. left her to use one of the telephones. While he was gone, Allyson kept up her furtive observation of Joan and Grant and pretended to be inordinately skittish. Joan, she noted, had called Grant aside and talked to him.

Presently, Grant positioned himself at the railing, and when R.T. returned from the telephones, they both looked up. Grant raised his hand in a mocking little salute to R.T.

"Oh, Lord," Allyson groaned.

After a moment, Steiger Tate arrived, on schedule and looking quite natty in his tuxedo. Joining them, he scoured the third-floor balcony and said, "Everyone's ready."

"I think Mr. Melbourne is getting antsy," R.T. said. "Should Allyson and I go up now?"

Nodding, the detective gave a signal of snapped fingers, and several dark-suited men appeared from the peripheries of the crowd. As R.T. walked Allyson to the stair, she laid her hand upon his braided sleeve and closed her fingers tightly upon it.

"Easy does it," he warned as they began to climb.

Higher and higher they climbed, and Allyson could feel the apprehension of Joan and Grant compounding. On the ground level, Steiger Tate was joined by more and more men.

"They've got security personnel at all the entrances and exits now," R.T. said.

"I think I'm going to be sick," Allyson moaned.

"Please turn your head the other way if you are."

Perspiration was drizzling behind Allyson's knees and her palms were sweating. Neither Joan nor Grant was watching them now, they were both staring at the cluster of men around Steiger Tate.

"Is he here, yet?" Allyson said. "I want to get a look at Joan's face when he arrives."

R.T. laid a hand upon her trembling, sweating one. "Then look."

As both she and R.T. turned to peer down, the federal security men stepped aside to form a loosely fashioned corridor. Through it walked Colonel Duane Hickson.

Joan's shock showed only for an instant before she replaced it with a hard mask.

"Boy, she is one cool bitch," R.T. said from the side of his mouth.

"It's not working," Allyson whimpered. "She's not alarmed. Maybe I made a mistake, R.T. Maybe I got bad information."

"Easy, easy. Give it time."

Wondering why she had let Steiger Tate talk her into this extremely iffy scheme, Allyson made an effort of steadying herself as they reached the third floor.

"Well," she said on a ragged breath, "the time to strike, they say, is while the iron is hot. I don't see it getting any hotter. After I introduce you, R.T., sort of drift away. Let me be alone with her."

His look was a loving, caring caress of eyes that reminded Allyson of all that had gone before, of the years when she had been the bright laughing girl who was in love with the bad boy.

"You're not afraid, are you?" he whispered as he memorized the curves of her eyebrows and the set of her mouth, the angle of her nose, the way her hair fanned back from her temples.

Allyson forced a smile. "Nah. When I throw up, I'll aim for Joan's punch bowl."

Laughter rumbled from his chest. "I knew I loved you for some reason." Kissing his own knuckle, he grazed it along her jaw. "I won't be very far, sweetheart."

Allyson didn't expect the introduction of R.T. to go smoothly. When she introduced R.T. to Grant, her ex-boss pressed his hand to his abdomen as if he were in pain. His features, normally handsome, were drawn, Allyson thought, and his hatred of her was so tangible, she could have closed her fist upon it.

"What've you done?" he demanded as champagne glasses clicked all around them and glitzy banter ricocheted from wall to wall.

Allyson gave him a look of utter confusion. With a purr of feigned delight, Joan moved to Allyson and breathed a kiss near her cheek. Allyson felt the woman's knowledge of what was happening like one feels a change of pressure before a storm.

"Darling," she cooed, holding Allyson at arm's length, "how lovely you look tonight. I adore your dress. Simply gorgeous."

"R.T. picked it out," Allyson said lamely.

"Really?" Joan's eyebrows lifted to R.T. "You can come live at my house any time, Captain."

"Major," R.T. corrected, and shook Joan's hand perfunctorily. "Excuse me, ladies, I think I'll get something to drink."

Grimacing at Grant, Allyson watched R.T. drift away to the table where other guests mingled. Returning to Joan, she shifted her weight from foot to foot. "Do you think the auction will go well?"

Joan's laughter drifted through the balcony like music. "Of course, darling. They always go well. Come, I want to show you a piece they're going to take down later. It's to be the surprise event of the evening. I expect it to bring a million dollars, at least."

As Allyson allowed herself to be cut free of R.T., she shivered. Grant, too, moved away, and she dutifully admired the huge Monet that Joan had acquired, a painting that had been hung in a stark white niche of the balcony, a bright, lyrical painting in which the air shimmered and the water seemed to be on the canvas, wet and inviting.

Allyson listened to Joan's nonstop spout of information—highly knowledgeable words that Joan had educated herself to say. After the brief treatise, the woman touched Allyson's wrist lightly and said, "That's all I wanted to show you. Unless you'd like to take a stroll downstairs with me and see if the feds brought their bloodhounds, too."

Allyson burned hot, then turned cold. But she managed to keep her head erect, and she forced herself to meet the older woman's eyes without a flinch.

"It was all in the computer, Joan." Her voice, though trembling, was distinct. "About how you've been defrauding the government all those years. We know about Duane

Hickson. We know that you used Daniel, then tried to hush him and lost him, and that you turned on me to get to Daniel. We know everything."

In the midst of her guests, Joan tipped back her magnificent head and gave a laugh so silver and so rippling, Allyson didn't know whether to pretend to laugh with her or burst into tears.

"Darling, darling, darling," Joan said when she had composed herself and signaled to her friends that everything was under control. "You are so pathetic in your little intrigues. Do you think that I haven't prepared for this day? You have nothing on me, and even if you did, you couldn't touch me. No one can touch me."

Adrenaline rushed through Allyson—violently—so that she weaved unsteadily. Her words would hardly move past the rage twisting in her throat.

"So you try to kill people, Joan?" she choked. "You send men after Daniel, and you wreck my apartment, frighten my child? I have the original Bolten file. The money you paid Duane Hickson is a matter of record."

"You little fool!" Joan hissed. "Do you think Duane Hickson frightens me? Look."

Allyson hadn't realized that Grant had walked down the stairway to the lower floor, but now she saw him below, making his way to the cadre of tuxedoed men. He spoke to Steiger Tate, and she saw Thurgood Lord approach. Both men looked grim as death. Grant gestured, then held out his hands, and Steiger Tate placed a pair of handcuffs upon his wrists.

Speechless, Allyson gripped the railing. Grant was turning himself in? Grant was taking the rap for Joan? But what . . . ?

Swiveling, she sought R.T.'s reaction, and Joan said with the sharp clarity of acid, "This is what happens when you screw around with me, darling."

Allyson wanted to hurl her glass as the Monet painting. She wanted to shatter it as R.T. had been driven to smash his glass in Honeymoon Cottage. She wanted to wrap her fingers about Joan's neck and choke the evil that was there.

Heartsick, she spun on her heel and made her way through the groups of beautiful people who were eating and drinking and laughing and didn't care. She didn't want R.T. to see how disappointed she was, how without hope she was.

She bumped someone and champagne spattered across her arms and her beautiful Sanchez dress. She reached the stairway and its downward spiral. She was struck with the doom of her own words to R.T. She was descending into hell!

From where he had watched the bitter exchange, R.T. adjusted his cufflinks and arranged a deadly smile upon his face. With a deceptive casualness, he drifted toward Joan Melbourne where she was watching Allyson hurry down the stairway. Did Joan not realize the precariousness of her position? That she had threatened the thing he loved most in life?

Sensing his presence, she turned, her eyebrows lifted in the first true uncertainty he had seen in her. "We're so flattered you could be with us tonight, Major."

"I'm sure you are." R.T. blandly placed his glass upon a tray as a waiter moved past.

He gave her his most chilling smile—a good smile, one of a sizeable repertoire that he'd collected when he'd had to scrounge on the docks for survival.

She averted her gaze to the men who were taking Grant away.

"He loves you," he observed softly.

"Yes," Joan agreed, her voice thin. "Poor Grant."

"Well, I don't love you."

She sought his eyes, a strange light coming from them. "Really, Major?"

"In fact, I'm not really impressed by this performance, Mrs. Melbourne."

The tiny lines at the edges of her eyes tightened. "You think you know me well enough to judge whether or not I'm performing?"

R.T. smiled nastily. "I know you very well. You may have everyone here fooled, but I grew up in one of the worst hellholes of this city. I saw women like you every day of my life. All that paint and all those jewels and all that money can't cover up the dirt inside you. I even know your old pimp's name. So don't put on airs with me, baby."

The trump card that Cocoran Gifford, Naval Intelligence, had placed in his hand had an effect that didn't come as a great surprise to R.T. Incensed, Joan's clawlike hand rose to strike.

R.T. didn't move a muscle. "Don't even consider it." His eyes were a furnace, and Joan, going pale, prudently lowered her hand.

He smiled. "That's better. I'm going to leave now, but there's something I want you to know. Allyson's nice, Joan, but I'm not. I wouldn't hesitate to kill you any more than you would have killed Daniel. Lest you doubt that, let me tell you that I could do it so that no one would ever know you didn't die in your sleep. Or, if you like it rough, I could throw you over the edge of this balcony right now. Personally, I like things neat. So, in parting, if anything should happen to Allyson—I mean, if she should get so much as a bruise from a slamming door—you're going to wake up one morning, Joan, and find your name in headlines across the front page—Joan Melbourne, Best Hooker on the West Coast. I'll come after you, baby. You know I mean that, don't you?"

Joan didn't have to reply. R.T. got his answer in the terror that turned her wonderful Elizabeth Arden complexion to the color of ashes. It occurred to R.T. that he should probably throw Daniel's own safety into the bargain, as well, but he had no fears on that part. Joan Melbourne might do many things before her death, but bringing harm to Allyson and Daniel would not be two of them.

Removing his cap from beneath his arm, R.T. fit it precisely upon his head. As a parting touch, he lifted Joan's hand in his own and brought it to his lips.

"I'll keep in touch," he promised, and turned on his heel and walked down the stairs.

Chapter 17

No matter how you played Life, Allyson thought when the next day's headlines declared Grant Melbourne's shocking arrest, it never let you get by with a single thing. It came full circle, always. The decisions you once congratulated yourself that you didn't have to make after all, stared you mockingly in the face.

"You'll know when the time is right to come to me," R.T. had said.

Well, she had made one decision about her life; she would leave Seattle and change it, she would put her mistakes behind her and move on. She would begin again.

The time had come to do it. Fortunately, she had never located Earl Kolpechy to inform him that she wasn't coming, so her lovely job was there, expecting her. Greg, her rascally, irresponsible brother, had even showed up on Kaye's doorstep and was, at this very minute, trudging back and forth to the U-Haul truck, loading her things.

"You'll know when the time is right to come to me."

R.T.'s words haunted her as she peered out the kitchen window and watched Greg carrying boxes and packages. She was caught in her own trap of good intentions. She

hadn't even been afforded an opportunity to be alone with
R.T. when the time came for goodbyes.

It had been her intention to make him regret having
shunted the decision back onto her shoulders, but all she
had done was stare at the toes of her shoes and mumbled,
"Our stars have never been in the right place, I guess."

*Please say, To hell with stars, come home with me, marry
me.*

But R.T. saw Michael hunched on the steps, his little face
large with unhappiness. Sweeping the boy up into his arms,
he hugged him and pressed his face into Michael's shoulder. R.T. loved Michael more than he loved her! And she
despised herself for being jealous of her own child.

Placing Michael on the ground, he kept the small hand
clasped in the large one. "You won't forget what I told you
about the Old Man, will you, son?" he said.

Tears spilling, Michael shook his head that he would not.

R.T. did kiss her before he left, very hard and very
quickly before turning to join his men before she could say
a word. Allyson watched him walk away, his jaw as grim
and disciplined as it had been that night in the motel when
he had refused to do things her way.

Was that it, then? Her brief encounter with R.T. was
nothing more than an interlude between the past and the
future?

"Will we go back to the farm, Mama?" Michael asked
when they returned dejectedly to Kaye's kitchen.

"Of course, darling," Allyson replied, and whispered to
a heartbroken ghost of herself, "Someday."

Margo had fixed them breakfast. Kaye had placed the
silver coffee service on the kitchen table, a thing she almost
never did. Allyson wanted to throw herself into her mother's arms and weep, "Would you talk to me like I'm a
woman, for once? Would you let me tell you how much I
have always loved him?"

"At first I didn't want you to go so far away," Kaye said
after they had laboriously suffered the ritual of eating. "But
I think this could be a real opportunity for you, Allyson.

You can build a good life in Atlanta. You'll meet some interesting people..."

"I know interesting people here, Mother," Allyson said dully as she helped clear away the breakfast dishes and place them in the dishwasher for Margo.

Greg poked his head into the kitchen and declared, "I'm nearly finished packing the truck."

Allyson told her brother, "I'll be there in a minute, Greg."

"You know what I mean," Kaye was saying. "You could meet someone, perhaps get married again. Have another baby, who knows?"

Frightened now that mere minutes existed between her and the point of no return, Allyson looked up from the sink and confronted her mother.

"Why don't you just say it? You're glad I'm going to Atlanta because I won't be involved with R.T. anymore. You didn't want me involved with him back then, so you married me off to Daniel. You don't want me involved with him now, so you... well..."

Kaye placed the top upon the silver sugar bowl with extreme care. Allyson thought of the plain plastic sugar bowl that resided in R.T.'s country kitchen.

"I know I pushed you too hard about Daniel," Kaye admitted. "But Allyson, look at the facts, darling. I know R.T.'s turned out to be good-looking and charming as they come, but he doesn't make enough to support you. And there aren't any prospects of things getting any better."

"You mean, because R.T. doesn't give parties at affluent museum auctions?"

"That's unfair, Allyson."

Michael slid off his chair and wandered to the front of the house. With a feeling of terrible loss, Allyson watched him go. She tried to shake the cobwebs from her head. She shut off the water at the sink, leaving her hand to rest upon the spigot.

Kaye was putting the silver coffee service back on the sideboard.

"My son has color in his cheeks now," Allyson mused, almost to herself. "For the first time since he was born, he doesn't pick at the food on his plate and he runs and romps and tumbles like a boy was meant to do."

"And you think R.T. brought that about?"

In surprise, Allyson found Kaye's eyes. "I know he has."

Kaye wrung her hands as genuine pleading found her voice. "He'd be gone all the time, Allyson," she reasoned. "He would never be there when you needed him. You'd be stuck out on that place...."

Allyson pushed a button on the dishwasher. R.T. didn't have a dishwasher. Liddy and Archie washed dishes at the farm.

"But when he was there," she told Kaye, "our time together would make up for all the other times."

Kaye covered her face in misery. She shook her head. "I can't believe you're saying these things. You're blind to how it would be. You'd never have a moment's privacy with all those people around."

"Don't confuse privacy with intimacy, Mother."

With a look of complete betrayal, Kaye mumbled that she had a going-away present upstairs for Michael. Allyson watched her mother go and wondered what had just happened between them. She had never intended to say the words that had come out of her mouth. But they were true, weren't they? Oh, yes, very true.

Michael wandered morosely back into the kitchen and climbed onto a stool beside the sink. He affixed his small bottom to two inches of the seat and dipped his head to his knees.

Allyson waited for him to speak, but he didn't. She lovingly threaded her fingers through his shining hair. "I'm never really sure what's going on in that muffin-puffin head of yours."

Michael looked at her with his disturbing adult's eyes. "I miss Manny."

"I'm sure he misses you." She laid the back of her hand upon his blossoming cheek. "Maybe we can go visit him sometime." When Michael didn't respond, she said, "You

know, darling, I imagine that R.T. would give you Manny
if you asked. We could take him with us. I don't suppose it
makes much difference to Manny if he lives in Washington
or Georgia."

Again, Michael shook his blond head.

From the front door, Greg shouted, "Do you want these
boxes in the living room to go, Allie?"

"Yes," she called back.

"It wouldn't be right," Michael told her gravely. "Manny's a farm dog. He wouldn't like it in town." His solemn
all-seeing eyes found hers. "He'd find his way back. Like
Lassie. It's best to be where you belong."

Kaye's steps sounded at the bottom of the stairs, and Allyson stood fingering Michael's collar, idly smoothing the
corner of it, running her fingertips over the back where Michael's hair grew too long at his nape. The truth was so
simple, she turned and gaped at her mother.

"You're right, Michael," she said in a faraway voice that
seemed not to belong to her at all. "It's best to be where you
belong."

You'll know when the time is right to come to me. Now
she understood why R.T. had dumped the decision back into
her lap—because she had never learned that one simple
truth that even dumb animals knew, and he had always
known it.

And what of Joan Melbourne, sitting in her multimil-
lion-dollar home? Should Allyson worry that the woman
would be plotting vengeance? Should she be afraid to send
Michael to school?

Life wasn't a matter of security. Life was a matter of risk
taking. There would always be things to fear.

Guessing that she would call herself a fool many times,
Allyson flew through the dining room door and across the
living room and down the sidewalk and out to the U-Haul
truck where Greg was packing the last items. She grabbed
her brother by the scuff of his denim jacket.

"Forget it," she gasped when he turned. "Don't pack
anything else."

Greg looked at her as if she'd lost her mind. "What d'you mean? I've just spent the past two days packing. Are you serious?"

"I was never more serious in my life. Just . . . leave everything. Go home, Greg."

"Go home? You're not moving?"

"Yes, but not to Georgia. I'm sorry, Greg." She left him mumbling, then turned from the front door and called brightly back to him, "Cheer up. I'll leave you a check with Mother."

Breaking the news to Earl Kolpechy on the day before she was due to report to work wasn't the easiest thing Allyson had ever done in her life. The man had only worked a small miracle to get her the job, and his anger blazed through the telephone wires.

She took her dressing-down with grace, for she deserved every word of it. She couldn't even explain, because she didn't know all the answers. She couldn't see the future, and she didn't know how it would work, only where she should spend it. Never again would she doubt that.

Her feet had wings as she flew to the kitchen and scuttled Michael from the table.

"Put on your jacket," she ordered. "We're going to the farm."

As Michael gave a yelp and ran to fetch it, Kaye exclaimed from the dining room door, "Allyson! You're ruining your life."

"No, Mother, I think I'm finding it at last. Don't try to talk me out of this. I'm going to marry R.T., if he'll still have me. I hope you'll give me your blessing, but if you don't, it's still something I have to do."

"But Michael? What about CNN?"

Taking Kaye by the shoulders as she should have done many years before, Allyson looked at her mother as one woman would look at another woman, not as a daughter to a parent.

"Mother," she said quietly, "there are some things that were meant to be. I like being with R.T. I—I love being with R.T. I belong with R.T. and always have. I know he's not rich, and he doesn't live like we do, but he's a good man, Mother. Michael needs him, and I need him.''

"Oh, no," Kaye wailed as Allyson hurried after Michael to get her own coat. "You'll never have anything, Allyson. You'll slave for the rest of your life and never have anything."

But that wasn't true. Allyson knew she would be blessed with wealth that her mother would never comprehend.

Bending his strength to the wire-stretchers, R.T. drew the strand of barbed wire taut and pulled the sagging fence back into alignment.

The afternoon was cold, but he was working hard, and he had stripped off his jacket and tossed it across the fender of the Beast. The sun was shining, and it played across the winter wheat, where the cows were grazing. The ground was saturated, too wet, really, to be stretching wire, but the fence was old here, and he didn't want the cattle trampling it down.

"Damn!"

The stretchers slipped and the wire skidded an inch, slicing through the top of his leather glove. Peeling off the glove, R.T. found a bleeding cut and drew a bandanna from the pocket of his jeans, winding it tightly about his hand and flexing his fingers.

He hardly felt the smart of it. He'd hardly felt anything since leaving Allyson and Michael upon Kaye Randolph's steps. She was probably on her way to Georgia by now, and he should be man enough to be glad.

But he wasn't. He hated it, and he hated the endless stretch of his life now, the hopelessness of it, the years of marking time that lay in store for him, going nowhere past Liddy and Archie and Kahn and the job that waited offshore for him.

His heavy leather workboots sucked softly at the wet earth, and he returned to the truck for a drink of water. Spinning the top from a juice bottle, he let the clear, fresh liquid sluice down his throat, and he wiped his mouth on the back of a glove.

From where he lay beside the rear tire, Manny lifted his head and whined.

"What's the matter with you?" R.T. asked. "You smell a grizzly or something? Some big mountain lion who wants you for dinner? A pole cat, more than likely."

Stooping, R.T. scratched the dog's ears, but the sad face reminded him of Michael, and that was something he couldn't afford to think about.

"And don't give me that look, either," R.T. said dourly, and rewrapped the bandanna about his hand, then brushed at his misting eyes with the back of it. "I can do without it."

The dog pricked up his ears. Smiling bleakly, R.T. let out his breath in a stream and pushed himself up. He was moving as though he were ninety years old. At this rate, he'd never get the fence mended.

Returning to the wire, he stooped and began twisting on the fasteners that kept the wire to the T-posts. After a dozen or so, he paused and gazed out across the rain-soaked fields. Far in the distance, he saw figures climbing the wood fence where the horses grazed.

He blinked to refocus, and his heart took a crazy plunge, then bounced into his throat. One was a tall, slim figure, and beside it, a short figure was churning to keep up.

Easy, you fool! he warned himself, and he slowly unfolded. *She could be coming out here for a dozen different reasons. After the cold shoulder you gave her, she'd be an idiot to want you or anything you have to offer. Which ain't much, Marine.*

But his legs were deaf to the good advice and they began moving toward the figures. His eyes strained to see the expressions on their faces. They were too far away, and a despair that he could usually keep hidden broke free in his lungs and made him utter sounds of panic.

Please, please, he found himself praying. *If you're up there, hear me just this one time. I haven't asked for much, and I haven't been given much. But this one thing, if I could have just this one thing . . .*

His boots began striking the ground hard and he felt as if he were running through a firestorm. He was running toward a child, and a woman was running toward him. But she wasn't screaming, she was laughing and crying at the same time. The dog sped past him, low to the ground, a streak of brown fur racing toward Michael, and he struck the boy so hard in the chest, they both toppled into the mud as Manny licked everything his excited tongue could find.

With a tortured pain in his chest, R.T. sought Allyson's eyes as he crossed the last throbbing feet between them. He found the beautiful young girl who could always turn his heart wrong side out, running across the beach toward him, twirling and laughing and tossing her face to the sky. He tried to see in her face the way she would grow old, but she would never be anything to him but the girl he loved.

She came into his arms as if she had come a long way. As she wept, R.T. didn't hold back his tears any longer. He wept for Eva Smith and he wept for Liddy and Kahn and Archie and all the children he had carried in his arms. He wept for this wonderful gift that he knew was being given him, and he raised his face to the sky and knew that something very right had happened. He would not question it, oh, he would not question it.

He found her lips salty with tears, and they, too, were wonderful. He held her face, and she held his bandaged hand.

"You've hurt yourself," she said.

"No, I haven't."

She pushed his cap back from his face and rose, smiling, to find his bleary eyes. "I don't know how we'll work out, R.T.," she whispered as Michael and Manny chugged toward them. "I just know we will. Somehow we have to find a way. We will. You'll see."

With a shake of his head, R.T. held her very close and smiled over her shoulder at Michael, who looked adorably funny in his bright red boots that were too big.

The boy returned R.T.'s look with one R.T. didn't entirely understand, and then R.T. pressed his face into the cold, spun gold of Allyson's hair.

"I know," he whispered, and he reached out a hand to the boy. "It's going to be all right, Cricket. Everything's going to be all right now."

*   *   *   *   *

Silhouette Sensation

COMING NEXT MONTH

WOLF AND THE ANGEL
Kathleen Creighton

Teresa Duncan knew Jack wolf was trouble the minute she saw him. Not for a second did she believe that he just wanted to help her get medical supplies to Baja, Mexico. Unfortunately, she needed him.

Jack's dangerous plans disintegrated a little more each day he spent with Terry. Soon he was just praying that he could keep Terry and the baby they'd been given alive. Revenge wasn't that important anymore. . .

JAKE'S WAY
Kathleen Korbel

She was everything he could ever want in life, but Jake Kendall knew Amanda Marlow would never be his. Jake's world stopped at his ranch's boundaries, whereas Amanda had the world at her feet. She would soon be moving on.

Jake Kendall was the most complex man Amanda had ever met. He spurned her at every turn, but she could see the longing in his eyes. What was it that held him back?

Silhouette Sensation

COMING NEXT MONTH

DESERT SHADOWS
Emilie Richards

Was rebellious Sister Felicia, the nun who stole cigarettes and went swimming in the nude, for real? Or was she a cool assassin, an impostor? Josiah Gallagher made his decision, but then he and the "sister" were stranded in the desert together, with only a slim chance of survival.

The desert trek told Gallagher all he needed to know about Sister Felicia, but there was no time to give in to passion. He was no saint and she was no sister, but they both had obligations to fulfil. Would they be in time?

HEAT LIGHTNING
Anne Stuart

Turner's Landing had never seen anything like Caleb Spenser. Handsome as sin and twice as mean, Caleb was rumoured to have killed a man. A smart person would keep out of his way.

Jassy Turner was usually coolheaded in a crisis, but nothing had prepared her for Caleb. He was like a fire in her blood and as dangerous as heat lightning. But what did he have against her family? Was he just using her?

TAKE 4 NEW SILHOUETTE SENSATIONS FREE!

Silhouette Sensations are thrilling romances for today's woman. A specially selected range of romantic fiction seasoned with suspense. You'll also find glamour, sensuality and daring in each thoroughly modern tale.

We're so sure that you'll enjoy you FREE Sensations that we've anothe treat in store! You could go on to have 4 Silhouette Sensations delivered to your door every month for only £1.85 each (we pay for postage and packing!).

No strings attached - you may cancel o suspend your subscription at any time.

EXTRA FREE GIFT
If you reply within 10 days
Post the Coupon below NOW and we'll send you this cuddly teddy PLUS a mystery gift!

To: Silhouette Reader Service, FREEPOST,
PO Box 236, Croydon, Surrey CR9 9EL

NO STAMP NEEDE

Please rush me 4 Silhouette Sensations and 2 FREE gifts! Please also reserve me a Reader Service subscription, which means I can look forward to receiving 4 brand new Sensations for only £7.40 each month, postage and packing FREE. If I choose not to subscribe, I shall write to you within 10 days and still keep my FREE books and gifts. I may cancel or suspend my subscription at any time. I am over 18 years. Please write in BLOCK CAPITALS.

Ms/Mrs/Miss/Mr _____ EP46

Address _____

_____

_____ Postcode _____

Signature _____

Offer closes 31st October 1993. The right is reserved to refuse an application and change the terms of this offer.
One application per household. Overseas readers please write for details. Southern Africa write to Book Services
International Ltd., Box 41654, Craighall, Transvaal 2024. You may be mailed with offers from other reputable
companies as a result of this application. Please tick box if you would prefer not to receive such offers. ☐